SUNNY DAYS AT THE COTSWOLDS CANDY STORE

HANNAH LYNN

Boldwood

First published in Great Britain in 2023 by Boldwood Books Ltd.

A CIP catalogue record for this book is available from the British Library.

Paperback ISBN 978-1-83518-819-4

Hardback ISBN 978-1-83518-822-4

Ebook ISBN 978-1-83518-820-0

Kindle ISBN 978-1-83518-821-7

Audio CD ISBN 978-1-83518-827-9

MP3 CD ISBN 978-1-83518-826-2

Digital audio download ISBN 978-1-83518-825-5

Boldwood Books Ltd
23 Bowerdean Street
London SW6 3TN
www.boldwoodbooks.com

To Sarn and Rob

1

Holly Berry lifted Hope out of the crib, rested her on her hip as she unclipped the stairgate and headed down the narrow stairs of the cottage. Her cottage. Sometimes she had to pinch herself to believe it was real. Holly and Hope had a home of their own.

During the first four months of Hope's life, the pair had lived at Jamie's. While living with a friend and her fiancé with a newborn baby was definitely not ideal, it came with the advantage of having Ben next door.

Holly and Ben had called it quits for good while Holly lay in a hospital bed with Hope in her arms. She had felt in her heart it was the right thing to do, but that didn't mean she wasn't terrified. After all, she had no idea how to raise a baby, let alone do it on her own. Though, as it turned out, most of her fears were unwarranted.

The set-up had been miraculously easy. On nights when Hope stayed at Ben's, Holly was only a door away and one ring on her phone was all it took for her to run downstairs, out the front door and be there, ready to take Hope and help Ben with whatever he needed.

There was the midnight feeding advantage, too. Holly had never realised the walls between Ben's and Jamie's houses were so thin until now, when Hope would stay next door. Holly's newly acquired sense of hearing meant the moment Hope's throat crackled with a cry, her dressing gown was on and she was ready to give Hope her night-time feed. Despite all their flaws, and the tempestuous end to their relationship, Holly and Ben were pretty fantastic at co-parenting. They could have probably hosted a podcast, given how smoothly everything had gone between them, and Holly could have probably stayed like that forever. But there was only so long they could live in Jamie and Fin's pocket.

'We don't mind,' they said every time Holly had broached the subject of moving. Holly was sure they'd meant it, but they were going to be married soon. It just wasn't fair on them to have her and Hope taking up so much space and not to mention waking them up in the night when she wanted feeding.

'I think it might do some good to put a little more distance between you and Ben, too.' Her mother, Wendy, was quick to jump onboard with the idea. 'You know, there's always room at your dad's and mine.'

'Thanks, Mum, but if I do this, then I want to be on my own. And I know Northleach isn't that far, but I don't want to take Hope out of the village. It wouldn't be fair to Ben. Not when he's been used to having her right next door all this time.'

'I understand. I'll keep my ear to the ground. Let you know if I hear of anything.'

As it happened, she was true to her word, and rather than finding out about the cottage through an estate agent, or even an online advert, news of the rental property came through her mother, via a neighbour who was friends with the landlord.

'They want to get it let as quickly as possible, apparently.'

'I doubt a semi-detached cottage in one of the most desirable villages in the Cotswolds is going to be in my budget,' Holly replied.

Bourton really was somewhere special. With its shallow river running parallel to the high street and its attractive, yellow-bricked buildings, it was a firm favourite with tourists year-round. At Christmas time, the village was alive with twinkling, white lights and a grand Christmas tree which sat slap in the middle of the river, while in spring, it was a cacophony of colour, with cherry blossom and daffodils blooming left, right, and centre.

Unfortunately, the village's desirability was reflected in the house prices.

'We should still see it,' her mother encouraged. 'If they want to rent it out quickly, maybe they'll let it go low. You know what these old cottages are like. It's better to have someone in them, making sure the heating doesn't play up, or that damp doesn't set in, that sort of thing.'

And so Holly agreed to see the place.

'What did you say the price was?' Holly said, as she turned up at the front door of the picture-perfect cottage, only three minutes' walk from the shop and less still to Ben and Jamie. Her mother had come with her to give an opinion, but also to help with Hope so Holly could have a proper nose around the place.

'Nora's friend thinks you can probably get it for seven-fifty if you're quick.'

'That can't be right.' Holly stepped back, trying to spot any obvious flaws in the place, but her mother was already unlocking the door.

'Oh Holly, come and look. It's perfect.'

Perfect was a word Holly didn't take lightly, but it was hard to think of a synonym to better describe the inside of the cottage. As she moved to join her mother in the doorway, she couldn't help but gasp. Downstairs, the small hallway opened into an open-plan living-dining room. The kitchen was also knocked through, meaning they had a clear view of everything downstairs.

'This would be perfect. You could cook in the kitchen and still watch Hope playing in the living area.'

Holly's heart soared as she took in the marble worktops and the clean, white walls. Deep down, she'd hoped she wouldn't like the place. That it would be unliveable, cramped or mouldy. Any fault that meant she wouldn't have to deal with the disappointment of not being able to afford it. But upstairs was even more perfect.

'There's only a shower, not a bath.' Holly had tried to find some negatives. 'And the second room is really small.'

'What are you on about? It's no smaller than the room you had as a teenager. Plenty big enough for a single bed and a chest of drawers. What more is Hope going to need for the next few years?'

Her mother was right, of course. It was exactly what Holly needed, but moving was a big step. In less than a year, she would have shifted from being young and carefree, living next to her boyfriend in a room rented from her friend to this: a single mum with her name on a lease.

When they left the cottage, her mother locked up and turned to Holly.

'So, am I getting Nora's friend to ring the landlord?'

Holly could still recall how in that moment, she had looked down at her daughter in the baby carrier and Hope had looked back up at her, her dark-blue eyes staring straight into her as if they held every answer Holly would ever need.

'As long as I can afford the rent.'

Four weeks later and she had unpacked her baking supplies into the kitchen cupboards, arranged her books onto the narrow shelves, and squeezed all hers and Hope's clothes into the wardrobes, while Hope lay on her back, kicking and flapping her hands at the toys hanging on the playmat. Now, that all felt like a lifetime ago and a lot had changed in those few short months. For starters, it was a lot harder to keep Hope on the playmat, and the previously sleek clean surfaces were now covered in everything from dirty muslin cloths to bowls with half-dried baby food, the latter of which Holly knew she needed to wash-up, although at that moment, they were miles from her mind.

She had barely reached the kitchen and flicked on the kettle when the front door opened. Her mother stepped into the house, coat on and bag over her shoulder, although rather than immediately grabbing Hope like she normally did, she stopped dead in the middle of the living area and stared straight at Holly.

'Why aren't you dressed yet? And where are all your bags? You're leaving for the airport in an hour.'

With a deep inhale, Holly looked from her daughter to her mother and back again.

'I'm not going.' She folded her arms as she spoke. 'I was thinking about it all night. I'm not going.'

'Like hell you're not,' her mother replied. 'Now get your bags sorted. You need to pack. Fast.'

2

Holly was panicking. A lot.

'Have you got the baby monitor? I can't find it.' She lifted the massive bag on her bed, tossing aside various babygrows and cuddly toys. 'I had the charger a minute ago. I know I did. It must be here somewhere.' Giving up looking on the bed, she turned to her bag, pulling out dresses and underwear which had been meticulously packed only an hour before. 'Where the hell is it?'

'Doesn't Ben have his own baby monitor?'

Having fixed them both strong cups of coffee, her mother was now upstairs in the bedroom, sitting in the corner of the room in a wing-backed chair, bouncing Hope on her knee. Hope, who, in just three hours' time, Holly was leaving for four days. Four whole days and nights she was going to be parted from her baby and it was turning her into a wreck.

'What does Ben do when he stays at hers during the week? Doesn't he have his own baby monitor then?'

With several tops still crumpled in her hand, Holly paused. Yes, Ben had his own baby monitor. He had his own cot and bouncing chair and bottle steriliser and every other item of paraphernalia that went with having a baby. That had been a downside to co-parenting: the need for two sets of everything and the cost of it all. She was still mid thought when she saw the glint of a glass screen behind the lamp on the bedside table.

'There it is.' She reached over and grabbed it. 'I'll put it in, just in case his stops working.'

While she packed the baby monitor, along with a new set of pyjamas and several spare nappies, her mother stood up and placed Hope in the wooden cot. Then she crossed the room, slipped her hand down to the bag, and took the monitor back out again.

'You need to stop worrying. Ben has had Hope hundreds of times before now. In fact, he's had her almost as much as you.'

'But never for so long. And never when I've been in a different country.'

'He'll be just fine. You're panicking. It's like when you moved out of Jamie's and you thought everything was going to fall apart because you were further away from Ben's – a three-minute walk! And look at how well everything has turned out.'

It was difficult to deny. The move might have been the right decision, but that didn't mean Holly hadn't been a wreck about it. She'd timed the walk between the new cottage and Ben's place at a leisurely stroll, a moderate pace, and then an out-and-out sprint before finally signing the contract.

'You're right.' Abandoning the packing, Holly bent down and picked up Hope. 'You're right. Ben will be completely fine. He's always completely fine. Me, on the other hand...'

'You're going to have a lovely time.'

'Four nights, Mum. In another country. And I've got to fly to get there. I don't think planes and I are a good mix.'

'This is a chance for you to switch off and relax.' Her mother skilfully ignored Holly's anxiety. 'Have fun.'

Holly hummed. Wasn't the whole thing about becoming a

parent that you could never switch off again? And the same could be said for running her own business.

'I meant to ask.' Her mother turned away before she spoke. 'Have you heard from Giles recently?'

With a sudden surge in heart rate, Holly stopped what she was doing and stared at her mother's back.

'Why would I have heard from Giles?'

'Oh, no reason, really. I just didn't know if you had. You know, now that Ben and you have properly broken up.'

With a purse of her lips, Holly tried to keep her voice as level as she could.

'The fact that Ben and I separated had nothing to do with me and Giles.'

'You're still sticking with that line, are you?'

It had been a long time since Holly could remember getting cross with her mother, but at that moment, she was biting down on her back molars and choosing her words very carefully. Her mother had developed a soft spot for Giles since he had helped tow their car out of a ditch many moons ago, but recently, she had started bringing him up even more. Perhaps it was because she thought he was the only man that might give Holly a second glance, now that she was on her own with Hope.

'You know me and Ben breaking up was the right thing to do. It had nothing to do with Giles at all. Anyway, none of that matters. I think I should stay. You know Hope's due to start her next sleep regression any week now. The last thing Ben wants is to have to face that all on his own when he's got so much work to do.'

At this, her mother turned around and faced her again.

'You know, that sounds remarkably like an excuse.'

'It's not an excuse. It's a very legitimate reason.'

Her mother's gaze narrowed.

'Fine,' Holly huffed, then got back to her packing.

It wasn't that she didn't want to go away. Part of her was relishing the idea of uninterrupted sleep and actual lie-ins for the first time in eight months. Even on the nights when Ben had Hope, Holly still woke up early and found herself unable to get back to sleep. And getting to sleep without Hope in the room was harder than she'd anticipated. Though she was managing a lot better now.

Those first weeks after she'd moved into the cottage, she would roll over in her bed and open her eyes at random times in the middle of the night, only to bolt upright, panicking at the sight of the empty crib. Even when she realised where Hope was, she would have to fight the urge to text Ben and check everything was okay. Normally, it was an urge she lost, and no matter how amicably she and Ben navigated co-parenting, there was only so often she could text her ex-boyfriend at three in the morning to check on his parenting abilities and him not get annoyed.

Thankfully for Ben, she'd reined in the late-night texting now, but that was when she was in the same country. This was going to be a whole different kettle of fish.

'I need you to send me lots of photos,' her mother said, taking over the packing, re-folding various items of clothing that Holly had strewn over the bed. 'Do you even know where this villa is yet?'

'It's the south of France.'

'France is quite a big area, dear. And are you sure you've got enough money? Your dad and I can scrape together a bit to help you if you need.'

It was a lovely offer, but Holly knew exactly how much money her mum and dad had, and it was even less than her. Her father had upped his hours at the shop to help accommodate the time Holly needed to be off with Hope, but in contrast, her mother had dropped her hours cleaning to help with the babysitting. It had been a masterpiece of juggling, with Holly having Hope for two weekdays and one weekend, Ben cramming all the work he needed to do into four days a week so that he could have Hope for the extra weekday and the weekend and her mother filling in all the gaps. Somehow, they had made it work.

'Thank you, Mum, but I've got this covered.'

'Well, I'm sure we can help if you need. I don't want you to miss out on anything because you're worried about the cost. You need to enjoy this holiday. You deserve it after the last couple of years.'

It was true. Holly had been working flat out since taking over the sweet shop and having Hope, but this holiday was unlikely to be the lazy lounging on the beach her mother imagined.

Planning for Jamie and Fin's joint hen and stag had started less than a month after Hope had been born.

'Ben and I can't both go,' she'd told her former housemates when they'd proposed the idea of going on an adventure trip abroad. 'Even if we're getting on well, one of us needs to stay with Hope. It wouldn't be fun for you guys having a crying baby on your holiday.'

'We wouldn't mind that,' Fin replied graciously, but even if it was the truth, it wouldn't be fair to the other guests.

'I've already spoken to Ben about it,' Jamie cut in. 'And he's not that keen on going. I mean, there's going to be a lot of focus on water sports and you know what Ben is like with water.'

Holly knew exactly what Jamie was talking about. She'd found this out when she unknowingly booked their second date together at a water obstacle course, only to discover that Ben couldn't swim and had to be rescued by a bunch of teenagers. Yes, she could easily believe that kind of holiday wasn't his idea of fun. But that didn't change the fact she'd have to leave Hope. And then there was the other factor.

'I appreciate what you're trying to do.' She looked at both Jamie and Fin as she spoke. 'I really do, but even if Ben has Hope, I don't think there's any way I can afford it. Not with the extra salaries I have to pay at the shop now.'

She had thought that would be the end of it. Her friends would have to accept she wasn't going to be able to make it, but that's when Jamie gave the real kicker.

'It's not going to cost you anything.' She grinned.

'What do you mean?'

'Fin's best man is covering the accommodation.'

'What? You can't mean for everyone? He hasn't even met us.'

Jamie shrugged, as if someone paying for half a complete stranger's holiday wasn't a big deal. 'Oh, he earns crazy money in London.'

He must be half crazy too, Holly wanted to add. Maybe he was one of those loner types who used his money to buy friends. Although that didn't seem likely knowing Fin.

'There's still the flight to get there.' Holly had never been to the south of France, but she could imagine it wouldn't be cheap. Rather than trying to convince Holly it would be all right, Jamie looked to her fiancé. Sheepish grins spread across both their faces.

'That one's on me,' Fin said. 'Or at least, my frequent flier account.'

'What do you mean?'

'Fin has loads of airmiles,' Jamie said, taking Holly's hand. 'Literally tonnes, from his skateboarding days. And they need using up. He's already said he'll use them to cover your flights. Right?'

'Of course,' Fin replied. 'We need you there.'

'Hope will be fine with Ben,' Jamie continued. 'And we will have an amazing time. You never know, there might even be a holiday romance on the cards for you.'

Holly scoffed at this remark. Romance was entirely off the table for now, but she had known then there was no way out of the trip. She would be going. Or at least, she had agreed to.

There had been six months between Jamie and Fin's announcement of the holiday and the date they were actually going, so Holly had assumed something would crop up or she would come up with a believable excuse as to why she wouldn't be able to go. But the six months had come and gone and now the day was upon her. In half an hour, Michael would arrive to drive her and Caroline to the airport, and Holly would fly off to a different country, away from Hope for the first time since she had been born. Just the thought of it was enough to fill her with nausea.

'You won't forget Mummy, will you?' She bent down and picked the child up off the floor. 'And be good for Daddy, but not too good, okay? I don't want him finding it too easy without me, so a couple of sleepless nights would be all right.'

Her eyes prickled with heat. Without a word, her mother came round behind and wrapped her arms around her.

'You are going to be just fine. Don't forget I'm still here. I'll be looking after her too. Just try to enjoy yourself, okay?'

Holly was about to reply how she didn't think that would be possible, but her words were cut short by the ringing of the doorbell. Feeling like her heart was about to explode, she pulled Hope in close.

'Well, that's it. I guess Daddy is here to pick you up.'

3

'We'll be down in a minute.'

While Ben chatted with her mother downstairs, Holly was double checking everything. She had packed Hope's favourite snuggly, although she knew there was one identical at Ben's house, plus an extra spare they'd bought in case tragedy struck and they lost them both. She had packed her a new tub of nappy rash cream, in case Ben had run out, not to mention the baby nail clippers. Nail clipping was her job, so that would be something she'd have to remind Ben about, in case Hope went through a rapid nail growth spurt in the four days she was gone. Still, it felt like she had forgotten something. Or rather, everything.

'Holly, are you coming?'

Knowing she couldn't avoid it forever, she grabbed the baby monitor and shoved it into the side pocket of Hope's bag before she trudged downstairs.

Ben was sitting on the sofa, though he stood up the moment Holly appeared.

'How are you feeling?'

'Terrified,' she admitted.

'You'll be fine. We both will.'

To an untrained eye, Ben's smile looked perfectly relaxed, though Holly could see the terror flitting away behind his pupils. Throughout the last eight months, they had tried to parent as evenly as they could, and Ben had never shunned any of his responsibilities, but his frequent days and nights working away in London, combined with Holly breastfeeding until only a month ago, meant he'd never had Hope for more than one night. So this trip away was likely to be a steep learning curve for them both.

'I thought it might be a good idea if we did a quick scan of the checklist before you leave.' She reached for a piece of paper on the sideboard. 'Just to go through the routines and make sure we've got everything.'

'You mean the checklist you sent me last night?'

'I think it would do us both good, just to make sure I didn't forget anything.'

Ben's lips twisted.

'I know the routines, Holly. Hope is my daughter, remember?'

She could hear the tension in his voice and normally she would know that was a sign to drop matters, but there was no way she'd be able to relax if she didn't go over a few last-minute details.

'I know you get the routines, but there are a few things that are different. I've written it all down, but I'm not sure if my instructions are clear so, maybe if you could read them through before you leave and then we can address any questions you might have?'

Ben nodded slowly and looked at the piece of paper. She had handwritten it originally, but then worried it might be hard to decipher, so had typed it out, at which point she decided it was probably sensible to get it laminated just in case Hope spilled anything on it. However, judging by Ben's face, the lamination may have been a step too far.

'I do have one question, actually.' He placed the instruction leaflet on the side table and picked Hope up from the ground.

'You do?' Holly felt both relieved and terrified. If he had questions this early on, it didn't bode well for the rest of the trip.

'Are you going to switch off at all this week? Because Jamie is going to need to give you a sedative if not. For her sake and mine.'

Out of the corner of her eye, Holly saw the smirk twist on her mother's lips.

'I think he has a point, darling.'

It was hard not to feel ganged up on, but before she could respond, her mother had moved forward and was squeezing her tightly.

'I should get going and leave you to it,' she said. 'It doesn't help to have a third person in here. As lovely as your home is, there's not exactly room for all of us.' After squeezing Holly's hands again, she moved across and kissed Hope on the forehead. 'And I shall see you tomorrow, my little one. Be good for your daddy, won't you?'

'Thank you, Wendy.' Ben offered a slight peck to her cheek. 'I'll be in touch later today.'

'There's no rush. We're all going to be fine, aren't we?'

When her mother reached the doorway, she offered a final farewell, blowing Holly one last kiss. 'Have fun, my darling. And please try to relax.'

The front door clicked closed and a moment of silence descended.

'You've really made this place home.' Ben's gaze lingered on the mantelpiece, which was filled to bursting with photos. The frames were a hodgepodge of styles Holly had picked up at charity shops, but the photos had a very clear theme running through. There was Hope on her play mat, Hope and Holly, Hope and her grandparents, and even a photo of the three of them – Ben, Hope and Holly – on a family day out to Birdland.

That photo was the first Holly had put up when she moved in. It felt important it was there, prominently, showing Hope that the three of them were a family, even if they weren't together in the traditional sense. She always felt strange about Ben seeing it, though.

'So, shall we go through the checklist?' she said, breaking the silence.

For the next fifteen minutes, she bombarded Ben with facts about Hope and her routine, all of which she was absolutely certain he knew, but he listened nonetheless. He listened when she told him about the bedtime routine that he had done himself hundreds of times. She repeated the importance of naptimes, particularly the morning nap, and also gave him strict instructions to keep the television volume on low while Hope was asleep in case she woke up. This point was definitely unnecessary, as Ben listened to the television on the lowest volume possible, so much so that Holly had always needed the subtitles on when she'd watched TV at his. Still, she needed to reinforce the point, just in case there had been a dramatic change in his habits since she had moved away.

'Okay, that's it from me.' Rather than the flood of relief Holly had expected at finishing her list of do's and don'ts, she was now even more nervous than before. After all, reciting the checklist meant she was one step closer to leaving. 'Is there anything else we need to go over? My phone should work, and I'll message you as soon as I'm there to check. If not, I'll send you the number of Fin's friend who rented the villa and the landline of the villa too, assuming it has one.'

'Holly, it is fine. Hope and I will be absolutely fine.' She nodded, about to double check with him which type of formula he had bought, when he spoke again. 'Actually, there is something I'd like to ask you about. Not a question so much... yes, actually... I suppose it is a question... I think.'

He dug his hands into his pockets. Holly's insides surged with fear. Digging his hands into his pockets was one of Ben's nervous actions. Her throat closed shut in sudden panic. Perspiration beaded on the back of her neck. Was he going away to London? That was the first thought that struck her. He was about to tell her he had to go on a trip to London, and planned on taking Hope with him, dragging her to meetings and restaurants at all hours of the day or night. Or worse, expected her parents to look after Hope, without first asking them about it. Holly could feel her temperature rising as she fought her fury down. A tendon twitched on her jawline and she was a split second from calling the trip off when Ben spoke again.

'I wondered if it would be okay to introduce Hope to Georgia?'

'Georgia?' Holly paused, the fury that had been about to burst open, suddenly cut short by this unexpected request. 'As in, Georgia that you work with, Georgia?'

'Yes, that Georgia.'

Holly's eyebrows rose with a slight crease of confusion forming between them.

'I guess. I mean, of course you can. You can introduce Hope to whichever of your colleagues or friends you want. I don't have a problem with that.'

'That's the thing...' Ben's lips pressed tightly together as his words drifted into silence. A new sense of confusion was prickling Holly as she tried to work out why Ben would act so strangely. It wasn't as if Georgia was some seedy character. Of the little Holly had seen of her, she seemed perfectly fine, if a little too attractive...

Ben's eyes were trained on the ground where Hope was playing, and when he lifted his gaze, his attention went to the picture of the three of them on the mantelpiece.

When he finally looked back at Holly, his neck and face had coloured with a deep red blush.

'The thing is, I don't want to introduce her as a colleague,' he said. 'I want to introduce her as my girlfriend.'

4

'I realise this is probably quite a shock.'

Holly stood mutely in front of Ben, her jaw hanging open.

Shock didn't come close to it. She was floored. So much so that she realised she was holding on to the back of the chair, probably to keep herself from toppling over.

It wasn't that she was angry; she was too surprised for that. Ben had been single for years and years before getting together with her, yet he was now so comfortable in his new relationship he wanted to introduce this woman to his daughter after only a few months. No, it was pure and undiluted disbelief that was making it impossible for her to respond.

'Maybe this wasn't the best time to bring it up.' Ben edged away from her by a half-step. The minute movement was all Holly needed to bring her back to the moment.

'Congratulations!' She blurted the word out so loudly Hope jumped. But that wasn't the worst of it. Before she knew what she was doing, she was taking Ben's hand and shaking it repeatedly as if it was part of some bizarre job interview and he had just been offered the position. And along with the handshaking, came the babbling.

'That's wonderful news. Wonderful. I am so pleased for you. You must be ever so happy. I want to hear all about it.'

'You do?'

'Of course!' Holly wished she could stop talking. Of course she didn't want to hear about her ex-boyfriend's new woman. She already knew Georgia was impossibly beautiful, held an extremely impressive job, and undoubtedly had her life far more together than Holly did. Yet her tongue, which only moments ago had struggled to make a single sound, was now on overdrive. 'You and I are friends. Of course I want to know these things. I'm happy for you. Happy you're happy. Happy Georgia's happy. It's just happiness all round. I couldn't be more pleased.' She lifted her hands into the air emphatically as if about to go for a hug, while simultaneously praying the world would open up and swallow her whole.

'Well, I'm glad you're okay about it.' Thankfully, Ben stepped back to avoid any awkward embraces.

'Of course, of course. Now, why don't you tell me all about it while I get Hope's bags together?'

Twenty minutes later, after Ben had finally left with Hope and her belongings, Holly was sitting at the bottom of her staircase, banging the heel of her hand against her forehead.

Why had she asked to hear all about it? She didn't want to know how long they had been together, or how fantastic Georgia had been about the situation with Hope. She didn't want to know any of it, but now she did. Ben had a girlfriend, and it opened a torrent of thoughts she couldn't avoid.

What was Hope going to call Georgia? That was one question she couldn't shake. She hadn't even started saying mummy or mama yet. Was it possible she would skip Holly entirely and say Georgia first? Unlikely, given the difficulty in her name, but then maybe Hope would call them both mum. Perhaps Georgia would be so good at the stepmother role that Hope would prefer her and call her mama instead?

The thoughts somersaulted around in her head, one after another, each more ridiculous than the last, and yet she couldn't stop them from spiralling. It was only when her phone buzzed on the step beside her that she realised what the time was.

'We're outside,' Caroline said the instant Holly picked up. 'You need me to come and help with your things?'

'Sorry, I'm just coming.' Holly raced up the stairs to grab her little black suitcase. 'I'll be fine. I'll just be one second.'

With the suitcase in her hand, she dashed back downstairs and double checked the hob and all the windows before finally heading outside.

Despite not coming on the do, Michael had offered to drive both her and Caroline to Bristol airport, while Jamie and some others were going to meet them there. There were a few people Holly didn't know going on the trip, too. Two of Jamie's old school friends were flying in from up north and Fin had buddies who were travelling all the way from the States, as well as someone he knew from London. Assuming there were no delays or major mishaps, they were all supposed to arrive in Nice at the same time.

Although as she climbed in the back seat of the car, Holly couldn't even think about the holiday. She had much more pressing thoughts on her mind.

'Did you not hear us beeping?' Caroline twisted around from the passenger seat as Holly slammed her car door shut.

'Did you know?' Holly couldn't stop the words coming out of her mouth.

'Know what?'

'About Ben and Georgia?'

A frown line formed between Caroline's brows. 'Georgia? The woman he works with?'

'Four months. They've been seeing each other for four months. You swear you didn't know?'

Holly had known Caroline long enough to read her expressions pretty well, and from the way her eyes widened, this was as much news to her as it had been to Holly.

'Wow, that's crazy. But I swear, Hol, I would have told you if I knew something like that. You know I would've done.'

Wordlessly, the two women looked at Michael.

'You have to be joking?' He scoffed. 'You know no one tells me anything, right?'

As much as Holly wanted to talk about something different, like the plans for the next four days, and what Jamie and Fin's friends were like, every time the conversation shifted, her mind would bring it straight back to Ben again.

'It's serious isn't it?' she said, as they turned onto the M5. 'You don't introduce someone to your child unless it's serious, do you? But when's he been seeing her? That's what I want to know. I mean, he's either away working, or he's got Hope overnight. It's not like he has endless free time.'

'He works nights away in London.' Michael kept his eyes on the road. 'Sounds like a perfect excuse for hook-ups, if you ask me.'

Without missing a beat, Caroline bent over from the passenger seat to thump him on the shoulder.

'Ow! What was that for?'

'Because.'

Holly couldn't even muster a smile because as much as she didn't want to think about it, Michael was probably right. Late nights in London with someone in the same job as you, attending the same functions, all dressed up and glamorous, were bound to bring people closer together. All while Holly was at home covered in sicked-up milk and dubious coloured sludges.

Silence filled the car, although, as was often the case in such situations, Caroline was quick to fill it. She twisted over her shoulder to look at Holly.

'You know I don't like to ask this, but you're not... you know...'

'Not what? I don't know what you're saying.'

'You know, regretting stuff. Regretting how it ended with Ben?'

Holly sniffed. She and Ben may not have had the easiest ending, but she had never once doubted that it was the right decision. And while she couldn't deny there was this niggling feeling eating away at her, it wasn't so much about the fact that Ben had moved on, but more how easy it had been for him to do so. No matter how much she would like to believe it, finding someone else to spend time with wouldn't be so straightforward for her. The sweet shop wasn't exactly a hub for single men and even if Mr Perfect strode into her life right now, she wouldn't even have time for him. Until this week, she couldn't even remember the last time she'd shaved her legs – although judging from the state of the bath afterwards, it had been a while. The truth was, she didn't feel like she'd ever have time for anything in her life besides Hope and the shop for a very long time.

'Remind me who else is going on this hen and stag do again?' Michael's over jovial tone was a clear attempt to distract from the fact that Holly still hadn't answered Caroline's question. 'Anyone I know?'

With a deep breath in, Holly forced her thoughts away from her eternally single future and answered.

'Besides Sandra, Jamie's mum, I don't think there's anyone any of us know,' she said. 'It's going to be strange, hanging out with so many people we've never met before.'

'I can't wait to meet Jamie's old school friends,' Caroline joined in, having dropped the comment about Holly and Ben. 'I can't imagine what they're like. Jamie says they're nothing like her, but they've been best friends since primary school.'

'Nothing like Jamie,' Michael responded. 'That could mean anything. Girly, quiet...'

'Hey!' Caroline thumped him for the second time.

Holly laughed to herself. She really had landed on her feet with finding friends in Bourton. Two years ago, she hadn't even known Jamie; now she was flying off to the south of France for her hen do. And reconnecting with Caroline had felt like one of the best turns of events she could have taken.

Her head was still filled with soppy sentimentality when her phone buzzed with a message from Ben.

Her heart spiked as she fumbled to open the text. She hadn't even been gone an hour and he was already messaging. There was no way he would manage four days away.

'Crap, this can't be good.'

Steeling herself to tell Caroline she wouldn't be coming, Holly swiped right to open the message – an image of Ben standing in the middle of the river paddling Hope's feet in the water.

Have fun Mummy

'Everything all right?' Caroline asked.

Holly continued to stare at the wide smiles that shone up at her through the glass of her screen. Ben, with his nephew and niece, and countless young cousins, had already had far more experience with young children than she had when Hope was born, and it all came so naturally to him. They were going to be fine. They were going to be just fine.

She, on the other hand, was a different matter entirely.

5

They reached the airport just before ten and had strict instructions from Jamie to head straight through to departures and meet them at a café for brunch. However, first they had to drop off their luggage. Given what a luxury this trip abroad was, Holly had considered buying a new suitcase. She and her ex, Dan, had never been big on holidays and had never needed proper luggage. As such, the only suitable suitcase she had was the one she'd taken to university over ten years ago. But the wheels still worked, and it was big enough to fit everything she needed in, so there was no need to spend extra money when she didn't have to. And so she rolled her small, black and moderately scratched suitcase to the baggage drop.

'Aren't you checking anything in?' Holly gestured to the small bag slung over Caroline's shoulder.

'No. I think it's travelling with three kids. I never have room for any of my stuff. Besides, I've got a swimsuit and extra bra in my coat pocket and two extra vest tops on under this T-shirt and I filled my jean pockets with socks.'

Holly didn't know whether to be amazed or alarmed.

Unlike Caroline, Holly had needed her entire suitcase. Between her swimsuits, flip-flops, books to read and a couple of nice outfits for the evening, she had been amazed at how much space she'd used. Still, it wasn't like she was going to do this again for a long time and the last thing she wanted to do was regret not having a certain top or dress. She had even purchased a couple of small items too, her favourite of which was a silk sarong she'd found in a charity shop in Moreton-on-Marsh. The delicate, teal fabric was embroidered with beads and was something she'd never have considered buying normally, but she was going on a proper holiday and she was going to enjoy it, even if she did spend half the time worrying about Hope.

'Now that Ben's dating, have you thought about doing the same?' Caroline said as Holly lifted her suitcase onto the conveyer belt and watched it disappear out of view. 'You never know, maybe one of Fin's friends will be single and good looking and, you know, super into new mums.'

Holly turned around to face her friend. This time she was the one who did the shoulder thumping.

'Hey! What was that for?' Caroline frowned, looking far more wounded than the soft thump warranted. 'A holiday romance could be fun.'

Trying to choose her words carefully, Holly took a deep breath and placed her hands firmly on Caroline's shoulders.

'I know you and Jamie and every other person have all these wonderful intentions when you talk about me moving on. But please don't. I'm not there. I don't have room for it, not in my head or my heart, or my timetable. All I want is a few days where I can close my eyes, read my book or swim in the pool, and not have to worry about anybody but myself. Romance is not on my mind. Full stop. So even if one of Fin's friends is attractive and single and absolutely perfect in every way possible, I will not be interested.

Please, please tell me you understand that. I do not want a relationship.'

'I hear what you're saying, but...'

Considering how good her speech was, Holly expected Caroline to agree immediately, and possibly apologise for bringing the subject up, but instead, her frown tightened and her lips twisted.

'What? What is it?' Holly had known Caroline long enough to know this look meant she had a strong opinion she wasn't sure she should be sharing.

'Nothing, it's nothing.' Caroline waved her hand flippantly, then turned around and marched away at a pace, leaving Holly scurrying behind.

'Just spit it out.'

'It doesn't matter. You don't want to hear it.' They were walking away from the baggage drop now, towards the security. As they reached the queue, Caroline stopped in her tracks and looked Holly square in the eye. 'Fine. I was going to say that I can't help wondering if you swearing off romance has something to do with... you know... the other one.'

'The other one? Really?' There was no point in Holly playing ignorant; she knew exactly who Caroline meant. Giles Caverty. The one-time shop saboteur with whom her relationship had dramatically transformed during her pregnancy. Giles had become a secret staple in her life during those months before Hope's birth. They'd secretly met on their weekly food shops, where he had helped lift the heavy items in and out of the trolly and poke fun at her ever-growing bump. But it had been more than that. Giles had been there for her, emotionally, when Ben hadn't. When Holly's father had his heart attack, Giles had driven her to the hospital and waited to rescue her from the pouring rain. Giles, who had rushed to the hospital the moment he heard Hope had been born.

No matter how much she had tried to avoid it, Holly knew she'd

probably felt more for him than she should have, given her relationship with Ben at the time. And Giles had made it abundantly
clear how he felt for her. But with Hope's arrival, she had been
forced to consider her priorities and her daughter had to come first.
That was who she chosen. Herself, and Hope.

As such, she hadn't heard from Giles for nearly eight months.
The last time she'd had any contact with him at all was when she
received a large bouquet and a giant pink bunny rabbit for Hope,
two weeks after Hope's birth, signed with two words.

Be Happy

Only a couple of months ago, just thinking about that note
made her eyes well up, but she'd put it down to hormones. Now,
though, the words felt like a dull ache behind her ribs, which she
tried assiduously to ignore. It was for the best. She hadn't been in a
position back then to consider starting a new relationship, particularly not with someone as flaky and untrustworthy as Giles Caverty.
But that didn't mean she didn't miss him. She missed the ease of
their conversations and the way he would speak to her even more
bluntly than Jamie and Caroline combined. They were incommuni-
cado, and that was the way it was meant to be.

But she wasn't going to say all that to Caroline.

'No, this doesn't have anything to do with Giles, or the fact that
Ben is seeing Georgia, or any other man, woman or creature in the
universe.' She glowered at Caroline with all the force she could
muster. 'This is to do with the fact that I am perfectly fine on my
own. I like my life exactly as it is. I have Hope. We have our beautiful, tiny family and I don't need or want anybody else to come in
and mess up the good thing we have going. So before you start
sussing out which of Fin's friends are single, can we just keep that in
mind?'

It wasn't often that Holly managed to silence Caroline. In fact, she couldn't think of a single time it had happened since her return to the Cotswolds. And yet for a split second, Caroline remained utterly mute.

'I guess that's me told.' She slipped off her coat and put it on a tray to roll through the scanner. 'So I assume that means I shouldn't mention that this friend of Fin's who's sorted out the villa is single? And apparently exceptionally eligible?'

Holly shook her head. Sometimes she wondered how she could both love and want to throttle her friend so much at the same time.

'You can mention it all you want. It doesn't mean that I care.'

'Fine. Then I won't mention it again.'

Holly hummed to herself. Not for one second did she think it was true.

They waited their turn to pass through the scanners. For Holly, it was a chance to people-watch. There were all sorts. Young couples. Old, solo travellers. And several lone parents with a toddler in tow. She looked on at these with a sense of awe. Some days, even taking Hope as far as Cheltenham was a mission, and she couldn't even walk yet. The thought of getting on a plane and travelling to an entirely unknown country with her caused Holly's stomach to twist into knots. Thankfully or not, it wasn't something she'd have to worry about soon. Not with their current financial situation.

The pair were just on the other side of the scanners, stuffing their belongings hurriedly back into their bags, when their phones pinged simultaneously. As Holly was still trying to cram a clear plastic bag of toiletries into a pocket – it had previously fitted in perfectly – Caroline was the one that read the message aloud.

'So apparently they are at the champagne bar. We've got to meet them there.'

'The champagne bar?' Holly looked down at her wrist. 'But it's just gone ten. They can't be drinking already, can they?'

A quizzical expression clouded Caroline's face.

'It's the airport...' she said, as if it were obvious.

'And...?' Holly said, unsure what difference that made.

'So it doesn't matter what time it is. You can always have a drink at the airport.'

'You can?'

'Definitely. It's a universal rule. I thought everyone knew that.'

Still doubting the validity of Caroline's comment, Holly considered the implications of heading to a champagne bar. It didn't matter what time of day it was; it was still going to be expensive, even if she had a soft drink. Perhaps, she hoped, she would be able to get away with a glass of tap water. Besides, drinking at this time didn't seem a good idea, particularly as she hadn't had breakfast yet.

As they weaved their way through the duty-free perfumes and oversized boxes of chocolates, Holly's mind wandered back to what she had said to Caroline about being fine. It was true. Despite everything that had happened, she had reached a level of independence she would never have dreamed of three years ago. She was no longer stuck waiting for a future that wouldn't exist, in a relationship with a man who didn't appreciate her or in a job that sucked her soul dry and left her with no energy to enjoy life.

That didn't mean it wouldn't be nice to share her future with someone, but if she did meet someone now, they would have to fit in around her life, and not the other way round.

As she rounded the corner, she caught sight of the group sitting together on the stools next to the bar.

'Over here!' Jamie was on her feet waving at them, with Fin by her side. But Holly's attention didn't stay with them for long. Her eyes were drawn to the man topping up Sandra's glass with a bottle of bubbles. And once she'd seen him, she couldn't take her eyes away.

'Damn.' Caroline's gaze was trained on the exact spot as Holly's. They were staring, but it was impossible to draw her eyes away. If it hadn't been for the fact he was talking to Sandra, Holly wouldn't have believed he was with their group, but there he was.

'Damn indeed,' she said eventually.

6

'We need to stop staring,' Caroline whispered, aware that Holly was as mesmerised by the figure next to Jamie as she was.

'I'm not staring. I'm just not able to move right now, that's all.'

Given her speech only moments before, Holly was more than a little embarrassed by her opened-mouth ogling, yet thankfully, Caroline was in the same position. In all her life, Holly couldn't remember gawking at a man the way she was now. She'd seen attractive men before, of course. The office in London was full of sharply dressed Henry Cavill wannabes, with their slick hair and tailored waistcoats. There were the joggers who went running around the village, headphones on and entirely topless, knowing their perfect six – or sometimes eight – pack was on display. But that was the difference. Those men were trying to be noticed. This one... this one didn't have to try.

In a plain grey T-shirt and pair of jeans, he looked like he belonged on the cover of a magazine rather than here in an airport lounge topping up Sandra's drink. His sharp cheekbones and square jaw were unfeasibly symmetrical, and while his thick eyebrows would have swamped some people's features, on him they just highlighted the bright blue of his eyes. Saying that this man was attractive was like saying an Irish Wolfhound was a big dog: an understatement of the greatest proportion.

'See, Mum, you owe me a tenner.' Jamie patted her mother on the back, before grinning at Holly. 'Mum said you wouldn't come. She made me bet that you'd get cold feet about leaving Hope. But I had faith in you.'

At the realisation of how much she'd been staring, a hot blush coloured Holly's cheeks. She crossed the bar quickly and embraced her old housemate.

'No cold feet here,' Holly said, to which Caroline quirked an eyebrow. 'Okay, maybe slightly cold feet, but I pushed past them. You know I wouldn't miss this. I'm excited.'

'I think we're all pretty excited.' The voice was a deep, American drawl that resonated right into Holly's chest. With her heart beating unfeasibly fast, she turned her head towards the speaker.

'Holly, Caroline. This is Evan Roth. Evan, this is Caroline and Holly.'

'Glad to meet you. Here.' He gestured to a bottle in his hand. 'I assume you two are drinking?'

Holly scanned the group. While Fin was nursing a luminous green smoothie, both Jamie and Sandra were sipping away at drinks from tall champagne glasses, and they weren't the only ones. The bar was packed full of people drinking everything from cocktails to bottled beers.

'See.' Caroline read Holly's expression of disbelief perfectly. 'Any time is drinking time in an airport.'

'I'll take it that's a yes.' Evan promptly filled up two glasses with prosecco, though Holly hesitated before taking one. Until now, her nerves about Hope had been enough to supersede her worry about flying. But the closer they got to boarding, the harder it was to ignore just how anxious she was. Looking down at the glass, she decided that perhaps a drink to take the edge off things wouldn't be so bad. Maybe that was why airport bars were so popular.

'Cheers.' Evan lifted his glass, prompting the others to do the same. A collective clinking followed before Holly took a sip.

'I hadn't realised you were American.' Caroline lowered her glass before she spoke. 'I thought you lived in London?'

'Caroline, right?' He confirmed her name, as well as confirming to Holly the depth of his drawl. 'I live in London now. But Fin and I go way back. I'd already moved over here when he quit the competitions to do his boards full-time. I was looking to move into a different market and he needed someone to help set up the business side of things, so we ended up working together for a couple of years. Kind of serendipitous, you might say.'

'Very serendipitous.' Caroline's eyes glazed and Holly was worried her friend might physically swoon, but before that happened, she shifted her stance and gestured to her side. 'Oh, and this is Holly. She runs her own business too.'

It couldn't have been any more obvious. Holly wouldn't have been so annoyed if they hadn't just been extensively discussing how she didn't want to be pushed onto any of Fin's single friends. As such, at this moment, her nerves were overridden by her sense of irritation.

'Jamie already introduced us, remember? About two minutes ago.' It wasn't the politest response, but she had been aiming her annoyance solely at Caroline. Only when a silence spread between the group did she realise just how rude she had come across. Clearing her throat, she forced herself to smile.

'Sorry, Evan. Thank you so much for paying for the accommodation. It's really generous. I feel like I should give you something towards the cost.'

The way Holly had been brought up meant she'd never forgive herself if she didn't offer to pay her way, but she wasn't exactly sure what she would do if Evan suddenly agreed to split the cost. She could only hope they were staying somewhere cheap.

'It's really not a big deal.' His slight smile caused his eyes to gleam even brighter than before. 'I've actually just bought the villa, so us going out together gives me a chance to see it. And figure out how much work the place needs.'

'You just bought a villa in the south of France?' Holly spoke slowly, just to make sure she had understood him fully. 'But you haven't seen it yet and you don't know if it needs to have work done on it?'

She had not intended to be humorous. If anything, she was simply checking his sanity, but the chuckle that resonated from Evan was so deep, his vocal cords could have been made of double bass strings.

'Don't worry, I'm not crazy. Well, maybe a little. I had a reputable estate agent involved. And I've had plenty of video calls to see the place. Not to mention a buddy of mine checked it out a couple of times, too. The area is good, and I know it's not crumbling down completely, so how bad can it be?'

Once again, that smile glinted, yet the nerves Holly felt at flying were now joined by the deepest sinking feeling.

'How bad indeed?' With a long sip of her drink, she hoped to cover her expression. Not only was she spending four days away from Hope for the first time ever, but now the owner of the villa they were staying in didn't even know how bad the place was going to be. She could see it now: the algae-filled swimming pool, with frogs hopping in and out of it. Creaking fans rattling on the ceiling and holes in the plasterboard as big as her fist. Bedbugs, fleas, mouse droppings, rat-chewed furniture...

With another long gulp, she finished the drink in her hand.

'Here, you need a top up.' Evan reached for the bottle in the wine cooler, only this time, Holly glanced at the label. A new level of tension surged through her. Champagne. No wonder it tasted so damn good. It probably cost more than half a dozen bottles of the plonk she normally bought.

'I shouldn't,' she said, covering her glass with her hand.

'It's on me.'

'Really, it's not necessary.'

The bottle remained hovering at an angle over her hand.

'Half a glass?'

Before she could refuse his offer again, Jamie was leaning over her shoulder.

'You can't tell me you're refusing free drink?' Jamie thrust her own glass forward, at which point, Evan promptly moved the bottle to top it up. 'This is a celebration. You need to switch off. Relax.'

'I have switched off,' Holly lied. 'But I haven't eaten yet today, that's all. I don't want to make myself ill on the plane.'

Jamie's eyebrows rose.

'She's having a top up,' she said, taking Holly's glass and holding it out to Evan. However, rather than immediately topping it up, as she expected him to do, he didn't move.

'Are you sure? I can order you something else if you'd rather. They do food here too. We've got time to get something before the plane goes if you need to eat?'

Whether it was all the other pressures of the day, or the fact that she couldn't remember the last time she had looked an attractive man dead in the eye, Holly didn't know, but as their gazes locked on one another, her heart rate took an upward turn. A large lump forced its way up her throat. When she finally swallowed it down, she could feel herself turning crimson.

'Another drink would be lovely,' she said.

7

Despite the fact the group had arrived at the airport with plenty of time, when they headed to the gate, they saw a mass of people already awaiting the first boarding announcement. Caroline was deep in conversation with Sandra, while Jamie and Fin were sharing what was likely to be one of many intimate moments, giggling as they rubbed their noses together. For most people, Holly would've thought a mixed hen and stag do would have been a disaster waiting to happen. The type of thing a couple with major trust issues did. But for these two, it was the perfect idea. They were both active and outdoorsy and enjoyed the same things. And when you looked at the pair of them together, it was obvious there was no one's company they enjoyed more than each other's. Which, Holly figured, was the way it should be if you were planning to spend the rest of your life with that person. When viewed like that, it was surprising that more people didn't do joint events like this.

'I like her. I wasn't sure I would, but I do.'

There was no mistaking the deep, American drawl, though the three early-morning glasses of bubbly meant it took Holly a second to realise Evan was speaking to her.

'Sorry, I was miles away. What did you say?'

'Jamie. I wasn't sure I would like her. But she's great. Really great.'

Holly cast her eyes to her old housemate, who was currently resting her head on Fin's shoulder, a broad smile still on her face although her eyes were closed.

'She is,' Holly agreed. 'She's the best. Though since we are being honest about friends, I should probably confess that I wasn't a fan of Fin when I first met him. I thought he was way too hippy, and that they were moving way too fast.'

'Crazily fast! You have no idea how much I warned him against it. Going on holiday together after a month? That was ridiculous. At least I thought so. I assumed she was a gold-digger.'

'I assumed the same of him!' Holly laughed. It felt weird talking so openly – and somewhat meanly – about Fin to a man who was one of his closest friends, but Evan had an incredibly relaxed demeanour. Besides, he had started the conversation.

'You thought Fin was a gold-digger?' His eyebrows rose in disbelief. 'Did you not know who he was?'

'Do I look like much of a skateboarder to you?'

'Hey. I've seen skateboarders of all types. I'm not judgemental.'

Judgemental wasn't a word that Holly had ever used to describe herself, and though he hadn't done so directly, there was still an implication, which Holly didn't like.

'I wouldn't say I'm judgemental,' she said with a sudden urge to defend herself. 'As it happens, I've already agreed that Fin can teach Hope to skateboard as soon as she can walk.'

'Hope? That's your daughter? Fin mentioned her. You were living with Fin and Jamie when she was first born, right?'

'Yes, I was.' The ease that had previously flowed through their conversation was dissipating fast. Holly wasn't sure why this stranger knowing about her and Hope made her awkward. Was he judging her? Probably. That was likely the reason he had called her judgemental in the first place. Judgemental people always did that, didn't they? Reflected what they were thinking. Here was a man who could buy a villa in France and bottles of champagne at extortionate airport prices. Even if the villa was as shabby and dilapidated as Holly feared, he still owned a property somewhere. That was a life goal she looked unlikely to achieve any time soon.

'I was living with Jamie before Fin was.' The need to defend herself was likely spurred by the early-morning drink, but the last thing she needed was people making assumptions about her. 'I moved in with her when I first came to Bourton, before she'd even met him, and long before Ben and I got together. And I asked them if they wanted me to move out, several times. But Ben, Hope's dad, lives in the house next door, so it made sense that I stay with them, at least when she was first born. But then this cottage came up to rent, and it was a great price and closer to the shop, and I knew that Jamie and Fin needed their space, even though they insisted they were fine and liked having us live there. So yes, I lived there with them when my daughter was first born, but I don't now.'

'Wow.' Evan expelled a long breath. 'That's a lot of detail to take in from a question I'd just expected a yes or no answer to.'

Holly clamped her mouth shut. One day, she would learn not to babble like a fool every time she was remotely nervous.

When she finally got a hold of herself, she looked at Evan, and found herself unable to read his expression. His eyes were narrowed ever so slightly, with the tiniest smile twisting at the corners of his lips.

'I babble.' She once again found the need to defend herself. 'It's a thing I do. I babble when I'm nervous, and I babble when I've had a drink and right now I'm nervous about flying and leaving Hope, and I've had a drink, as you know, because you were the one who bought it. See, I'm doing it again. Babbling.'

His smile twisted higher. 'I never knew babbling could be quite so cute. You know, Fin said I'd like you. I see why.'

For a split second, Holly was stunned into submission. 'I... I...'

Once again, she was staring at Evan's perfectly chiselled jaw, but it was more the way he was looking at her that was sending her adrenaline sky high. That coy grin. That playful glint in his eyes. Was he flirting with her?

The colour in Holly's cheeks reached a new fluorescent shade as she struggled to work out how to respond. For a second, she considered explaining that she had a child – a baby – and was therefore not in the market or mindset for anything as simple as a bit of harmless flirting. But he already knew that. They had been talking about Hope less than a minute before.

With her brain on overdrive, she knew that any second, the babbling was going to start again. She opened her mouth, preparing for whatever stream of nonsense was about to spew from it, when a voice spoke over the top of them.

'We are now inviting rows one to twelve to board at gate fourteen.'

Grateful for the distraction, Holly looked down at her phone, which displayed her boarding pass. A sigh of relief flew from her lips.

'Looks like this is me.' She held up her phone and waved it just close enough to Evan's face so he could see she was telling the truth. But rather than just believing her, Evan caught the phone between his thumb and finger. A wide grin stretched across his face. Reaching down, he pulled out his phone and flicked it open.

'What do you know? Looks like we'll be sitting next to each other.'

8

Holly was panicking. Again. An orderly queue was forming in front of the gate as they waited for the air stewards to check their passports. And Holly was meant to be in it, ready to board, only she couldn't. She couldn't get on the plane and spend the entire time sitting next to a man who had been so openly flirting with her. Not one as good looking as he was.

'We should probably get in line.' Evan nodded to the queue, but rather than moving to join it, she smiled tightly.

'I'll just be one minute.' Without pausing, she turned around and scampered to where Caroline was behind her, in a deep conversation with Sandra.

'Caroline,' she hissed. 'Caroline. I need you to swap seats with me. Sorry Sandra.'

Interrupting conversations wasn't something she normally did but needs must. Her heart pounded in her chest as Caroline broke off her conversation and turned to Holly. She frowned, each of her reactions infuriatingly slow.

'What's wrong with your seat?' she asked.

'Nothing's wrong with it. I just don't want to sit in it, that's all.'

Caroline scoffed, before offering Holly a withering look, crossing her arms over her chest. It was undoubtedly a tried and tested pose she used with her children. 'I'm hardly going to swap with you if I don't know what's wrong with your seat.'

'I'll swap. I'm not bothered,' Sandra said. 'I've got an aisle seat though—'

'No, don't swap with her. Tell us what's wrong with your seat first,' Caroline pressed.

Holly gritted her teeth. There was no way she wanted to tell Caroline the real reason. If she did, her friend would turn it into this whole thing about Holly finding Evan attractive, and the entire break would be a nightmare as she engineered situations to get the two of them together.

'I just don't like middle seats, that's all.'

Before Holly could say any more, Caroline took Holly's phone from her and entered the password, the way only a true friend could.

'You don't have a middle seat. You're in seat C. It's in the aisle. You'll be fine.' She shrugged as she handed the phone back.

Throwing a quick glance over her shoulder, Holly noticed Evan now queuing up, and he was looking at her expectantly. There would only be so long that she could stand here talking to Caroline before it became obvious what she was doing. Against all her better judgement, she took a steeling breath and spoke again.

'Fine. I'm sitting next to Evan.'

'You are?' This time Caroline turned back to her immediately, her eyes wide and gleaming with mischief.

'Please. I just don't want to have to deal with any small talk at the minute. I just want to read my book in peace. And I've got enough to worry about with Hope and Ben and Georgia and the fact that I don't think anyone truly knows how a plane stays in the sky. I mean, it's weird right? It just floats there. It's not natural. I can't deal with all that, and with sitting next to Evan.'

'Why? Because you fancy him?'

As a grown up, Holly knew it was 100 per cent wrong to slap a person under any circumstances. Even – or possibly especially – someone that was a dear friend. But as a smirk spread onto Caroline's face, so did a sense of burning fury within her.

'I guess that's just fate,' Caroline said.

Holly sucked a deep breath in through her nose. 'It's not fate. It's random number allocations. Please.'

'Nope.' Caroline folded her arms across her chest once more. 'I like my seat and I like the idea of you having to make small talk with the gorgeous Evan for two hours. And there's no point asking Jamie or Fin to swap with you, either. It's been Fin's plan to set you two up since they organised this thing.'

Holly clenched her fists at her side so tightly, it was a miracle she didn't crack her phone.

'Please, Caroline. I'll do whatever you want. I'll babysit. I'll babysit once a week for a month. Two months. Anything.'

She was begging, she knew that, but she couldn't see any other way out of it. The champagne that had felt like such a good idea at the bar was now churning in her stomach and the thought of the take-off alone was turning her dizzy. All she wanted to do was sit on the plane, bury her head in her lap, and close her eyes until it was all over.

'Name your price, I'll do it.'

It was the last offer she could give, but it wasn't enough.

'I'm sorry, Holly, but there are some things you can't put a price on.' Caroline smirked.

The tannoy crackled overhead, once again repeating the request for Holly's rows to board. In one last-ditch effort, she offered Caroline her most desperate, pleading look.

'As my best friend?'

'My conscience just won't let me. Go. Have fun. You might find you like chatting with him. What's the worst that can happen?'

* * *

As it happened, there were quite a few things that could go wrong on a short flight. Particularly when you were as unaccustomed to flying as Holly.

'Is everything all right?' Evan asked when she finally joined him in the queue.

She glanced over her shoulder to where Caroline and Sandra were now giggling conspiratorially with Jamie and Fin.

When she got back to Bourton, she decided, she was going to make a concerted effort to make some new, less interfering friends.

'Yes, fine. I just wanted to check something with Caroline before we boarded.'

'That's good, because for a minute, I was worried you were deliberately trying not to sit next to me.'

Holly laughed. It was high pitched and nasal and made her sound like a complete and utter fool, though thankfully, he only smiled.

'No, nothing like that,' she lied and took a deep breath in.

While boarding was fine, Holly's first issue occurred when she went to lift her bag into the overhead luggage compartment.

'Do you want me to help you with that?' Evan asked in his drawl, which Holly had now determined was both incredibly attractive yet mildly grating, though merely because of its attractiveness.

'Thank you, but I can do it.' Her small handbag was perfectly light – she had packed all her clothes and heavy belongings in her suitcase – but still, she didn't want to keep the bag down by her feet.

It wasn't a matter of leg room either – she wasn't tall enough to worry about that. What she wanted was zero distractions. After eight months of barely being able to catch her breath, she intended to use any spare time to catch up on some of the reading she had missed out on since Hope was born. Besides, she figured Evan would be less likely to chat if he saw she was reading. So she slid her phone into the top pocket, placed her book on her seat, and lift the bag up into the locker once more.

'You know, I can put it up there,' Evan said again.

Given how succinctly she had replied to his previous offer of help, Holly didn't think he warranted a second answer. Ignoring him, she got back to pushing the bag into place.

The problem – along with her lack of height – was the fact that the bag was such an awkward shape. After trying it at one angle, she pulled it back out and tried again. This time the end slid in; all it required was a little bit of jamming in.

It was hard to explain why she didn't simply ask Evan to help her push it in that last couple of inches. With his height, he would have no issue in ensuring it was securely in place. But it was a matter of pride. He'd already called her out for not wanting to sit with him, and then there was the whole thing about calling her cute. Like she was some little, helpless kitten. No, she was certain she could do it herself.

Her bag was three quarters in when Holly stepped back to give herself a little more leverage. Another inch was all it needed to be fully inside, but as she went to push it, someone at the other end of the compartment shoved their oversized suitcase in next to it, making the whole thing that much harder. With an agility she didn't know she possessed, Holly jumped forward and pushed her bag back into place. It bent slightly and then, with just a fraction more pressure, slid in.

'There,' she said, as a smug smile of satisfaction rose on her lips.

Brushing her hands together, she turned and looked to Evan, for no other reason than to confirm she had not at any point required his help, but as she twisted her hips, and took one final glance up, she noticed that all the pushing back and forth had forced the zip on the top to come open. She was staring straight at the bag, wondering if it would be okay, or whether she needed to reach up and try to close the zip, when the shape of the shadow inside seemed to change. She barely had time to register what it was when her phone dropped straight from the gap and hit her squarely between the eyes.

9

The pain seared through her skull, sharp but fleeting, and was immediately replaced by a dull throb that spread out behind her eyes.

'Jeez, are you okay? Holly?'

She blinked, taking a minute to recall exactly what had happened.

'My phone?' She looked down at her feet, her heart lurching. If something happened to Hope, hers would be the first number Ben rang. She needed her phone.

'Don't worry, I've got it.' Evan bent down and picked it up. When he stood up to face her, concern etched in his face.

'Is it broken?'

'You mean the phone? No, the phone's fine. But that was quite a knock you took there. Are you sure you're okay?'

'I'm fine. I'm fine.' Holly already wished she could disappear on the spot. But the humiliation wasn't over yet. Her accident hadn't gone unseen, namely by the person who had shoved their bag at the other end of the luggage compartment. The passenger was a woman with thick, black eyeliner and excessively long nails, which

Holly could see all too clearly as she was currently covering her mouth in shock.

'I'm so sorry.' Her eyes bulged as she stared at Holly's head. 'Are you all right?'

'It's fine,' Holly insisted. 'Honestly, it was just a little bump.'

As Holly was the one who had felt the knock on the head and therefore considered herself in the best position to determine how severe the situation was, she thought that was that.

She expected the woman to accept her answer, but instead, she called, 'Is there a medic aboard?' Her voiced shrilled above the noise of the bustling passengers. 'We need a medic. And ice. We need an ice pack.'

'We don't. We don't need a medic or an ice pack.' Holly's cheeks burned hotter and hotter by the second. 'Honestly, I'm okay. It was just a bump.' The woman was bouncing on her feet, scanning up and down the plane, seemingly oblivious to Holly's pleas. 'We really don't need an ice pack. I'm fine. I'm fine. It's just a bruise.'

She was about to shout over the woman again when a hand pressed against her shoulder. With all the commotion the woman was causing, Holly had almost forgotten Evan was even there. With his eyes on hers, he lifted his hand, and hovered his fingers above the spot where she could feel a bruise blooming.

'It was a big knock you took.' He touched her forehead with his fingertips, causing her to wince. 'I know you British hate a fuss of any sort, but I think she might be right. Maybe it would be better to be safe and have someone check you out.'

'I just want to sit down.'

His eyes locked on hers with the type of intensity that made her skin turn clammy, and for a split second, she thought he was going to refuse and join the woman in yelling for a medic. But he nodded and stood back against his seat, giving her room to get past.

As she clipped on her belt, Holly sat down and had just opened her book when the air steward arrived.

'Yes, that's her.' The woman with the nails pointed at Holly. 'She had a bump on the head. I think you need to check it out before she flies.'

Two minutes later, Holly was having a torch shone in her eyes while simultaneously having to follow an index finger back and forth.

'You've got quite a lump coming up there,' the steward said when she'd stopped waving her fingers about. 'Tell me, any dizziness. Nausea?'

'I mean, the whole thing is so embarrassing, it's making me feel sick, if that counts?'

'What about your vision, any blurriness?'

'Other from the champagne I had before boarding?'

The crew member stiffened. 'Madam, are you intoxicated?'

'No, it was a joke.' Holly cursed her ability to say exactly the wrong thing in the attempt at humour. 'I mean, I had a little champagne, but no, honestly, I am fine. My vision is fine. I don't feel sick. I've just got a bruised head, and bruised ego. That's all.'

'And you feel fine to fly?'

'Better than fine. Well, no, not better. I want to fly. I can fly. I am fine to fly, that's what I'm saying.'

The woman studied her for a moment longer, before standing up and moving into the aisle.

'I'm all right with you flying, but I need you to let me know if anything changes. Any dizziness, sudden sickness. And try to stay awake just in case there is any mild concussion.' The steward turned to Evan. 'Are you travelling together?'

'We are.'

'Then I would ask you to keep a close eye on her and inform us if there are any worrying signs.'

'That would be my pleasure.'

Finally, Holly was left alone to let out a long sigh of relief.

'You know how to make a scene, don't you?' Evan's eyes glinted.

'Not intentionally. Believe me, all I want is to read my book and get through this flight without any more drama.'

'I'm sure that's doable. No more drama. Easy.'

'Exactly. Easy.'

* * *

It was a sign, she thought as she cradled her head in her hands. A sign she should have stayed at home.

'Surely this isn't normal?' she said as turbulence knocked her forwards, then back in the seat. Her stomach churned with each jolt of the plane and her fists were so tightly clenched, her nails had dug divots into her palm. By contrast, Evan was reading an ebook, as relaxed as if he were in a rocking chair.

'It's not unusual. We're probably just flying through some thunder clouds. I doubt it will last long.'

Fifteen minutes later, and Holly's head was between her knees, a paper bag open and any scrap of dignity gone.

'Are you okay there, miss?' The air steward who had dealt with her head was back, holding on to Holly's seat to keep herself steady.

'I am fine,' Holly said at the exact moment that another bout struck. She dived for the paper bag and remained with her head there until the steward left again.

Five minutes later, when the plane was finally smooth again, she took a sip of water and let out a long groan.

'Next time, you should bring some sweets to help,' Evan said. 'I think ginger's meant to be good for sickness, isn't it?'

'I have no idea.' Holly wished his voice was quieter. Something about the deepness of it seemed to resonate into her very skull. Unfortunately, he seemed to be in a mood for conversation.

'You own the sweet shop, don't you?'

'Yes.'

'That must be incredible. I mean, it's a dream, right? From what I've heard Fin say about the place, it's a big kid's paradise. Chocolate hedgehogs, marzipan squirrels. I never liked marzipan growing up, but I've got more of a taste of it now that I'm older. Though I'll always be a chocolate man deep down. Chocolate truffles, ice cream. The lot.'

'Can we please not talk about sweets right now?' A deep breath in caused the taste of bile to sting the back of her throat. 'Or anything else, for that matter?'

She rested her hands on her head. The positive side of the travel sickness was that she had gone a half an hour without worrying about Ben, Hope or Georgia. Also, any hope that Evan still found her cute was well and truly gone. If the massive bruise on her head hadn't done it, then the horrific noises and foul aromas that came from her emptying her stomach into a paper bag would have done. How he still wanted to make conversation with her was, in her mind, a miracle.

'Don't worry.' He placed his hand on her arms. 'When you get to the villa, you can have a dip in the pool. That'll make you feel better.'

Mention of the pool caused images of brown sludge and warty toads to sweep into Holly's mind. Reaching for the bag, she ducked her head and let out another low moan.

10

The rest of the journey was smooth enough until the landing. Despite seeing the ground growing closer and closer through the window, the thud of the wheels hitting the tarmac caught Holly by surprise. Gasping, she reached out and grabbed the arm rest. Only it was already in use, and what she grasped instead was Evan's arm.

'Sorry.' Her hand sprang up away from him.

'It's fine. I hate take offs and landings, too. The rest of it I'm fine with, but it doesn't matter how much I fly; I don't think I'll ever like this part.' He smiled softly before the expression dropped. 'How are you feeling? How's your stomach?'

'Empty, but I think that's a good thing.'

'And what about your head?'

Reaching up, Holly touched the tender spot below her hairline.

'It's fine. Annoying. I'm not normally the clumsy one.'

'Just the one who babbles?'

His eyes caught hers, and she found herself needing to look away. Even then, she could feel him watching her.

The instant the plane stopped, passengers rushed to stand, despite the seatbelt sign remaining on.

'This drives me mad,' Evan said. 'No one can get out until they open the doors. I don't know why everyone stands up so soon. I prefer to sit and wait. It gives me time to think.'

Given how disastrous the flight had been so far, Holly waited in her seat. The fewer bags in the overhead compartment, the less chance of being hit by one. Although it meant sitting next to Evan for even longer. Thankfully, he quickly turned his attention back to his e-reader.

Deciding she might as well do the same, she stuck her nose into her book and began to read again.

'We should probably think about moving?' Evan's voice caught her by surprise, as did the fact that Holly looked up from her page and found the plane only a third full. 'And at the risk of sounding like I don't think you're capable, can I get your bag down for you? It's an entirely selfish request. I'm not sure my French is good enough to deal with a hospital if you knock yourself out this time.'

Standing up, Holly offered him a grateful smile.

'Thank you. That would be helpful.'

While Evan brought the bags down, Holly scanned up and down the plane, searching for the others. Considering how few people were left, they should have been easy to spot, yet there was no sign of them.

'I guess the others have got off already,' she said, taking her bag from Evan. 'I didn't see them pass.'

'They probably went out the back door. Don't worry, we'll see them at immigration.'

He stepped back, allowing her to slip out of the seat.

Just as Evan had said they would, they found the rest of the group in the immigration queue, though they were too far ahead to manage any sort of conversation. And although Evan was right beside her, Holly had bigger things to worry about than small talk.

From the moment they had entered the building, she had tried to send a message to Ben, but it wouldn't go through.

'Sometimes it can take your phone a while to get a signal, that's all,' Evan said, as Holly swore at the screen. 'And there's Wi-Fi at the villa. So you can call them on that. But you can use my phone now if you want? I travel a lot, so I know it works.'

Holly was about to refuse. Using a strange and attractive man's phone to message her ex didn't feel like a good thing to do, but she quickly changed her mind. After all, it wasn't as if there was anything going on with them; she just wanted Ben to know she was there safe, that was all.

'That would be great, thank you.'

Evan held out her phone, though he kept his fingers on it, even when she had taken a hold.

'I think I better keep an eye on that bump on your head. That's twice you've accepted my help now. So either it's a head injury, or you might be starting to like me?'

Holly pressed her lips together and tugged the phone from his grasp. 'Definitely a head injury,' she said, before firing off a message to Ben.

It wasn't until they had made their way through passport control and were waiting by the baggage conveyer belt that she found the others.

Immediately, Caroline tugged her off to the side.

'So, how was your flight?' she asked conspiratorially. 'Two hours sitting next to the beautiful Evan? Not that I'm trying to push you into anything. I'm just saying if I was single, I would go there.'

'Don't. Just don't.'

Caroline went to grin, only for her expression to change as she viewed Holly more closely. 'What happened? It couldn't have been that bad. What did you talk about?'

'It was difficult to do a lot of talking, with my head in a paper bag and everything.'

Caroline's hand didn't quite cover her gasp. 'Oh no. And what happened to your head?'

'Is there a mark?' Holly groaned. So much for thinking the embarrassment was over.

'A mark? If that's what you want to call the massive bruise on your head, then, yes, there's a mark. Did you knock it on something?'

'I'll tell you later,' Holly said, her stomach sinking. So now everyone would be able to see the evidence of her clumsiness. This holiday was just getting worse and worse and it hadn't even started properly. 'Let's go get our bags. I need a nap and food.'

The luggage took its time tumbling out over the conveyer belt, giving the others a chance to go over the plans yet again. There was a lot of nattering and a fair bit of yawning. But while the rest of them chattered away, Holly turned in a circle, trying to take this small airport in. She hadn't even stepped outside yet, but so much about the room was new, exotic even: the different languages on the signs, the different uniforms of people that worked there. This was only Holly's fourth trip abroad ever and one of those was a school trip on a ferry.

If nothing else, it was fascinating to see the range of suitcases people had. Plain black ones like hers were a rarity. There was one covered entirely in Disney characters, several with polka dots, and one that was decorated like a Van Gogh painting. At least half a dozen were completely covered in cellophane, and while Holly could appreciate the extra safety of wrapping up a suitcase like that, she couldn't help but wonder how difficult it was to get off.

'It drives me insane how people stand so close to the belt,' Jamie said loudly, as someone shoved her to the side to stand in front of the yellow line. 'If everyone just stepped back a bit, everyone could see, and there wouldn't be the need for all this pushing and shoving.'

'That's mine!' Sandra leaped into action, shoving several people out of the way. Behind her, Jamie stifled her growl. Another minute and it was Jamie and Fin's joint, oversized holdall that appeared.

'Just you and me left,' Holly said to Evan, who had moved to stand next to her as the others backed away with the trolly.

'Just you,' he replied. 'I brought hand luggage only. I needed to order a ton of things to the villa, so added a few clothes to the delivery. I'm just standing here to keep you company. Assuming you want it.'

Holly wasn't sure how she was supposed to reply, so she didn't. Instead, she stared at the conveyer belt, praying her suitcase would come soon, while wishing Evan would go join the others so the silence didn't feel so awkward.

Thankfully, she didn't have to wait long.

'That's mine,' she said, as the familiar, plain suitcase appeared on the belt.

Now that so many people had already collected their luggage, no pushing or shoving was required. Still, Holly dashed towards the bag and the moment it was in reach, grabbed the handle.

'Jeez.' She yanked it off the conveyer belt and onto the ground. The way it had been moving when she went to pick it up made the suitcase feel substantially heavier than when she had packed it. She let go of the bag to reconsider her angle, only to change her mind and immediately grab the handle again. The last thing she wanted was for Evan to think she was unable to pick her own bag up. That would truly cement her as the hopeless female, and there was no way she was having that. With a sharp intake of breath, she hoisted it up, then, refusing to show even a hint of the effort she was exerting, dragged it towards the trolley. Only when she lifted it up did she notice the large new dent on the bottom corner. A flicker of annoyance flitted within her. It was a good job she hadn't bought that new suitcase after all, if it was going to get bashed about like this.

'Let me help you with that.' Holly had barely wheeled the suitcase two feet when Evan swept in. 'I don't want anyone leaving here with broken toes.'

Holly was forced to grit her teeth. This role he played – the handsome, humorous, overly helpful saviour – could wear thin. At some point, she was certain his facade would crack. Still, she was surprised to see him flinch as he lifted the suitcase onto the trolley.

'Wow, what did you pack in here? It's heavy.'

'To be honest, I thought I'd packed light. I guess swimsuits and flip-flops were heavier than I thought.'

With a light grunt, he hauled it upon to the trolly.

'Is that it? Has everyone got everything?' Jamie said as she and Finn approached, her sitting on top of the trolley Fin was pushing. The appearance of her sunglasses implied she was more than ready for the holiday.

'I think so,' Holly replied, not wanting to speak for everyone else.

'Great, because we need to head outside and wait for the others. They should be arriving soon. And I can't wait for you to meet them all.'

11

Thankfully, the suitcase was a lot easier to push on the trolley, as Holly walked through the airport, still trying to take everything in. Though she didn't get a lot of time to do so. Once they were through into the departure hall, Holly had barely figured out where they needed to go next when the scream shot out from the other side of the hall.

'Jimjam!' Holly turned her head to see two women of a similar age to her, racing straight towards them, dragging their suitcases. 'Happy hen do!'

One woman was short with pale skin, the other was tall and dark skinned, but both were dressed entirely in hot pink. Under their pink dresses, they wore bright pink leggings, accented with pink legwarmers, pink trainers, and even pink headbands. And around their middles they sported bright pink sashes with the words *Hen Party* in bold letters across them.

Jimjam was, evidently, Jamie.

'Nay! Zai!' Jamie embraced her old school friends. 'When did your flight arrive? You told me you didn't get in until later than us.'

'We told you that because we wanted to be here before you.'

The shorter of the two lifted Jamie up in a massive bear hug before letting go so her friend could take her place.

'Obviously Fin was in on it,' the second said. 'Considering we've never met the guy, he did pretty good at keeping shtum, although less good at making sure you were ready for your hen do.' After exchanging a brief glance, the pair stepped back. Their eyes scanned Jamie up and down before they looked at one another.

'This will not do at all.'

'Nope, we are ashamed to be with you in this state. You call this a send-off?'

Holly didn't need to know anything about the women to know that the grins spreading across their faces were a sign of complete and utter mischief.

Jamie saw it too.

'Whatever you have planned, you should know this is an entirely respectable weekend. My mother is here.'

'Sandra!' Another barrage of hugs and kisses followed, this time as the girls descended on Jamie's mother, before they turned their attention back to the hen.

'Now where were we? Of course, we were talking about how utterly terrible you looked. At least, in hen terms.'

Although Holly wouldn't have thought it was previously possible, their grins widened further, as they delved into a plastic bag one was holding and pulled out a fistful of pink headbands.

'What is on those?' Caroline whispered in Holly's ear.

Just like Holly, Caroline was standing back from all the action, although it was difficult not to be intrigued. As such, Holly took just a small step closer, at which point she was close enough to see what was on the headbands. Tiny penises.

'Time to get you properly dressed for a hen do.'

'Zahida, there is no way I am wearing this.' Jamie stepped back from her friends. 'This is a classy stag and hen do. An adult trip.'

'Yeah, right. You do remember how long we've known you, right?'

Nai – or Naomi as Holly knew her actual name to be – stood beside her friend and for a second, Holly thought she might be about to come to Jamie's defence. But instead, she began clapping her hands and chanting.

'Wear them. Wear them!'

'Wear them! Wear them!' The women had the chorus down to an absolute tee, which attracted the attention of several passers-by. Not to mention the small tourist police box positioned at the edge of the building.

'Should we maybe move away from this area?' Holly said, gesturing to the police officers nearby.

'Why? Do you think there's a law about wearing penises on your head?'

'There probably is if they're not plastic ones.'

Finally, Jamie snatched a headband and held it down by her side. 'Fine. I shall wear it in the villa, in private.'

'No. Where's the fun in that?' Naomi stopped her chanting to speak. 'How about this: if you wear them now, in the airport, then we won't make you wear them out?'

Jamie's lips disappeared into a straight line as she contemplated the deal.

'Fine, I'll wear them. But only if these guys do, too.' She nodded to Holly and Caroline.

'Please no,' Holly whispered to herself as she momentarily closed her eyes, but from the grins on Naomi and Zahida's face she knew that there was no escaping it.

'Obviously. We bought plenty for everyone. Sandra, we got one for you too.' And just like that, they reached into the bag and pulled out a handful. 'We even got them for the boys.'

With all of Jamie's side now present, all they were waiting for were Fin's three college friends, who were due to get off their flight any minute. As they still needed to get through passport control, Evan suggested they move over to the café and take a seat while they wait.

'Or you can go sit on the chairs over there, and I'll grab us all a croissant,' he offered. 'Assuming nobody here is gluten intolerant?'

'I'm tolerant of anything you want to give me,' Naomi replied, her lips twitching.

Holly felt a pang of relief. If Naomi had her eyes on Evan, perhaps that would keep Caroline off her back about this whole holiday romance thing. Not that Evan could consider her cute any more. Not after the flight they'd just had.

As Holly watched Naomi scurry after Evan, she felt her phone buzz in her pocket. A release of tension flooded through her; Evan had been right about it taking time to get some signal. That was a good thing. Assuming the message would be from Ben, perhaps with another photo of Hope, she opened it nervously. But instead, it was her mother.

How's it going?

How was it going?

The embarrassment of being treated for a near concussion on a plane, vomiting endlessly, and now being made to wear penis-decorated headbands, while they waited to stay in what could well be the most shambolic accommodation anyone had ever stayed in. That was how things were going.

Holly looked at her mother's message. She couldn't say any of that. She replied with,

All going well.

'Everything okay?'

The voice made her jump. When she turned around, Holly found Evan standing with his hands outstretched. 'One croissant. I got you a lemonade too. It always used to make me feel better when I got travel sick.'

'Thank you. That's really kind.'

'I'm a kind guy.' His smile caused an unexpected fluttering to erupt within her.

Taking hold of the drink and croissant, she looked past him, hoping that perhaps Naomi might be there, ready to swoop in and take his attention. But instead, their group was on their feet and looking through the arrivals door.

'Please tell me these are for us,' Naomi gawped.

A group of three men were walking directly toward them. Three men who made Evan look averagely attractive. If they had been chosen for a magazine advert, then every straight woman's taste had been accounted for: dark hair, blond hair and a redhead. Two with bulging biceps, the other gorgeously geeky, and each with straight white teeth that couldn't possibly be natural.

'Please, Holly, please.' Caroline sidled up next to her and whispered in her ear. 'I have to live vicariously. Please, give me something. Don't let this all go to waste.'

'Finley! Dude.' The one with the red hair was first to speak and he must have stretched each syllable out for a full five seconds as the three hurtled towards them, arms wide open. The closest one ducked down into a rugby tackle pose and a second later, he struck Fin squarely in the waist and lifted him up, as if they were on a sports pitch, not in an airport surrounded by various people pushing trollies loaded with luggage. Not to mention children.

'Jamie,' Fin said when he finally regained both his footing and his breath. 'Meet the guys. Tyler' – he gestured to the blond one, then the redhead – 'Eddie' – and finally to the dark-haired man – 'and Spencer.'

With his arms once again wide open, Tyler went straight for Naomi, ready to pick her up in the same fireman's lift he had given Fin before Fin corrected him.

'Wrong one,' he said, then pointed at Jamie.

A series of loud shrieks and rugby tackles followed. The type that would have left Holly wholly embarrassed, but Jamie could handle herself just fine, although by the time the boys had put her down, one of the headband penises was bent at a very painful-looking angle.

Stepping forward, Evan shook the gents' hands before addressing the rest of the group.

'As much as I know we all want to catch up, the minibus is waiting for us outside.'

'Woohoo,' Spencer said, fist bumping one of his friends. 'Time to check out this villa we've heard all about.'

12

For Holly, the word minibus evoked memories of school trips. Grey seats with holes in and bits of chewing gum stuck down the side of the chairs. Not to mention the aroma of sweaty children and packed lunches. Though as they stepped outside and into the warmth of the day, it became clear that this minibus was nothing like that.

Leather seats, ample legroom and cup holders filled with chilled sparkling water awaited them.

'This is fancy,' Zahida said, as she popped a headband on the top of a headrest.

'Very fancy.' Slipping off her own headband, Holly dropped into a seat. While compared to Caroline, Holly was concerned she had over-packed, seeing Zahida and Naomi's suitcases had put her mind at ease. Naomi's in particular looked big enough for a family of four to travel for a full week.

'Are you okay?' Caroline slid into the chair next to her. 'You look stressed. Please don't tell me you're worrying about Hope already. You know she'll be fine.'

'No, it's not that...' Holly paused. She didn't know how to word it without coming across as ungrateful, but she was sure Caroline had to feel the same way. It wasn't as if she and Michael were rolling in money. 'I'm worried about how much this is costing. And who's paying for it all? Even if the village is only a thirty-minute drive away, a van like this is going to cost a fortune. Has Jamie mentioned money to you at all?'

With the rest of them having piled in, the car door slammed shut. Caroline lowered her voice.

'I've already brought this up with Jamie. She knows Michael and I are on a tight budget. And she's fully aware of your situation too. She wouldn't put us in a position that made us feel uncomfortable, neither would Fin. You have to trust them.'

As Holly fixed her belt in place, she tried to take comfort in what Caroline was saying. After all, Jamie and Fin were two of the most generous people she had ever met, and it wasn't like Evan had even let any of them see the bill at the champagne bar before handing over his credit card. But there were several trips and activities involved in their getaway, and trips cost money.

'You are allowed to enjoy yourself this holiday.' Caroline squeezed her hand. 'I know what it's like with the mummy guilt. It's hard to let go, but you deserve to have some fun. You're still your own person, even if you are a mum now, too.' Instinctively, Holly cast her gaze down at her phone and the screen saver of Hope chewing on her favourite plastic giraffe. Something tugged behind her sternum at the realisation Caroline was right. It was guilt that had been churning away at her, not just today, but for months. Ever since she'd agreed to go on this trip. Guilt not just because she was going away from Hope, but because she needed this time. She needed time without nappies and nap schedules, so she could hear herself think again. And it made her feel like the worst mother in the world. Tears pricked behind her eyes.

'We all need time to recharge every so often.' Caroline squeezed again. 'But think of it this way: if you don't enjoy yourself, then – and don't take this the wrong way – there's no point you being here. It won't take long for the others to pick up on how you're feeling, so you need to make a decision now, before we get to the villa. You need to decide to enjoy yourself. Please.'

There was more than just a prick of heat behind Holly's eyes, and several stray tears escaped. Before she could even sniff the rest away, Caroline had a tissue out.

'You're right.' She took the offered tissue and mopped up the rest of the tears. 'Of course you're completely right. This is Jamie and Fin's time, and I'm not going to let anything ruin it. Including me.'

'That's my girl.'

'And I deserve this time.'

'You do.'

She took a deep breath in, trying to fill her lungs with Caroline's confidence. There was no way she was going to let her feelings interfere with Jamie and Fin's break. She was about to assure Caroline that she was fine one last time when Spencer's voice blasted out from the front of the minibus.

'Evan, dude, how far away is this place of yours? Are we nearly there yet?' He sounded like a child, but Holly was grateful; she had wanted to ask the same question herself.

'It's about a twenty-minute drive,' Evan replied. 'The coastline is pretty impressive, though.'

Pretty impressive was an understatement. The roads wound up and down, with a view of the sea out on the left, unlike anything Holly had ever seen. The crystal blue expanse was dotted with ships, from pristine white sailing boats, all the way to full-on cruise liners.

'If we were staying longer, we could have headed to Monaco,'

Evan said from the row in front of Holly. 'But we've got a pretty packed schedule as it is. Maybe next time.'

'Does he mean Monaco as in *the* Monaco? With all the casinos, and the crazy sports cars and ridiculously wealthy people?' Caroline hissed to Holly.

'I think he might.' Her tension loosened by a fraction as she found herself grateful that they hadn't had time to add that excursion onto the trip. There was no way she could afford a night outing at a casino.

The conversation turned quickly to flights. How long it had taken everyone to get there, what the food was like, and if anybody besides Holly had suffered from sickness. Apparently, she was the only one.

'I used to get travel sick as a kid,' Evan said. 'Not on planes, but cars. And crazily bad. My parents didn't take me on a vacation one year. They left me with my aunt and uncle instead, because they were driving up to these lakes in Ohio, and knew I was going to get travel sick.'

'That's terrible. They didn't take you on holiday?'

'I probably made that sound worse than it was. My uncle and aunt lived on a farm. Well, a ranch I suppose. Tractors, horses, proper wild-west set up. I probably enjoyed that more than I would have with them. And one of my sisters got food poisoning while they were away, so I think I lucked out if I'm honest.'

'I get seasick.' Naomi joined in the conversation from the front row of seats. 'So I'm not looking forward to the boats. I figured I'll drink my way through it.'

'I'm pretty sure the drinking will make it worse,' Zahida replied.

'We'll see.'

As the roads continued to twist and turn, Holly's eyelids struggled to stay open. She hadn't woken up particularly early that morning, but it had hardly been a restful sleep. Not that she had anyone to blame other than herself and her own anxiety. Hope was a dream at bedtime. And with all the worry stories she had heard at the mummy-baby groups, Holly knew just how lucky she was with a baby who slept six hours solidly from four weeks old. But the nerves had kept her awake. Covering her mouth, she allowed herself a yawn that stretched out far longer than expected.

'Why don't you close your eyes?' Caroline said in her amazingly motherly voice. 'They'll be plenty of time to see the view when we get there.'

As much as Holly wanted to stay awake, she knew Caroline was right, and using her jumper as a pillow, she rested her head against the window and was fast asleep within minutes.

* * *

The shaking on her shoulders was confusing. As was Caroline's voice, telling her she needed to wake up. For a split second, Holly assumed she was at the shop and had fallen asleep upstairs while weighing out sweets. It wouldn't have been the first time since Hope had been born that she'd done that, but as she felt the softness of the seat beneath her, she realised that no chairs in the sweet shop were this comfortable. Blinking herself awake, the morning came back to her with a rush of excitement and fear. Today was the day she was leaving Hope. No, she remembered, she had already left Hope – and the UK. She was on holiday.

'We're at the villa.' Caroline was still shaking her arm. 'You're gonna wanna wake up and see this.'

The villa. Once more, Holly's stomach dropped. Did she really want to see the hovel they were staying in for the next four nights? Not particularly. As the dread settled, she remembered what Caroline had said to her before she fell asleep. This wasn't about her. It was about Jamie and Fin and, whatever state things were in, Holly was determined to be positive. And perhaps even enjoy herself.

With one more steadying breath, she forced her eyes open and looked out of the window.

'Crap.'

13
<hr />

'Don't worry about your bags. I'll get Hugo to bring them in.'

Evan stood outside the villa as he spoke, although Holly was barely listening. Instead, she was staring at the gargantuan twists of metal and wood that made up the front door. If you could call it that. It was more like a gate to a fortress. Something you would see on a Hollywood set marking the entrance to a home of a billionaire tech wizard or a mafia drug lord. Actually, she thought, as she drew her eyes away from the door and scanned the rest of the building, the entire thing looked like it belonged on a Hollywood set.

Rather than a normal electric doorbell, it had a large, physical, cast-iron bell with a heavy rope which dangled down. A wrap-around balcony swept around the entire first floor and large, curved windows displayed a glimpse of the world inside. Overgrown plants cascaded over the red-brick walls, allowing glimpses of the vivid, yellow flowers hiding within the foliage.

'Hugo? Who's Hugo?' Holly tuned in to what Evan was saying, realising she had missed some important information while she was asleep.

'He's the driver,' Caroline caught her up.

'He's more of an all-around handyman,' Evan added. 'He's going to be with us for the entire trip to drive us to places, like the water-skiing and the yacht. He's planning on tidying up some of the garden as well. As you can see, it's overgrown a lot. And he cooks too. He's in charge of dinner tonight.'

'Wow. Okay.' When Evan turned back to the door, Holly whispered into Caroline's ear. 'Does that mean we've got our own chef?'

'I think that's what it means. Yes.'

Still struggling to wake up fully, Holly took a deep breath in and held it in her lungs before releasing a long sigh.

'We probably need to sort out rooms first.'

In Evan's hand was a large bundle of keys, held together on a thick, metal hoop, and it was clear from the way he was struggling that he wasn't sure which one opened the door to his house. Still, he covered his difficulties well, as he continued to speak.

'I know this isn't your average hen and stag do, but I am afraid we're going to need to split the lovebirds up. Unless there is a great objection?'

'Too right. We need some man space!' Spencer lifted his hand into a high five, which he aimed at Eddie, only to be left hanging. If Holly was to go on first impressions – which she tried not to – Eddie was the only one of the new men she could see herself having a conversation with. Other than Evan, that was.

'It's more a case of room logistics than anything else,' Evan added. With an unexpected click, the lock on the door popped open. 'So, this is it, guys.'

Holly held her breath as she stepped into the white, marble hallway.

'He owns this place?' Caroline whispered. 'How?'

'I have no idea.'

While Holly had watched plenty of millionaire real estate programmes in her time, she had never accepted that real people could actually own those homes, or anything like them. And certainly not the type of people she knew.

'Jamie, I thought you and your mum might want to take the top floor.' Evan pointed at a staircase to the right. 'The suite up there has got a great balcony looking out over the sea.'

'That sounds perfect.' Sandra sighed in delight.

'Then there are two bedrooms on the first floor that the rest of the ladies can take, and us gents can use the ones in the basement.'

Caroline elbowed Holly firmly in the side.

'We want to make sure we've got a decent room. I bet at least one of them has a sea view.'

Holly was only half listening. Instead, she was watching Evan and how he was tapping the side of his trousers with a slight hint of nervousness. There was no way around the fact he was taking his role as host seriously and wanted to make a good impression on everyone.

It was sweet, Holly thought, before pushing the thought away. Even if he was charming and helpful and had more money than one individual person should probably possess, she was absolutely not interested in a holiday fling.

His eyes caught hers and for a split second, she was terrified he knew what she was thinking, but before she could move her gaze away, he was speaking again.

'Okay, well, I'll head downstairs and show the boys their rooms and you ladies can sort out which you want to take.'

It was as if somebody had fired a starting pistol but not told Holly. The instant Evan finished speaking, Naomi, Zahida and Caroline darted towards the bedrooms; Caroline and Zahida went one way, Naomi went the other.

'We're in this one!' Caroline and Zahida yelled in unison.

'It's fine. We're having this one,' Naomi yelled back from her room. 'Zahida, we want this room.'

'But this one has a sea view.'

'So does this one.'

'And a walk-in-wardrobe.'

'Snap.'

It was only when Holly took the time to check both rooms slowly that she found they were identical. They were perfect mirror images of each other, even down to the same style abstract acrylic painting above the bed.

With the window open, a strong, briny aroma of the sea wafted into the room. Holly stared out at the vista.

'You can see for miles.'

Never had she stood before such a view, where the only thing between her and the deep blue sea were lush green trees tumbling down a mountainside.

She was still standing, lost in the warmth and the ripples of sunlight, when Hugo appeared. How on earth he knew which bags belonged to which person, Holly wasn't sure, but it was hers that he rolled in as he knocked on the door.

'I will make a light lunch,' he said in flawless English with only the slightest hint of a French accent. 'Nothing special. A salad and breads for before your trip. I will have it ready in thirty minutes.'

'Thank you. Thank you very much.' Holly wasn't sure how she was supposed to behave in such a situation. In the movies, they always tipped people who brought their bags and made their food, but that was in hotels, not a house. The etiquette of how it all worked was utterly beyond her.

'Thirty minutes until food? That sounds like just enough time to check out the pool.' Caroline pulled her swimsuit out of her coat pocket before she disappeared into the bathroom.

It took more effort than Holly expected to lift her suitcase onto the bed, although, she reasoned, it probably shouldn't be a surprise. She'd barely eaten all day. When it was secure, she entered her code into the small, embedded padlock.

The dials jangled a little under her fingers, but the lock didn't ping open the way it normally did.

'Crap.' She looked again at the bump on the side. It was bigger than she'd first thought and clearly it had done some damage. Alongside were several other smaller scrapes and bumps that hadn't been there before. By the looks of things, her luggage had had almost as rough a journey as she had.

With a hard thump, she smacked the top of the case, just above the lock, and tried it again. Still no luck.

'This. Is. Not. Good.' She spoke in sync with whacking the suitcase, though even that didn't help the lock budge.

'Everything okay?' Caroline stepped out of the bathroom, already dressed in her swimwear.

'No. My suitcase won't open. I think the lock jammed when it got dented.'

Without waiting to be asked, Caroline came to her side and jiggled the lock a bit, though, as Holly suspected, it still didn't move.

'Are you sure you've got the code right?'

'Positive. I've had it since university and I haven't changed it once. I don't know how to.' It was probably not something Holly should have admitted, but it was the truth. After a couple more thumps, Caroline stood back and folded her arms.

'Well, in that case I think we're gonna need to use a little more force.'

Two minutes later, Holly and Caroline were downstairs, the suitcase on the living room table. Evan and Tyler had joined them, and the latter was holding a large penknife in his hand.

'I'd really like to avoid breaking the suitcase entirely.' Holly said, with more than a slight flicker of annoyance. 'I will need it to get my things home.'

'There are a couple in the storage room here,' Evan responded. 'The previous owner must've left them. Worst-case scenario, you can take one of those back.'

'Thank you.'

'Let's hope you don't need it.'

Her eyes met his again, and an unexpected calm ran through her. Even if there weren't suitcases in a cupboard somewhere, she suspected Evan would make sure she had one, anyway.

'So, just so you guys are aware, doing things like this, I'm normally stronger than I realise.' Tyler flexed his muscles, then clicked his neck from side to side. 'You guys might want to stand back a bit.'

From the few words they had shared, Holly was growing more and more certain that Tyler was not her type of person. Still, if he got her suitcase open, she would be infinitely grateful. As such, she did as instructed and took a large step back.

'The secret to opening locks like this is to use the thinnest blade you can find.' He slid the knife into the gap beside the lock with scary expertise. 'Yep, that's it. I can feel it. Just another second. Here we go. Here we go.'

The pop was like an audible version of the sigh of relief which rushed through her mouth.

'We just need to open it up, check nothing is jammed on the inside.' Tyler reached towards the case—

'That's fine,' Holly said quickly. Her packing was relatively tidy, but the last thing she wanted was her five-year-old underwear on display. 'You've sorted the lock. If there's anything else, I'm sure I'll be able to fix it.'

'Don't be daft. Might as well check it all opens completely before you take it back upstairs.'

It was a good point, Holly conceded. And there wasn't anything exciting in there, just clothes and swimsuits. Even her undies were packed right at the bottom. And so she remained quiet as Tyler slipped open the suitcase. Though as the top half folded open onto the table, she gasped.

'What the hell?'

14

The four adults stared in silence at the open suitcase. Someone had to speak first, but Holly had lost her voice.

'Is that yours?' Caroline took the pocketknife from Tyler's hand and prodded at the top of the suitcase. The penknife was currently in contact with a series of magazines. The type of magazines found on the top shelf, normally with black plastic obscuring the cover images.

'Of course they're not mine,' Holly said indignantly. 'I've obviously picked up someone else's suitcase.'

'You seemed pretty sure it was yours before.' Tyler mocked.

Ignoring him, Holly grabbed the penknife from Caroline and used it to shift the magazines over onto the other side of the suitcase, displaying the contents beneath. Using the end of the blade, she picked out two pairs of red speedos, a selection of Hawaiian print shirts, and some other items that were far less wholesome.

'I guess handcuffs are heavier than you would have expected,' Caroline smirked. 'Looks like someone was planning on having some fun on this trip.'

'Someone who probably has my suitcase.'

'Please put that down and wash your hands before you touch anything else in this house.' Evan spoke to Tyler with a tone of deadly seriousness. 'We need to put all this back and contact the airline. Hopefully your suitcase is still there. I'll ring them now.'

As Evan packed up the mystery person's belongings, Caroline rested a hand on Holly's shoulder.

'You okay? I'm sure Evan will sort it.'

'I know. It's a pain, that's all.'

Holly didn't want to feel so crestfallen, but she had packed her nicest things in that suitcase. They may not have been designer brands, or particularly expensive, but a couple of those dresses she'd had for years, and they had more memories attached to them than any other outfits she owned.

'Come on.' Caroline took Holly's hand and pulled her towards the stairs. 'I'm sure between the five of us girls, we can mix and match enough stuff for you to get by until your luggage shows up. Also, I think I might need a shower after seeing all that.'

While Caroline and Holly weren't the same size, Naomi was almost an exact match. Never, Holly decided, would she judge someone for over-packing again.

'I plan on wearing these two when we go out on the yacht,' Naomi said, taking two dresses and corresponding swimsuits from the pile and promptly hanging them up in the wardrobe. 'But help yourself to anything else you want to wear.'

Holly studied the garments. This wasn't the first time she'd picked something to wear from a selection of clothes that were well out of her budget. The same thing had happened on her first Christmas back in Bourton and that time, the clothes in question had been ball gowns, belonging to a fiery old lady called Verity. A friend who had now passed away.

Shaking off the memory, Holly focused on the task at hand.

'Is it okay if I borrow this one?' She picked up a plain black bikini with a low-cut neck. It wasn't a style she normally chose, but given the situation, beggars could not be choosers.

'Sure. You might as well take another one too.' After a brief rummage, Naomi handed Holly a canary-yellow number. 'I packed six more. And don't forget some sun dresses. You're going to need some for waterskiing later.'

'You packed seven bikinis?' Holly questioned, skipping over the fact that waterskiing in a sundress sounded both impractical and possibly dangerous.

'And three bathing suits. Dress for your mood, right?'

'I guess so.'

Once dressed, Holly headed downstairs, intending to check out the pool, though when she reached the bottom of the stairs, Evan was there, waiting for her.

'So,' he said, 'do you want the good news or the bad news?'

'Bad news first, always.' It was a rule she lived by. After all, there was no point in getting good news first, if the whole time you were wondering what the bad news was going to be.

'Okay so the bad news is that your bag is not there. It seems that the owner of this one made the same mistake as you and took yours with him.'

'And there's good news?'

'The good news is that the person I spoke to at the airport says when things like this happen, people normally return the suitcase within a twelve-hour period. I've ordered a taxi already to take this one back to the airport, and the woman there has my number so they as soon as the other one is returned, they will call us, and I can send another taxi to pick it up.'

Twelve hours still felt like a long time away, but that didn't diminish the gratitude Holly felt. 'Thank you so much.'

'It's no problem.'

'It's a lot of effort that you had to go to.'

'I really don't mind.'

A moment formed between the pair in which Holly faced the overwhelming desire to give him a hug. She would have hugged Fin in such a situation. Or Michael. But she didn't know Evan like that and so instead, she stepped backwards, aware of the tightening in her throat.

Evan broke the silence before it could settle. 'I think it's time we checked out the pool, don't you?'

'Definitely. The pool sounds good.'

Given her delay in getting ready, Holly had barely opened her book when Hugo called that lunch was ready.

'I thought he said he was doing us a light snack?' Naomi echoed Holly's thoughts as they stared at the spread laid out on the table in front of them.

'Just a few different things: bread, olives, cheese, a tomato salad, a goat's cheese salad. A caprese.'

During the meal, Holly found herself sitting next to Spencer on one side, who was mostly calling over to his friends, and on the other was Zahida, who she learned was a pharmaceutical engineer, about to take a six-month sabbatical to work with orphaned orangutangs.

'That's amazing,' Holly said.

'I know, it is, isn't it?' Zahida grinned with a positivity that was immediately infectious. It was no wonder she and Jamie had been such good friends for so long. 'I tried to talk myself out of it for years. You know what it's like; you have these big dreams, but then you give yourself all the reasons about why it's not possible and why you have to be sensible. But then I was like, I'm single. I have no commitments. My employers love me and I know they'll take me straight back again. So why am I not doing this? Why am I not embracing life and living it to the fullest?'

'You don't need to convince me. You're talking to someone who bought a sweet shop in a spur-of-the-moment decision.'

'I heard about that. It's incredible. I should have been down to visit. I'm so sorry. It feels ridiculous that we're only just meeting like this when Jamie's spoken so much about you. I feel like I already know you.'

'I feel the same.'

The rest of lunch went by in a constant stream of chatter and laughter, and though Holly was faced with the constant urge to check her phone, she felt herself relaxing more than she had done in months. She could certainly envision herself back on a sun lounger with a cocktail in hand.

She was busy imagining what sort of drink she would have when Evan stood up and addressed the table.

'As fun as all the lazing about is, I'm sure you know that we came here to do more than just sit around. I'm afraid it's time we all get ready. We will be leaving for waterskiing in twenty minutes.'

And just like that, Holly was tense all over again.

15

'Have you ever been waterskiing before?' Holly asked Zahida as the group drove away from the villa.

Since bonding over lunch, Holly was hoping to continue the conversation and so had taken a seat next to her on the minibus. At some point, she hoped to talk some more to Naomi too, although the second of Jamie's friends had planted herself firmly in between Spencer and Tyler on the front row of seats, and didn't seem quite so bothered about mingling with the girls. Sandra and Eddie, meanwhile, were deep in a conversation about electric cars.

'You know, I see myself as a sports car.' Sandra leaned forward slightly as she spoke. 'Sleek and efficient, and I always get you to your desired destination.'

'That's actually not true of electric cars,' Eddie replied, somehow oblivious to Sandra's blatant flirting. 'The mileage range of electric cars varies greatly. Even fully charged, some can't go much over a hundred miles, unless you plan to visit recharging stations on route.'

'Then I guess I'll just need a bit of spark to keep me going.'

Holly forced herself to stop listening. The conversation was more cringeworthy than she could bear. Thankfully, Zahida was still happy to chat away.

'Nope. I've been skiing before, but never waterskiing,' Zahida answered Holly's earlier question.

'I've not even done that.' Holly had been too preoccupied with worrying about Hope to think about the activities she was going to have to do, and now the apprehension was beginning to get the better of her, though Zahida was quick to put her at ease.

'Don't worry. I was terrible. I spent my whole time on the beginner slopes with the children. I tried to do this surfing thing once too. It was on this weird plastic slope and the water just kept coming and coming. But again, I was useless. I kept face planting. So I'm hoping I'm better at this. I'm pretty sure I broke my nose on the surfing thing.'

'I'm not sure you're making me feel any better.' Holly laughed, though she did feel slightly less concerned that she wasn't going to be the only terrible one.

'Is anyone going to teach us how to get up on these water skis?' Caroline asked. 'I feel like I'm going to need a lot of tuition.'

'Don't worry, I did my instructor's training years ago.' Evan turned around from the front of the minibus. 'And the guy who owns the boat has done it for years. He's the best in the business. He was in the World Championships at one point. Though that was a while ago. Between us, you'll be fine.'

Zahida leaned in to Holly conspiratorially. 'Can I check this is right? He's good looking, really, really rich, super organised, super generous and also a waterski instructor?'

'Jamie really has a way of finding these people, doesn't she?'

'I'd be happy if I could find a guy who ticked only one of those boxes.'

Holly smiled. As much as she liked Evan, she couldn't help but think how she'd already had a man who ticked rather a lot of those boxes. Two men, in fact. Super organised, super generous and good looking: that was Ben to a tee. While really rich and super generous also hit Giles on the head. And now she had neither of them.

But she had Hope, who was a million times better than any man could ever be.

'Okay guys, we're here.'

Here turned out to be a marina. Squinting against the sunlight, Holly stepped off the minibus. Bright-white boats shone out under the cerulean sky while the chime of clinking metal accompanied the soft flapping of sails. Small cafés spilled out to the waterfront, with metal tables and chairs occupied by elegant women and pristinely dressed men, sipping at their coffees, while a row of shops extended down the other way. Holly got the impression this wasn't the type of place where she could pick up a cheap cuddly for Hope, or a box of chocolates for her mum. But it would be nice to have a look around.

'Monsieur Evan!'

The group's attention was drawn down one of the jetties, where an elderly man with white hair was waving his arms. If this was the man who had competed in the World Championships for waterskiing, Evan wasn't joking when he said it was a while ago.

'Gabriel.' Evan greeted the old man with a kiss on either cheek and a hug that Holly thought would have been far too long for a man like him. He seemed like someone who was used to a swift handshake. 'We've got a perfect day for it.'

'I picked the weather just for you,' the old man said kindly. 'It has been a long time since you were on the water. Can you remember 'ow?'

The way Gabriel dropped his aitches make Holly smile. It added such a beautiful lilt to his voice.

'Don't worry about me,' Evan responded. 'How's the boat?'

'She is perfect. As you will see. Come, we should go.' He looked past Evan to where the rest of them were trying to look inconspicuous. 'This is your group?'

'It is, and I've promised them an amazing time. You won't let me down, will you?'

'Never, Evan. You know that.'

'Then we should get going.'

Puddles covered the wooden planks of the jetty, and as Holly walked over it, with its constant rocking motion trying to throw her off balance, terrified of slipping, her eyes didn't leave her feet. It reminded her of her second date with Ben, where he had taken every step of that water obstacle cause with absolute caution. As quick as she could, she pushed the thought from her mind. The last thing she needed to think about was people needing to be rescued. Then again, maybe if she slipped on the jetty now, it would save her the humiliation of having to waterski.

'Look at the size of that yacht,' Naomi said. 'It's bigger than my house.'

Holly threw it a quick sideways glance. Not enough to unbalance her, but more than enough to know the boat dwarfed their cottage, too.

She had just reached a notable damp patch when Gabriel and Evan came to a stop in front of a small speedboat. Small, at least, compared to the yachts they had passed.

'Take your time getting on,' Evan said as he stepped with ease onto the back of the boat. 'We don't want anyone getting wet yet.'

'Can you to hold my hand?' Holly whispered to Zahida and Caroline, who were on either side of her, but they clearly didn't hear, for before she could step any closer, Caroline had grabbed Evan's hand and was already aboard, with Zahida following. While Sandra and Eddie also required Evan's help, Jamie and the others bounded on without a second's pause, leaving Holly the only one standing on the jetty.

'Don't worry, I've got you.' Evan stretched out his hand.

The last thing Holly wanted was to look like she was incapable, but she wasn't that keen on falling in, either. Reluctantly, she stretched out her hand and grabbed hold of Evan's. She had expected him to be there, simply to hold on in case she started to slip, but instead he tugged at her arm, yanking her up with far more strength than she expected. Her pulse skyrocketed, the ball of her foot landed on the boat, but it wasn't enough. A slight rock and she would topple back and into the water. Using all the momentum Evan had pulled her with, she lurched herself forward, only to land straight on his chest.

Gasping with both shock and relief, she righted herself and stepped to the side, ensuring her feet were firmly on the boat.

'I'm sorry,' she said, her nostrils still filled with the sweet, musky scent that had emanated from his shirt.

'It's fine. I'll always catch you.'

As he held her gaze, Holly felt the heat rising through her.

'Come on you guys, what are we waiting for? We want to get out there!' Spencer shouted.

Swallowing back the sudden dryness that filled her throat, Holly found herself a seat.

Caroline smirked as Holly sat down next to her. 'Everything all right there?'

'Don't say a thing.'

A swarm of butterflies filled her stomach, a swarm which only increased as she looked at Evan. With a deep sniff, she tore her eyes away and focused on the view instead. She was not going to have a holiday romance. She was not.

Father time. Jesus was the mannered to give it a go,' she said traitorous.

'If you don't want me to try, then I would be...I am going to try,' he affirmed.

Before he could react, he grabbed, who is seated, and Evan stood up.

'This is wonderful, my niece. That's what I – you. We'll see...' he continued.

16

Holly was having trouble believing this was her life. She was sitting in the back of a speedboat, surrounded by her friends, watching as white clouds sped above her. This was something she had wanted for so long. A real adventure.

The boat rode the waves with varying levels of smoothness. Some moments it was like gliding across ice, without the slightest bump, but the moment Holly thought she had figured out a pattern to it, they were tossed into the sky by an oversized wave. So much laughter rattled up around them, it was impossible not to smile. So much so that Holly's cheeks ached.

'At least you don't get seasick,' Evan said as he took a seat next to Holly. 'How are you feeling about the waterskiing? Are you going to give it a go?'

They had been travelling for about twenty minutes and all that time, Evan had been occupied talking with Gabriel or the rest of the men. As such, Holly's butterflies had diminished so much, she thought she may have imagined them. But now he was back beside her and expecting her to speak.

'I didn't know there was the option not to give it a go,' she said truthfully.

'Of course you don't have to. But it would be a shame not to try, don't you think?'

Before she could reply, the boat drew to a stop, and Evan stood up.

'This is it, everyone. It's time to see what you've got. Who wants to go first?'

* * *

With each person she watched on the water skis, Holly's fear increased exponentially. Given it was their special break, Jamie and Fin were first – and second – into the water. Without so much as breaking a sweat, they put on an impressive display, each standing straight up and slicing through the waves as they held on to the thin rope that pulled them from the back of the boat. Next went Spencer and then Tyler, who were even more impressive. After which, Evan asked for another volunteer.

'I'll go next.' Caroline was on her feet.

As a Park Run addict and Zumba class enthusiast, Caroline could be considered a sporty type, but given all the time she'd spent truanting PE lessons at school, Holly had never previously thought her so. Yet there she was on the skis, whizzing through the water, her hair spraying out behind her as she laughed.

'See, it's really not that hard,' Jamie said, nodding to Holly. 'You've just got to work with the boat, not against it.'

Holly wasn't sure how she was meant to work with a massive hunk of metal, but her fear had decreased fractionally. If Caroline could do it, so could she. Or at least she could try.

'It's so much fun,' Caroline said as she clambered back into the boat and took her life jacket off, ready to pass on to the next person.

'I mean, I'm going to feel it in my arms tomorrow. And my thighs. You really need to focus on keeping your legs together so you don't do the splits. But the water really isn't that cold at all. Holly, do you want to go next?'

She held out the life jacket, causing all of Holly's nerves to return in one overwhelming rush.

'I... I...'

She didn't have to do this, she reminded herself. Jamie and Fin had said repeatedly that the holiday was all about fun and no one should feel pressured into anything. Sandra had also made it clear that she wasn't going to have a go and had taken the role of group photographer instead. But Sandra was twenty years older than Holly and had waterskied several times in her youth. For Holly, there wasn't likely to be another chance. It was now or never. And if she meant what she said about wanting a bit more adventure in her life, this would be a great place to start.

'I'll go,' Naomi said, standing up and grabbing the life jacket from Jamie's hand before Holly could reply.

'I thought you got seasick?' Jamie commented.

'I guess I grew out of it. Now, how do I do this thing up?'

'I'll go next,' Holly said, as Jamie looked at her with a mixture of apology and concern. 'It's fine. We've got ages.'

Unfortunately, Naomi going first eradicated the tiny bit of confidence that Holly had garnered. It was painful to watch, although, Holly suspected, not half as painful as it was for Naomi. Unlike the others, who had all started on their back the way Evan had instructed, Naomi struggled to get into position, constantly twisting the rope around the skis. A couple of times, she had started moving and even stood upright for a second. Then, just like Caroline had said, the skis pulled her legs apart, and she performed a gymnastics worthy split before tumbling into the water.

'One more go. I'll get it this time.' She waved enthusiastically as she bobbed up and down in the water.

'You might want to give it a rest,' Evan called back. 'Give your arms a bit of time to recover, then try again.'

'No. I've nearly got it,' she insisted. 'I can feel it. This time, I'm going to get up. One more go. Trust me.'

So Evan nodded to Gabriel and Naomi took hold of the rope yet again. Everyone's breath was held as they watched and waited. Despite Naomi's confidence, the fall that followed was the worse one so far. Her legs flew up in the air only for her to belly flop down, though somehow she still managed to hold on to the rope. The result was her being dragged forward face down in the water.

'Let go!' Fin, Jamie and Evan cried simultaneously, but whether Naomi was being utterly stubborn or she could just not hear through the crashing of the waves, she ignored them. When the boat slowed to a stop, she was still there, holding fast.

'I nearly had it,' she said, as Spencer and Eddie pulled her back onto the boat. 'One more try and I would have been up.'

As she spoke, she took off her life jacket and handed it to Holly.

'Guess it's you next.'

With her pulse pounding against her eardrums, Holly moved to the edge of the boat and gazed down at the water below her. The sea had looked so blue from the villa and the car. Even when she looked out in the distance, it was brilliant azure, but beneath her feet, it was a deep, swirly mass of grey and black. Foreboding. That was the word that stuck in her head, as she looked down at the water. Foreboding.

'You really don't have to go if you don't want to,' Jamie said. 'No one will mind.'

But others had words of encouragement.

'You'll be fine. It's not that bad.'

'Just take your time and don't rush. Use the rope.'

'Stay on your back until you're stable. Try to keep your knees together.'

Too many instructions were being fired at her. She squeezed her eyes closed and tried to block them out when she felt a hand on her shoulder. A soft but firm grip than had an unexpectedly calming effect.

'The first thing you need to do is swim out and get the rope. It's going to be a nice, slow start,' Evan said. 'And that's only if you want to. But there's no harm in having a dip, right?'

Maybe it was the American charm, or that he spoke at a volume she was sure no one else could hear, but Evan's words eased her nerves enough to finally think.

'I'll just swim to the rope,' she said.

'Sounds perfect.'

Before she could second guess herself, she dropped into the water.

'Wow! That's cold!' The words flew from her mouth. How come no one mentioned it was utterly freezing? She pulled in a deep breath and allowed herself one deep shiver.

'Swim to the rope,' Caroline called. 'You'll warm up by the time you get there.'

With each stroke Holly took, her mind swirled. Where their sharks here? There probably were. There were sharks everywhere. Or stingrays. But couldn't they be equally dangerous? Although they were normally on the seabed, weren't they?

'I'm sorry, Hope,' she said, as she continued to swim.

What was she thinking? She was a mother now. This was the worst time in her life to be taking up extreme sports. It was reckless and selfish. She'd decided to turn around and swim back to the boat when the rope handle appeared.

A series of cheers went up behind her, even though all she'd done was swim. Still, just as they said, the cold had all but gone and a sense of adrenaline was starting to fill her.

'Sod it. I'll give it one go.'

One attempt, one face plant, and she could happily admit that she wasn't made to do this. Then she would climb back on the boat.

Holding the rope as she'd been shown, Holly lay back with the tips of the skis poking out of the water and her heart knocking at three times its normal pace. She waited for the roped to go tight. With her eyes once more squeezed shut, she imagined the pain of impact while trying to remember everything the others had said. Her arms quivered as the rope went tight. This was it, she thought. This was the moment she was going to face plant into the water. At least Naomi hadn't broken anything, but maybe Holly would be the first. She was going to ruin the rest of the holiday by needing to go to the hospital.

Her eyes were still tightly closed, and she was busy considering what she was going to tell Ben when she arrived back on crutches, when the whoop of cheers ringing up from the boat distracted her. For a split second, she wondered what they could be cheering about. Most of the cheering that day had been when people got up on the water...

And that was when she opened her eyes and saw it for herself.

Holly Berry was waterskiing.

17

Holly loved waterskiing. It was something she never thought she would say, but it was true. She loved it. She loved the feel of the wind whipping through her hair, and the saltwater spray rising from the sea. She loved the feeling of freedom as she shifted her weight from one foot to another and cut the waves behind the boat and moved from side to side. No wonder people got addicted to things like this, she thought as the boat swung her around in a fast arc. It reminded her of the rush she got as a child, flying down a massive slide or pushing herself extra high on a swing just so she could jump from the top.

Once, she even went one-handed, so she could wave to the others on the boat, although the sudden misbalance that nearly toppled her meant she didn't try that again.

Had it not been for her arms, she would have kept going even longer, but after nearly ten minutes, it felt as if she had spent the last month in the gym, and she was finding it harder and harder to keep a decent grip. When the boat drew to a stop, Holly swam back towards it.

'That was amazing!' She hoisted herself back onto the boat, the heat of excitement helping to block out the cold.

'You are amazing,' Caroline said as she pulled her up to standing then handed her a towel. 'You definitely put me to shame.'

'That's not true.'

'It is. You were a complete natural.'

The high of being on the water hadn't faded, and hearing the others congratulate her only made it even better. 'I have no idea how I did it. It just felt natural. And I've never been into a sport before. This is a sport, right? Yes, of course it's a sport. It's a water sport.'

Holly could hear herself rambling but it was an excited rambling. Goosebumps had spread across her arms, but she didn't even feel cold. Instead, she was just desperate to get straight back on it again.

As she looked out onto the water, Zahida was strapping herself onto the skis, ready for her first turn. Before the boat started moving again, Holly dropped onto a seat. She barely had time to catch her breath before Evan came and sat beside her.

'Are you sure you've never done that before?'

It was a cheesy line, yet Holly couldn't help but grin.

'Positive, but I need to do it again.'

'Is there somewhere close to you where you could do it?'

'Like a beach? No. But there's a water park in South Cerney. I think they do it there. I might book lessons when I get back.'

'Wow, you got the bug fast.'

'It's a little different out here in the sun than it is on one of the lakes back in the Cotswolds.' Jamie joined the conversation. 'You'll probably need to get yourself a wetsuit.'

Even the thought of shivering away in a cold lake didn't dampen Holly's enthusiasm, although she might have been a bit pre-emptive with the idea of lessons. Even if she could arrange them for the afternoons when Ben had Hope, there was a minor issue of cost. With the annoyance of reality sinking in, she was even more determined to make the most of her time in France.

'We're gonna have time for another go, right? We don't have anything planned for the rest of the afternoon, do we?'

Evan laughed. 'I guess we're not going back to the villa just yet.'

As the boat moved, they turned their attention to the water, although there wasn't much time for waiting. Zahida quickly decided that waterskiing wasn't for her, and Eddie also declined the offer of a go due to an issue with recurring ear infections and saltwater.

Holly managed another three turns out on the skis before she had to call it a day. She hadn't wanted to. She'd wanted to stay out there until it was too dark to see any more. And even then, she'd wondered whether night waterskiing was a thing. But her arms ached, although ache probably wasn't sufficient to describe the unceasing throbbing that pulsed through her muscles. Still, even her last attempt, where she'd only managed to stand up for a couple of minutes before she had to let go, didn't erase the rush and sense of pride she was feeling.

'Any chance we can come back tomorrow?' she said to Jamie as they headed to the marina. 'Or Thursday? Or any day where there's a spare hour in the schedule?'

Jamie laughed as she roughly towel dried her hair. 'No chance, I'm afraid. Tomorrow, we're going for a hike. All the reviews say this viewpoint is stunning, and I don't want to miss it. And then we've got the yacht.'

A hike and lying with nothing to do on a yacht or waterskiing? To Holly, there was absolutely no question as to which she'd prefer. But it wasn't Holly's hen do, and so she relented. Perhaps the hike would be shorter than they thought.

By the time they arrived back at the marina, Holly was almost dried off.

'Okay, let me just tie her up before you guys get off.' Evan hopped from the boat to the jetty with the assurance of a man who had done it many, many times before. 'And be careful. It moves, so the gap can be wider than you think.'

One by one, they filed off the boat. Once again, Spencer and Tyler were the first off, and Eddie helped Sandra and Zahida down. After that, it was Holly's turn.

Evan stretched out his hand, though this time something made her hesitate. It could have been the swarming butterflies that had attacked when she'd got too close to him before, or it could have been the newfound confidence that had come with her current status as a successful amateur waterskier.

'I'm sure I'll be fine,' she said.

'I have no doubt you will be.' Evan's eyes locked on hers. It was a far more intense meeting of gazes than Holly had expected and it caused a somersault in her stomach more violent than some of Naomi's face plants. Swallowing down the heat building in her, Holly stepped forward, not noticing the puddle of water right where she placed her left foot. It was a mixture of bad luck and lack of concentration, for no sooner had Holly shifted her weight towards the jetty than the wake from a leaving yacht caused their speed boat to lurch upwards.

Before she could even reach out her hand to grab hold of something, Holly plummeted straight into the water.

18

Holly's arms flailed around her and the sudden iciness caused her to gasp aloud, though she had barely hit the water when two pairs of arms grabbed her.

'We've got you. We've got you.'

Having taken an arm each, Fin and Evan hauled her up and onto the jetty, where they dropped her onto the wooden planks. The entire thing couldn't have lasted more than thirty seconds, and yet her body was trembling from head to foot.

'What happened? Are you okay? Did you hurt yourself?' Caroline was beside her in an instant, brushing up and down her arms as she checked her over. 'Tell me, where does it hurt?'

'I'm fine. I'm fine.' Holly flapped her hands as she tried to push the attention away. As if falling in wasn't bad enough, having everyone staring at her while she was dripping wet was the last thing she wanted.

'Can you stand?' Evan's calm and quiet voice was a complete contrast to Caroline's fussing.

'I'm sure I'm fine.'

Hoping that it was merely her pride that was bruised, Holly

went to stand, but the instant she put her weight on her left foot, her ankle buckled and searing pain shot up through her leg. She toppled forward, where Jamie was thankfully waiting to catch her.

'I think I just stood up too fast,' she said optimistically.

Freeing herself from Jamie's hold, she gingerly put her foot down on the wooden planks again, only to feel the same pain bolt upwards to her knee.

Before she could say anything else, Evan had hooked himself under her arm and took her weight.

'Eddie, you speak French, right? Can you go to one of the restaurants and ask them for some ice? We'll put that on it until we get to the villa and we can have a proper look. I can always call the doctor if we need.'

'No problem,' Eddie said, already walking towards the marina restaurants, with Naomi hot on his heels.

'It's really not that bad.' Holly tried again to take a step on her own, only to flinch the minute her foot touched the ground. There was no denying it. Her ankle hurt. And not the type of hurt where you could rub it better and forget about it after a couple of hours. A lump formed in the base of her throat as she realised that her holiday was about to take a very different turn. Tears pricked her eyes. 'Maybe a bit of ice would be good.'

As they travelled back from the marina, Caroline, ever the dutiful friend, held the ice pack to Holly's ankle – the whole way – and then helped her onto the sofa, where they inspected the joint for the first time since the fall.

'I think it's unlikely you're going to do the hike tomorrow,' Caroline said as she stared at Holly's foot.

Caroline was right. While the swelling had stopped, there was no chance of Holly being able to get her foot in her hiking boot and the purplish tinge of a bruise was blooming across the surface of the skin.

Groaning, Holly tossed the ice pack to the side. Her level of self-pity multiplied with every passing second. 'Of course it would be me. And of course it would be on the first day.'

'We got ice on it quickly. It might be better in the morning.'

As much as Holly loved Caroline's optimism, she suspected it would take more than one night before she was doing any more outdoor activities, and she was about to say as much when her phone buzzed.

Pressing her lips together, she fought the tears that pricked her eyes as she picked up the phone and accepted the video call.

'Look who it is. It's Mummy! Say hello to Mummy.' In the tiny rectangle of her screen, Hope was bouncing up and down on Ben's lap, frowning at the camera.

'Hope, how are you, my baby girl?' At the sound of her voice, Hope's face lit up and the tears that Holly had been battling once again threatened to appear.

'She's good, aren't you, Hopey?' Ben replied, upping his bouncing. 'We've just got back from the village. And we've had a nice bath, so I thought we'd give you a ring to see how your day has gone before we head to bed. Are you having fun?'

'Fun?' The word came out with more of a hitch than she'd planned. Most people probably wouldn't have noticed such a small inflection, but Ben wasn't most people. He spotted everything. And they may have split up, but Holly knew that didn't stop him from worrying about her.

'What happened? It was waterskiing, wasn't it? I knew it was dangerous. I was going to tell you it was dangerous, but I didn't want to be overbearing. You had an accident waterskiing, didn't you? Is that what the bruise on your head is from?'

'No, that was at the airport. And I did not have an accident waterskiing,' Holly said forcefully.

A look of relief washed over Ben.

'Thank goodness.'

'I did, however, have an accident *after* waterskiing.' She switched the camera around so he could see her swollen ankle. Somehow it looked even worse on the screen, the bruises even brighter than in real life. 'I slipped after getting off the boat.'

'Have you iced it?' Ben's face was a crinkled mass of concern. 'And kept it raised? You should keep injuries like that raised, you know. And take some anti-inflammatories.'

'It's iced, it's raised and Evan has gone to the shop for some painkillers.'

Ben's frown was still in place as he nodded, although he was no longer bouncing Hope, all his attention on Holly.

'What about a doctor? It could need an x-ray.'

'She's going to be fine.' Without warning, Jamie appeared and placed her hands on Holly's shoulders. 'She did it on purpose so she gets an entire luxury villa to herself rather than having to spend the day walking.'

Holly's lips twisted into a smile.

'When she says it like that, it really isn't that bad at all.'

Despite the pair of them trying to lighten the mood, Ben's concern lingered. For a second, Holly regretted telling him, but it was better this way. If she'd kept it hidden, he would have found out when she got back, and then he'd accuse her of keeping things from him, which was something they didn't do. Or rather, she didn't think they did that. This news about his relationship with Georgia meant Holly wasn't quite so sure as she had been.

After blowing a kiss at the phone, Jamie disappeared and joined the others, leaving Holly to continue the conversation.

'Look at it this way: I'm injured now. It's happened. You don't have to worry any more.'

'We weren't worrying about you,' Ben said unconvincingly.

'So.' Holly was keen to move the conversation on. 'What about you two? Any exciting plans for tomorrow?'

Ben shook his head as he recommenced his bouncing.

'I've got to work tomorrow,' he said. 'But on Wednesday, we're going to the animal park, aren't we? They've got rhinos, and otters, and even a sloth you can walk right up to.'

'Not close enough to touch, though?' Holly was momentarily distracted by the thought of Hope grabbing hold of a giant sloth.

'No, not close enough to touch.'

'Good, then that sounds like a lot of fun.'

She wanted to ask if this was where Ben was going to introduce Hope to Georgia. A nice day at an animal park felt like the perfect venue, but she could hardly pretend she wasn't bothered if she was the one who mentioned it.

'I should let you get her to bed,' she said, breaking the stream of thoughts spiralling in her head. 'I don't want to mess up the night-time routine.'

'We were just going to have our last bottle, weren't we?'

Holly stared at the screen, wishing she could give her daughter a bed-time hug. She hadn't even been gone a day, but it still hurt.

'I'll get your mum to give you a ring tomorrow,' Ben said. 'I'm dropping her off fairly early.'

'Don't worry. It's not like I'm going to be going anywhere.'

'Take care of yourself.'

'I'll try. Love you loads, Hope. And Ben?'

'Yes.'

'Thank you.'

Then, before the tears could start, Holly hung up the phone.

It was ridiculous. She had had one of the most fun times she could remember in years, and was, by all accounts, in paradise, but it didn't change the fact that whenever she was away from Hope, she felt like something was missing.

'Are you all right?' Sandra stood in front of her, two glasses of wine in her hand, one of which she held out to Holly.

'I shouldn't. I need to take some painkillers.'

'More for me then.' Sandra took a seat next to her. 'The first time being away is the hardest, but she's completely fine.'

'I know, I know.'

'You just need a distraction, that's all.'

Changing her mind, Holly reached out, took the spare glass, and took a long draw. French wine, she discovered, really was as good as they said.

She was nearly half a glass in when Evan appeared.

'How's the patient doing?'

Having gone straight from the villa to fetch painkillers, Evan hadn't got changed, or even dried himself properly, and so his hair was tousled. Holly couldn't help but notice how he looked even better like this.

'I'm doing just fine,' she said.

'Sure. Do you mind if I have a look at it?'

'Go ahead.'

He moved straight to her ankle, where, with the gentlest of fingers, he pressed lightly against the swollen flesh of her foot.

'Looks like you've got a perfect distraction just there,' Sandra whispered into her ear.

19

As naturally talented as Holly had been at waterskiing, the same could not be said for her skills at beer pong. Perhaps unsurprisingly, the game had been suggested by Tyler and Spencer, confirming their frat-boy status in Holly's mind.

'I don't get how they bounce it in so accurately.' Naomi crossed her arms in a sulk as Tyler landed his eighth shot in a row.

'An extremely misspent youth – and adulthood,' Fin replied. 'Right, I don't know about anyone else, but I'm gonna call it a day. I still want to be able to do this hike in the morning.'

'What's wrong with you, old man?' Spencer yelled, then landed yet another shot without even looking at it. 'You can't go soft on us. It's your stag do.'

Maybe if she'd been in a different frame of mind, Holly would've joined in the games more, or at least added some supportive cheering, but as she could barely put any weight on her left foot, she had quickly given up spectating. So instead, while the rest of them continued to play, she had skulked back to the sofa and sighed in relief as she lifted her foot onto the coffee table. Closing her eyes, she drew in a deep lungful of fresh sea air and allowed herself to relax.

'You don't mind if I disturb you, do you?'

Evan stood beside her, a glass of water in his hand.

'It's your house,' she replied, only to realise that probably sounded ruder than she intended. 'No, of course I don't mind.'

Placing his drink on the table, he slid in next to Holly on the sofa, and she couldn't help but pick up on a sense of nervousness rising from him – though what a man like Evan could ever have to be nervous about was beyond her.

'I'm glad I've got you on your own,' he said. 'I wanted to apologise.'

'Apologise? For what?'

'I should have been keeping a better eye on the jetty. I could see that the boat was about to swing out again and I should have warned you. Or at least been there to grab you.'

'If anyone should have kept a better eye on things, it was me, not you. It's typical of me to do something like this that would mess up the entire holiday.'

'Hey, the holiday is nowhere near messed up. Think of it this way: you get to be waited on the entire time. And sure, you're going to have to miss out on the hike, but did you feel how hot it was out there today? If I'd realised that slipping over would get me out of charging over rocks and scrub in the scorching heat, I probably would've beaten you to it.'

Even though she knew he was saying this to make her feel better, Holly couldn't help but laugh.

'If it's possible, I'd really like to apologise properly,' he carried on. 'Perhaps I could take you out for dinner?'

'Honestly, there is nothing to feel bad about. Besides, we're all eating together, aren't we?'

'Then maybe it would have to be after the holiday. Maybe you could meet me in London, or I could come to the Cotswolds, if that's easier?'

'Now that really is going too far. I mean, you'd have to drive for hours. You wouldn't want to do that just to take me to dinner and apologise.'

'Well, maybe it's not about the apology at all; maybe it's just that I want to take you to dinner.' He was looking straight at her. Staring, almost.

Holly opened her mouth to object, only to realise what he had said, or more importantly, what he meant.

'You're asking me out?' she said, feeling the need for confirmation.

'I am. Is that all right?'

Despite the cool of the evening air, she could feel her cheeks growing hotter than they had done all day.

'I don't know, I mean... I think so. I'm not sure.'

'I've obviously caught you by surprise.' Evan pushed himself off the seat and stood up. 'Look, I better join the others before they notice I'm missing but perhaps, later on this trip, I might ask you again? When you're a little less surprised.'

Holly nodded, keeping her mouth tightly closed.

'Okay. I'll catch you later then,' he said before turning around and walking away.

First, Holly found out she could waterski, and now she was getting asked out by a multimillionaire. It was fair to say this holiday was not going the way she expected.

* * *

'My God, this might be the comfiest bed I've ever slept on,' Caroline said as she slid in under the sheet beside Holly. 'I might never wake up again.' She leaned over and flicked off the light switch, rolling back to face Holly. 'So, you and Evan, you were talking for a long time.'

'Were we?' Holly tried to sound as casual as possible. Any other time, she would have filled in Caroline and Jamie straight away. But this wasn't any other time. This was Jamie's hen do. And the last thing Holly wanted was to make things awkward. If she mentioned anything about Evan asking her out, they would all be waiting for that moment when they finally hooked up and, when it didn't happen, they'd all be disappointed.

'You know you were,' Caroline said. 'What were you talking about?'

'Nothing much. Just my ankle, that's all. We really weren't talking that long.'

'If you say so.'

Sometimes it was great having friends who could read your every mood; other times, it was just frustrating. Still, Holly wasn't giving in.

'You don't mind if I listen to a soothing sleep track, do you?' Caroline said as she flicked off the light. 'The kids can't sleep without it on, which now means I can't sleep without it on either. Trust me, with this bed, and my whale music, you're going to have the best night's sleep you've had in months.'

'Let's hope so,' she replied.

As it turned out, Holly did not have the best night's sleep. Having been woken at random hours in the night for the last eight months, she'd assumed she could sleep through nearly anything, though it turned out that was not the case.

Firstly, there was the issue with her foot. It didn't matter what angle she lay at; she couldn't get it right. Every time she shifted her body weight by half an inch, it sent the same pain shooting straight up towards her spine. That, combined with Caroline's whale music, the fact her friend needed to take up three quarters of the bed, and the impressive yet infuriating snoring that rose from the floor below meant that Holly had the worst night's sleep since Hope had been a newborn.

Covering her ears with her pillow, she tapped her phone to check the time, only to discover it was less than five minutes since the last time she'd checked.

'Jesus,' she gasped as Caroline rolled over yet again, her elbow landing square on Holly's rib.

At three-forty, Holly gave in. There was no way she could sleep next to Caroline, so, knowing the sofa was definitely large enough for her to lie out on, she decided to try that. Gritting herself against the pain, she grabbed a pillow, then hoisted herself up.

Her eyes watered, although once she was up, the pain lessened. Still holding the pillow, she limped her way across the bedroom and pushed open the door as quietly as she could before hobbling downstairs.

Hopefully, she thought, there would be milk in the kitchen and she could warm some up in the microwave. It was a sleep remedy her mother used to use, though Holly hadn't tried it for the best part of a decade. Still, with the travelling, the anxiety of missing Hope and the pain in her ankle, she was willing to try anything.

Groaning with relief, she reached the bottom of the stairs to discover the kitchen light was already on. There, sitting at the dining table, with his laptop open, was Evan.

'I guess I'm not the only one who can't sleep.' He smiled.

20

Dressed in a dark-grey vest and grey jogging bottoms, Evan had a pair of narrow reading glasses perched on the end of his nose – he pulled them off incredibly well – which he placed on the counter as he looked up at Holly, who was still slowly edging her way from the staircase.

'Let me guess, Tyler's snoring?'

Holly paused, regathering her balance and preparing her muscles for the last few steps.

'That, along with Caroline's non-stop turning, the fact she thinks she's the only one in the bed and she needs to listen to frog music to fall asleep.'

'Frog music? I didn't know that was a thing.'

'She says it's whale song, but there's no chance whales make sounds like the ones she's listening to.'

'That sounds intriguing.'

'Trust me, you don't want to hear it.'

Refocusing her attention, Holly glanced at the sofa, although it seemed rude to go straight there considering Evan had now struck up a conversation.

Wincing, she took a step forward, though she had barely moved before Evan was up out of his seat and rushing over to help her.

'I'm fine, I've got it.'

'I know. But there's no harm in leaning on someone else now and then. Jamie told me that about you. You don't like accepting help.'

The remark surprised Holly. Firstly, because it was hard to believe Jamie envisioned her like that. The two of them had first become friends when Holly needed help fixing the roof of the sweet shop when it flooded. Then again, Ben had been the one to call Jamie. The second reason she was surprised was because it meant Jamie and Evan must have discussed her at some point. Which caused a feeling that didn't sit quite right.

Deciding to ignore his comment, Holly gestured at the computer. 'What are you doing up at this time anyway? You can't be working, surely?'

'I was.' He pushed down the lid on his laptop. 'But mainly because staring at a screen is the fastest way to send me back to sleep.'

It was only when he laughed that Holly realised he had been attempting to make a joke.

'Maybe you can help me. I've bought this house to renovate in London. The whole place has been gutted. It's a shell. I just can't work out how to re-figure the two upstairs floors. Want to have a look?'

Holly glanced over at the sofa. There was no doubt it was big enough for her to sleep on and there was even a throw blanket hanging over the back that she could use. But Tyler's snoring was even louder down here than it had been upstairs, and so she decided that perhaps an hour of staring at a screen would help her drift off too. Besides, it didn't feel right, curling herself up and falling asleep while Evan was sitting at the kitchen table, practically looking right at her.

'Sure, why not?'

With a slight smile, Evan opened the laptop back up and revealed a floor plan of a three-storey building. The downstairs was mostly open plan, while the two upper floors were boxed in with various bedrooms. The first thing that struck her was the six ensuites, not just because of the implied size of the building, but because she couldn't imagine having a home that big and not having a single bath in it.

Even before Hope, she had adored a soak in a tub, and a shallow bath was a far more convenient set up for washing a wriggling little baby than a plastic tub in a shower. When Holly had first seen the cottage, there had been a shower, but the day she signed the agreement, the landlord had informed her they planned on refitting the entire bathroom, and Holly was allowed to choose the specification. She had rented properties from faceless landlords before, but they'd never been quite so accommodating as this one.

'You have to have a bath,' she insisted. 'If there's enough room, I'd definitely put one there, under the window.' She pointed to a square on the screen.

'Really?'

'Yes. Without a doubt. That way, you can lie in the tub and gaze out of the window.'

'Okay, so what about on the third floor? Would you leave those showers there?'

'I think I'd turn one of the rooms into an office.'

Holly had always imagined at some point she would get a chance to renovate her own home, and she'd use all the ideas she'd found from years scouring the internet. She dreamed of posting the perfect before and after photo of her transformations on her social media. But so far, she hadn't had the opportunity. And it didn't look like one would come along any time soon. The only renovations she had time to think about were the number of shelves on the shop floor, and even that had been pushed to the back of her mind recently.

'Do people still soak in baths?' Evan asked, bringing her back to the moment. 'It's not something I do.'

'Let me guess, you're the type of guy who only has time for showers.'

'Possibly.'

Together they sat and looked through various designs, Holly offering as many pros and cons as her limited knowledge of building would allow. Yet every time she made a suggestion, Evan looked at her with a face of complete appreciation as if he would never have to come up with the idea on his own. Which she was almost certain was untrue.

Once or twice, the conversation veered away from the images on the screen into other topics, like the upcoming wedding, or the differences between living in England and America.

His smile was only slight, yet incredibly endearing. How was it possible he didn't have a girlfriend, she thought, as she forced herself to look away. What was even more impossible was that he had asked her out on a date. Perhaps he envisioned the sweet shop as something grander than it was. Perhaps he thought she was one of these entrepreneurs who planned on opening an empire of chains across the country, rather than being content in her little corner of the Cotswolds. There was no way he could be interested in her, just the way she was, surely?

'Everything okay?' Evan's voice broke her thoughts. 'You look like you slipped away there.'

Holly's throat croaked as she tried to think of something to say, but the silence was making it hard to think.

'Do you hear that?' Excitement fluttered in her voice.

'Hear what? I don't hear anything.'

'Me neither.' Holly grinned.

It took him a moment, but a second later, Evan's eyes glinted with the same sense of excitement and relief.

'He's stopped snoring.'

'He's stopped snoring.'

The two of them remained there a second longer, revelling in the absolute silence that filled the room. It was so quiet, Holly realised, she could hear her heart beating away, and it was getting faster and faster the longer Evan looked at her.

'I... I should probably grab a couple of hours' sleep,' she said hastily. 'Assuming there's a couple of hours left until morning? I'm not even sure what time it is.'

She turned her head to the window. Outside, the sun had begun to bleach the darkness, illuminating thin wisps of cloud that would quickly be burned away by the heat.

'You're right,' Evan said, slipping off his stool. 'I should probably try to get a couple of hours, too. With all this walking Jamie and Fin have got planned, I suspect I'm going to need it. Not that I need that much sleep, really. Obviously, I need sleep, but you know, I get by on a couple of hours of kip normally. That's what you Brits call it, right? Kip?'

Holly pressed her lips tightly together, trying to suppress the smile she desperately wanted to show. He was right about one thing: babbling could be cute.

'I guess I should go up to my room,' she said, not entirely sure why she was still lingering.

'Of course. Absolutely. Will you be all right? The snoring might have stopped, but Caroline is still up there. She's probably taken the entire duvet in your absence.'

Holly chuckled lightly. 'I don't doubt it. I guess I'll have to get the sharp elbows out.'

'Good luck.'

Forcing herself away, Holly dropped down from the stool. The steps had been manageable, but all the chatter with Evan meant she'd forgotten about her foot, until her heel slammed against the hard marble floor. An involuntary gasp flew from her lips as she grabbed onto the worktop to steady herself.

'Let me walk you to your room.' Evan was on his feet.

'It's fine. I just jumped down too hard, that's all. It'll be fine in a minute.'

'Maybe I could escort you to the bottom of the stairs?'

He looked at her with puppy dog eyes, which would have been impossible to refuse at any time, but given that she actually needed help, there was no way she could say no.

'That sounds like a good compromise.'

He offered his arm to Holly, which she took, as though they were part of some formal dance. She wasn't sure whether she walked so slowly because of her foot, or because she didn't want to reach the staircase and head upstairs.

When they reached the bottom step Evan smiled. 'This is you.'

'I believe so.'

'Enjoy your frog music.'

'I will try my hardest.'

It was only when she noticed the ache in her cheeks that she realised how much she was smiling. With one last thankful look at Evan, she turned around and headed back up to the room.

Upstairs, Holly checked the time. Four forty-five. Jamie had wanted everybody up by eight to make sure they were ready to get moving before the day's heat hit. Thankfully, Holly thought as she climbed under the blanket and shoved Caroline over on to her side, she wasn't going to be included in that. It turned out there were some silver linings to this ankle after all.

21

When Holly rolled over and opened her eyes, she was alone in the bed. Morning light shone through the gaps in the blinds in tiny shards. From outside came the trills of birdsong, while from downstairs came the chattering of people.

Yawning, she stretched out as wide as possible, only to get a sharp surprise in the form of a pang of pain from her ankle. Lifting the duvet, she examined how it was faring after some more rest. The swelling had gone down, and the bruises had stopped spreading, too. Hopefully, it would all be fine by the time she headed home; she dreaded to think how she would run around the shop if it still hurt, bolting up and down the stepladder to fetch the jars of sweets from the highest shelves.

With a deep inhale, she pushed herself upright and swung her legs off the side of the bed. Thankfully, she could put a lot more weight on it now. Maybe another day of rest was all it would take.

Filling her lungs with the scent of the sea, she noticed another smell in the air. One that immediately piqued her attention. As someone who had baked their way through all of life's trials and tribulations, Holly was well versed in the aromas of fresh bread. And the smell she caught was good fresh bread.

Her stomach growled in reflex as she glanced at her watch. She faltered in surprise. It was already eight-thirty. The others would be leaving any second, and she wanted to say goodbye.

After a quick check in the mirror to ensure that her hair wasn't a complete crow's nest, she headed downstairs, pleasantly surprised by how easy walking was.

The group was gathered around the dining room table, although they were all on their feet, and most of them already had their boots on.

'There you are, sleepyhead,' Jamie said. 'I thought we were going to have to leave a note for you.'

'Sorry, I had a bit of a rough night's sleep.'

'I think most of us did.' A collected group glare followed, aimed entirely at Tyler, although Holly couldn't help but think that Caroline had some cheek in glowering at him considering how much she'd also kept Holly awake.

'Are you hungry?' Evan stepped away from the table. 'There are a couple of croissants, a pain au raisin too. I left them in the bread bin for you. I didn't want these gannets polishing all the pastries off.'

'A croissant would be amazing, thank you.' As she caught his eye, she couldn't help but smile again. Was this another moment passing between the pair of them? It definitely felt like it was another moment, but then it was probably the tiredness and smell of fresh bread that was doing it.

'Are you going to be all right here on your own?' Jamie said as Evan disappeared. 'Mum says she doesn't mind staying with you, but I know she'd quite like to do the walk too. The views are spectacular and I already feel terrible enough that you're going to miss out on it.'

'Honestly, it's fine. I've got a luxury pool and a book to read. And quiet for the first time in months. I will be fine. I'll be better than fine. I'm quite looking forward to it.'

'Which supports my idea that you might've slipped over on purpose.'

Holly gave Jamie a withering scowl.

'Fine, fine. Just make sure you look after yourself properly while we're gone.'

While the others ensured their water bottles were full and sunscreen suitably applied, Evan reappeared with Holly's breakfast.

'I was going to make you a coffee too, but I wasn't sure what you like best. There's a machine in the kitchen. All the pods are there to make whatever you want. Or if you prefer, there's ground coffee and a cafetiere. Help yourself to anything. And one of my business cards is pinned to the fridge if you need to ring me for anything.'

It was a lot for Holly to absorb in one go, especially as she'd only just woken up, but if this was how Evan treated people he barely knew, she couldn't help but wonder how spoilt she'd be if she was his girlfriend. The thought came out of nowhere, and even though she tried to quash it, she could still feel it lingering in the back of her mind.

'Oh, I forgot to tell you the best news of all,' he said with a new degree of excitement. 'The airline rang. Your bag's been returned.'

Holly made no attempt to disguise the sigh of relief that flew from her.

'That's amazing. Thank you.'

'They said they'll get a taxi driver to drop it off, although it probably won't be until later in the day.'

It was like a weight had been lifted off her shoulder. Soon, she would be hobbling around in her own clothes.

'Oh, and the taxi driver will need paying in cash when he gets here.'

Holly's previous good mood evaporated.

'I don't have any cash on me. I thought I'd just be able to use card. Is there somewhere I could walk to get some before he arrives?'

'You shouldn't walk anywhere on the ankle,' Evan said, reminding her. 'At least not for a while. And the nearest town is three kilometres away. It's fine. I've got plenty.' He took out his wallet and placed it on the table. 'Help yourself to whatever you need. It's not like I'm gonna need to take anything hiking with me.'

Holly stared at the visibly bulging wallet in front of her. Is this what all wealthy people were like? It certainly didn't fit the stereotype of the hard-nosed, rich folk she'd seen in films.

'Thank you, I'll pay you back. I'll get some money out when we go to the port.'

'You know you could pay me back in a different way?' The instant he finished speaking, Evan's jaw dropped in horror. 'I didn't mean like that.' A crimson flush drowning his cheeks. 'I... I, oh God. That sounded awful. I really didn't mean that. I just meant dinner. We could go for dinner. Please, please forget I said that.'

It was hard not to enjoy watching him squirm. Particularly as he looked so sweet doing it.

'It didn't sound as horrendous as you think.' Holly attempted to comfort him before changing her mind. 'Actually, it did. It made you sound like an absolute creep. But when you clarified, that didn't sound so terrible.'

The colour of his complexion was a tone brighter than it should've been and she met his gaze, a slight smile toying on her lips. Slowly, Evan's look of shame switched to one of intrigue.

'Is that you saying you'll go for dinner with me?'

Holly nodded. 'I would like that. But not here. This is Jamie and Fin's time. But if you'd like to meet up when we're back in the UK, that could be nice?'

'I would like that.' He grinned, causing an eruption of butterflies in her stomach. 'I would like that very much.'

'Evan, are you coming?' Fin's voice came from the hallway. Holly could already hear Tyler and Naomi whingeing about their headaches, and she could only imagine the bickering and sore heads would get worse when they started walking.

'I should get going,' Evan said, then leaned forward and kissed Holly once on the cheek before he disappeared to find the others.

As the front door closed and silence descended on the villa, Holly bit down on the side of her hand and released a silent scream. Had she correctly understood what had happened? She doubted for a moment that it had even been real. And yet the smell of Evan's aftershave still lingered on her skin and the fluttering within her had yet to lessen, either. There was no denying it. Holly Berry was dating again.

22

The French pastries were sublime. Every mouthful Holly took was a dream: buttery, soft, melt in the mouth and even better than the ones they sold at the bakery in Bourton. When she got back home, she fully intended on learning to master croissants again. Not that she would be able to make them like this. No, these were absolute perfection.

After polishing off the remaining pastries and feeling like she should do something to repay Evan's hospitality, she loaded the dishwasher and had a bit of a wipe around after which, she decided she'd done enough to deserve a break. Although taking some time for herself was easier said than done. After all, it had been a long time since she'd had nothing to do, and it was going to take some getting used to.

Standing on the balcony, she stared out at the view. Glimmers of reflected light sparkled across the sea, while the final clouds of the morning drifted off beyond the horizon. After checking her watch, she felt a pang of annoyance at not having asked Jamie how long the hike was going to take. They had marked it down on the events plan as all day, but they hadn't packed any lunch, or at least not that she saw. Maybe the rucksacks had been full of French baguettes and cheese. If that was the case, she could easily be on her own until mid-afternoon. Which meant she still had several hours in the villa on her own and no idea how she was going to spend that time.

The lack of anything productive to do made Holly surprisingly nervous. But deciding to make the most of the weather, she lay down on one of the sun loungers, opened her book and started to read. She was less than two pages in before she closed it again. Ben had sent a message saying they were up and well, but he hadn't sent a photograph, or tried to call. It seemed strange that he wouldn't have called at all, considering how long Hope would have been up. Holly's mind whirred with images of trips to A&E or Ben with a smashed phone so he could no longer contact her. Perhaps it was the opposite. That nothing bad had happened to Hope at all, but instead they'd both had so much fun with Georgia, stepmother extraordinaire, that they had simply forgotten about Holly altogether. With her anxiety building, she picked up her own mobile, preparing to call Ben, only to change her mind.

Everything okay?

she texted instead. After a minute of staring at the screen, the three dots of an impending message appeared, only to disappear again. Whatever Ben had written, he hadn't wanted Holly to see it. Her anxiety kicked up by another notch. What would he have written that he didn't want her to see? And why hadn't he called her when he'd promised they would speak every day? She was about to dial for a second time when a message finally pinged through.

Sorry, someone was up very early. Everything good here.

The text was accompanied by a photo of an exceptionally grizzly looking Hope and a pouting Ben.

Holly sighed with relief before lying back on the lounger and opening the book.

An hour later and Holly was near giddy with excitement. She'd just enjoyed sixty minutes of uninterrupted reading and she didn't need to stop. Only it was getting hot, and as the sun glimmered on the surface of the pool, it became harder and harder to ignore how appealing it looked.

With a crystal-clear swimming pool before her, a view over the sea and not a single person to see her, one thought sprang to her mind.

Skinny dipping.

Holly wasn't a person who had ever written a bucket list. Adventurous escapades, like climbing mountains or jumping out of a plane had always been too far-fetched for her to consider, though at that moment, she was feeling alive with possibility. After all, it wasn't like she was ever going to get an opportunity like this again.

With no time to second guess herself, she stripped off her clothes and slid into the water.

'I am skinny dipping.' She said the words quietly, relishing in their ridiculousness. Then shouted even louder. 'I am skinny dipping!'

Never in all her life had she envisioned a moment like this. Pushing away from the side of the pool, she swam into the middle. She could feel the tension melting away from her shoulders. All the stress and strain that had been playing on her mind since this holiday had first been discussed dissolved into the water as she lay on her back and closed her eyes.

Maybe this was a start of a new chapter of her life. One where she was bold and adventurous. After all, wasn't that what she wanted Hope to be like too? Fearless. Adventurous. The type of woman who grabbed life by the horns. Maybe writing a bucket list wasn't all that ridiculous.

With the sun beating down on her face, she imagined what items might be next on her list, when a sudden noise broke her concentration.

Opening her eyes, Holly stared straight up.

'Mademoiselle, you are having fun, yes?'

23

Holly ducked down under the water so the bottom of her chin was submerged. The man was standing on the other side of the pool with a giant pair of secateurs in his hand, which would have looked menacing at any time, but even more so given she was naked in an empty villa in a foreign country.

'Hugo. What are you doing here?'

'Gardening.' He lifted the pair of secateurs and gestured to the overground foliage that blanketed the brickwork and covered the flower beds. 'These bushes need a big trim. No?'

'Oh God. Oh God.' Holly could barely breathe.

Hoping that her fluorescent glow could be disguised as sunburn, rather than raw embarrassment, she forced herself to smile. 'Okay, well, I'm going to just... stay here. Swimming.'

'Very good. Very good.'

He smiled broadly, though it brought Holly zero comfort. Maybe he thought this was completely normal. Maybe it was extremely common here for people to swim naked when others were around. Maybe he would stand there until her skin became a shrivelled mass and she caught hyperthermia.

Panic had well and truly set in when Hugo dipped his head in a nod.

'I should work. Have a good swim, mademoiselle.'

The second he turned his back, Holly leaped from the pool, grabbed her clothes from the sun lounger and bolted upstairs, her sense of adventure well and truly quashed and the bucket list forgotten.

Only when Hugo's voice rang up through the house, bidding her farewell, over an hour later, was she brave enough to leave her room again.

This time, she headed back down towards the pool in a full swimsuit and took two towels, one to use on herself after another dip and the other to mop up the puddles she had left when she darted into the house earlier.

She had just reached the landing when the doorbell rang. Just as she'd noticed when she first arrived, this wasn't the average electric ding-dong like she had at the cottage, but was an actual bell, and resonated with a sonorous, metallic gong. Her initial thought was that Hugo had returned. However, given that he'd previously let himself in, that seemed unlikely. Which was when she recalled that she was expecting someone. Or rather something.

Her heart leaped. Being reunited with the suitcase was just the good bit of news she needed to perk up her mood. With the fastest walk she could manage, she raced downstairs and swung open the front door.

There, with his hand still by the rope of the doorbell, was a portly man whose head was as round as his belly, and wore a pair of aviator sunglasses that masked his eyes. Rather than the golden skin tone of Hugo, his complexion was red, while his small, white soul patch had the unfortunate effect of making his chin look even rounder. And on the ground beside him, with his left hand still on the handle, was her suitcase.

'Thank you so much.' She was near breathless at the reunion with her belongings. 'I am so grateful. Thank you.'

She reached out for the suitcase, only for the man to tug it back and away from her.

'English?' His accent was thick, though Holly understood it perfectly.

'Yes, yes, I'm English. Thank you. Thank you.'

She took a step forward to take the bag, but once again, the man wheeled it away from her. He was scratching his head, coughing out several sounds.

'Monday? Monday?' He repeated.

'Yes, I left it at the airport on Monday.'

'No. Mon... mond...' The man rubbed his fingers together in a universal gesture and suddenly it made sense.

'Money! Of course. You need money. Wait here.'

In the excitement of dashing to get Evan's wallet, Holly barely even noticed her ankle, except in that it wasn't hurting half as much as she expected. It looked as if this day was just getting better and better.

Upon grabbing Evan's wallet, she returned to the taxi driver.

'How much?' she asked.

He looked at her blankly and pointed to the wallet.

'Money.'

'Yes, I know, but how much do I give you?'

She lifted her fingers, trying to communicate her question, while all the while drowning in embarrassment. Why could she not remember a single word of French from school? She must've been able to ask how much something was back then, but her mind was blank. 'Un? Deux? Trois?'

The embarrassment rolled through her in waves. He was speaking to her, saying numbers no doubt, but it was all so fast. Holly just couldn't make sense of it. At school everything had been slowed down and clearly enunciated to help them understand. There was no enunciation here, at least not that she could tell. She opened the wallet, intending to remove some money, only to stop.

A thick wedge of notes was packed into the large pocket, but it was the denominations that surprised her. On the rare occasions that she carried cash, it comprised a couple of crumpled five- and ten-pound notes and a ton of heavily jangling shrapnel. But this looked like an entire day's takings at the shop, and on a good day.

Not knowing which note was which, she removed one, ready to work out what the value was, when she caught sight of a photo in the card slot. She knew it was exceptionally bad taste to look through anyone's wallet, no matter how well you knew them, but there was something about the top of the image that made it impossible for her to draw her eyes away. Still holding the note, she slipped the photo up.

Her throat tightened. In the image, Evan was smiling brightly, his arm around the waist of a woman and from the way she was looking at him and smiling, she was not just a casual acquaintance. And there wasn't only one photo. Removing the first revealed a second one beneath.

The tightening was replaced by full heart palpitations. How had she been so ridiculous? Rich, mature men who had their lives together would not be interested in her.

She would have stayed there for hours, staring at the photos had it not been for the taxi driver's hand moving towards her.

Only then did she remember the note she was holding and the fact she hadn't yet paid him. Glancing at the thin rectangle of plastic, she had barely noted its worth when he pulled it out from her grip.

'*Merci! Merci beaucoup.*' He swiftly turned and headed out the door, the two hundred euro note that she had been holding only a moment ago racing away with him.

'Hey!' Holly lunged to follow him, but the driver was already disappearing into his car.

'*Merci, mademoiselle. Au revoir!*' he yelled with a look of pure satisfaction.

24

Holly felt like a fool. Not only had she just let a taxi driver head off with two hundred euros for what was probably a fifty-euro trip, but she had genuinely believed Evan liked her when he clearly had a stream of girls at his beck and call. For all she knew, he was probably lining up dates with Naomi and Zahida, too. As she continued to look in his wallet, she found more small passport size photos, a couple of which looked as if they'd been taken in a photo booth, another one had been obviously cut down from a larger photo. Who would do that? Who would be so arrogant that they would flaunt their infidelities? Or conquests. That was probably a better word for it. Not that he was cheating on her. They hadn't even had their first date, but it was these other women Holly felt sorry for.

On a positive note, it was incredibly satisfying to be wearing her own underwear and clothes as she headed back downstairs, ready to while away a few more hours with her book. The sun was high in the sky, and the heat of the day caused ripples in the air, which led her to think about the others on the hike. It was doubtful whether there would be much shade to shelter them from the sun, although the sympathy she felt was conflicted by a hint of amusement as she wondered exactly how Tyler and Naomi were faring with their hangovers.

Not wanting to risk a sunburn, she decided against reading outside and instead headed for the large sofa.

Whether it was heat, or that the cushions were comfier than her bed at home, it wasn't long before Holly's eyes sagged. The last time she had indulged in a midday nap was when Hope was a newborn, and then it had been more a case of passing out from sheer exhaustion than consciously deciding to go to sleep. She closed her book, adjusted a cushion to a pillow position and lay down.

She was mid-dream about waterskiing on the river in Bourton when a loud bang jerked her back awake.

She jumped to her feet and turned in a circle, trying to find the source. Had one of the inflatables burst? The noise had sounded loud enough; however, a quick glance at the pool told her everything was all right there. Her heart hammered. Was it the front door? Had Hugo returned? If so, she wanted to make herself scarce again.

'Hugo?' Her pulse was abnormally high. This villa was far from the stereotypical location used in horror films, but it turned out that being alone in a big house could be scary, however modern and luxurious it was. She scanned the room, searching for an item she could use to defend herself, before deciding that hiding might be the better option.

She was still debating whether she could squeeze in the gap under the sofa when Evan's voice called out.

'Not Hugo. Just me.'

Relief flooded through her and she rested her hand on the arm of the chair, although that relief was quickly replaced with annoyance. Annoyance at herself for overreacting and even more annoyance at Evan. From the lack of chattering, she could only assume he had returned on his own, meaning she would have to speak to him one on one, which was the last thing she wanted to do.

'You're back early.' She kept her voice as neutral as possible. 'Everything okay?'

'Not that early. It's three.'

'It is?' Holly checked her watch in surprise. So much for a quick nap. Shaking off the feeling, she turned back to Evan.

'Where's everyone else? How come they're not back yet?'

'The others just had the viewpoint to get to. I've already seen it enough times, so I thought I'd head back. How are things here? Has your bag arrived yet?'

'Yes. And Hugo came too. He did some gardening.' She left out the part about him catching her skinny dipping; Evan imaging her naked was the last thing she wanted.

'I should have told you I expected him. Everything was okay, then?'

'Yes. Fine.' No matter how much she wanted to stay neutral, she could hear her clipped tone, and from the way Evan frowned, he could hear it too.

'Is everything all right? You seem... tense.'

Tense. That was a good word to describe it, but Holly wasn't going to give him the satisfaction of letting him know she knew about his womanising ways.

'Everything's fine.' The words had barely left her lips when she realised it wasn't the entire truth. 'Actually, no it's not. There was a little confusion when I paid the taxi driver. I may have overpaid him. But I'll give you the money back, obviously.'

'It doesn't matter. It's fine.'

'No, it is not. It was my mistake.'

'How much did you pay him?' Evan tilted his head to the side.

'About two hundred euros,' she said hoarsely.

Evan covered his mouth with his hand as he coughed. 'You paid him two hundred euros? I bet he was laughing.'

'Well, I didn't exactly pay him. Rather, I got the money out of your wallet and he took it and I was confused because I didn't realise the value of the note immediately. But like I've said, I'll pay you back.'

'You've got your suitcase, that's what matters the most. Now I was going to make a cup of coffee if you want one? Or I've got some wine if you prefer. The previous owner left a well-stocked seller; you can take a look yourself. See if there's anything in there you like the look of.'

Never in Holly's life had she been asked to take a pick from a private wine cellar, and had he asked her previously, she would have probably accepted, but a lot could change in a few hours.

'I'm fine, thank you.' She spoke with just enough terseness for it to be noticeable, and once again, Evan's head tilted to the side. But this time, a deep crevice formed between his brows.

'Are you sure everything's okay? Apart from the taxi driver completely ripping you off?'

Holly pursed her lips. It would be so easy not to say something. The last thing she wanted was to make things awkward on the second day of the break. They weren't even halfway through yet. But this wasn't just about her. This was about all the girls he was stringing along. Maybe her calling him out would be enough to make him think twice. And it was better to do it now while it was just the two of them in the house than when everyone else was back.

With a bracing breath, she squared up to him the best she could, considering he was a good foot taller.

'I've met men like you before,' she started, not entirely sure where she was going. 'You're rich, charming and obscenely attractive in an overly obvious kind of way.'

'I don't think anyone's made that sound like such a bad thing

before, but I'm interested to see where this conversation is going.'
His lips quirked into a smile, but Holly didn't react. She wasn't
going to fall for his charms now. Not that she could see straight
through it.

'And you have this annoying ability of making me feel incredibly relaxed yet giving me butterflies at the same time, and I'm not
entirely sure how you do that.'

'I give you butterflies?' It wasn't a small smile; it was a full-on
smirk now. His eyes glinted with mischief, but Holly was determined not to fall into the trap.

'There's no point looking at me like that, because I'm not buying
it any more.' She paused for added emphasis. 'I saw inside your
wallet.'

Pushing her shoulders back with a newfound confidence, she
waited for him to respond. She had thought that sentence would be
enough to clarify her point, but instead his smile barely faltered,
other than to be clouded by a hint of confusion.

'I know you did. You had to open it to get money out.'

'I mean, I saw inside it. I saw the photos. Photos of you and all
those women.'

'Oh. Right.'

His nonchalance was enough to boil her blood.

'I bet you thought I was an easy picking. A single mum who's
probably got a terrible track record in love. Probably desperate for a
bit of attention. And you're right; I am terrible in love. I got pregnant and I'm not with Hope's father, but that doesn't mean I don't
deserve respect. That I can just be used for another notch on your
bedpost. I have more dignity than that.'

She waited for Evan to respond, only to notice how his former
confusion had gone and was replaced with a suppressed smile. If
she hadn't been angry before, she was furious now.

'Oh, of course you think it's funny. It's just a game for you.

Everything is just a game to you people. Just because you've got money, you think you can mess around with people like me. Normal people.'

'I can assure you, that is not what I think. But I will admit I find this situation rather amusing.' Her back molars ground together as Evan sauntered over to the cabinet and picked up his wallet, promptly pulling out the photos that she had seen and placing them on the table.

'I assume these are what you were talking about?'

It was even worse than she had first thought. There were six of them. Six photographs, although one of them was of Evan with an elderly woman she suspected was his mum.

Holly cleared her throat. 'That's right.'

'These are my sisters.' He stared at her, his expression unblinking, as deadpan as a person could be. Without waiting for him to say any more, she threw back her head and laughed.

'Really? You're really expecting me to believe that. You have five sisters.' She scanned the images. 'They don't even look alike.'

'I promise. I have five sisters. I'm the youngest of six.'

This time, Holly shook her head as she laughed. The lengths some men went to to cover their lies was ridiculous. She had already learned that from Giles, and she wasn't going to fall for it again.

'You don't believe me?'

'No, of course I don't believe you.'

'Fine then. I'll prove it to you.'

Part of Holly didn't want to bite. To play along with his ridiculous games. But this had her interest piqued. Besides, that smirk was so infuriatingly gorgeous, she would do whatever it took to wipe it off his face.

'You'll prove it to me? How?'

'Easy. You can speak to my mum.'

25

If nothing else, this was a holiday of firsts. First lost luggage, first holiday accident. And first speaking to a man's mother on a video call before they'd even been on a date.

'You can't be serious?' Part of her was still convinced that Evan was bluffing. That this was simply a way for her to drop the issue.

'Oh, I'm very serious.' He moved over to his laptop on the kitchen counter, opened the lid, went to video call, and selected, 'Mom.'

In barely a breath, the call was picked up.

'Evan, honey. This is a nice surprise. An early surprise, but a nice one. Is everything all right?'

Judging from her comment, it was early morning, and she was already wearing a full face of makeup, lashes, lipstick, the lot. This was a woman who clearly took pride in her appearance.

'Hey, Mom.' Evan's grin was wide and eyes bright as he spoke. 'Yes, everything's good. Really good. I'm at the new house in France. We went waterskiing yesterday, and on a hike today.'

His accent was far stronger now he was talking to his mother, and it was hard not to find it cute. That was, until he turned the computer around, so the camera was facing her too.

'Mom, this is Holly. She's one of Fin and Jamie's friends. Holly, this is my mum, Anne.'

This was up there with Holly's most embarrassing situations and, considering some things she had done in her life, that was no small feat.

'Hi, Anne.' She offered a little wave.

'How is my son treating you? Is he being a proper host?'

Holly's head span with the bizarreness of the situation. She was still standing a way away but felt rude speaking from such a distance. She came and sat on the stool besides Evan.

'Oh yes, absolutely. And the house is beautiful.'

'I'm sure. It's a bit hot for me at this time of year. Maybe I'll come out later when it cools down. Evan's stepdad is not very good with the heat either. And boy does he whine when it comes to flights. Why my only son would choose to buy a house all the way out there when we have beautiful beaches right by us, I have no idea.'

'Because that's not where I live.' His voice was clipped, leading Holly to believe this wasn't the first time they had shared this conversation, but before they could say any more on the matter, Evan was changing the subject. 'Mom, I'm ringing you for a reason. Holly here refuses to believe that I am one of six and that I have five sisters, and I thought, who better to get the truth from than my dearest mother?'

'This is why you called me at nine in the morning?'

'This is why I called you.'

With a grossly exaggerated roll of her eyes, Anne looked through the screen at Holly. 'Honey, if you're ever blessed with children, you should learn now that they are the most wonderful, torturous gift.'

'Actually, I already have a daughter. She's with her dad at the minute. I would have brought her, but she's just a baby, and well, it's an adult do, and Jamie and Fin really wanted me to come.'

'Oh honey, you don't need to tell me all this. I know what life is like. Like Evan said, I've got six of them.'

'How?' Holly responded with a fraction more disbelief than was probably polite, though thankfully, Anne chuckled.

'I must've asked myself that same question a hundred times a day for the last forty years. But I'd get that son of mine to fetch you a drink if I were you. This is a bit of a long story.'

'It's fine, Mom. She doesn't need a long story. In fact, she doesn't need any of the story.' Evan turned to face Holly. 'There, as promised, I have proven without a doubt that I am one of six, with five sisters, the photos of whom are all in my wallet. Thank you for your time, Mom.'

He moved as if to end the conversation, but Anne was having none of it.

'Don't you dare. I've raised you better than that. You can't ring me up at whatever time you fancy and ask me to tell half a story.'

'Technically, I didn't ask you to tell any of the story. Besides, Holly doesn't want to hear it.'

'Yes, I do, thank you very much. I want to hear all about it.'

Anne smiled. It was easy to see where Evan got his looks from. She was a beautiful woman. 'I like this one. She's not afraid to stand up to you. Now, let me tell you where they all came from. Cathy is my eldest. I got pregnant when I was nineteen, and thankfully, she didn't inherit any of her father's bad traits. Not that he was on the scene long enough for me to work out what they all were. He left the moment he realised that having a baby interfered with going to watch football games.'

'That's American football, by the way,' Evan interrupted. 'Most of my family are massively into it. They get very cross if you call your football, actual football, football, even though the players use their feet more, so it is far more aptly named.'

'I am not getting into this argument again,' Anne said. 'Lovely Polly here doesn't want to hear us bickering.'

'Actually, it's Holly, with an aitch,' Evan corrected, saving Holly the need to.

'Oh, I am sorry, dear. Blooming videos. Can't hear half as much as I want to. Anyway, I was telling you about the kids. So Cathy is my eldest. After that I met Jonathan. That's Evan's dad. Well, we had another girl. I would have been fine with two, to be honest, but he wanted a boy, so we kept trying. Along came number three, and guess what?'

'Another girl?' Holly offered the expected answer.

'Another girl. His dad was already outnumbered, so he convinced me to try once more. Anyway, what do you know? I'm pregnant again, and this time it was triplets. And Evan here was the last to poke his head out.'

Holly coughed in surprise. Even before Hope, she had been in awe of anyone with the tough job of raising twins – let alone triplets. Now she assumed they were superhuman. But how someone could do it with three other children to raise was beyond her.

'Oh, I know what you're thinking. It must've been a madhouse.'

'It was a madhouse,' Evan added.

'Ignore him. We had a lot of fun.'

'Apart from the fact that you liked us all to dress in matching clothes, so I spent most of my early life wearing pink.'

'And what's wrong with boys wearing pink, exactly?'

'I agree,' Holly chuckled. 'I happen to find it quite dashing.'

Evan offered her a sideways glance. 'In that case, perhaps I might start wearing it a little more.'

A moment of blushing past between the pair of them. Thankfully, Anne spoke before it could get too awkward.

'Well, I can't be standing around chatting to you two all day. You might not believe it, but I've got things to do. Your dad's convinced he's going to put a fountain in the garden and he'll be digging up my roses soon if I don't go and stop him. Ring again soon, won't you?'

'Will do, Mom. Love you lots.'

'Love you too, baby.'

A second later, the screen was dead.

'So?' Evan's eyebrows were raised as he awaited Holly's response. 'Believe me now?'

'Well, you do put a fairly compelling case forward.'

'Fairly compelling?'

They still hadn't moved since he had hung up. Both sitting on the high kitchen stools. Though at some point, their knees had shifted closer together so that they were now touching, and it was difficult to ignore how intently Evan was smiling at her.

'Why are you looking like that?' She was sure she should move away from him, but at the same time, couldn't bring herself to.

'Like what?'

'I don't know. Strange.'

'Strange? Well, I guess this is what I look like when I want to kiss someone.'

26

The butterflies had overtaken every other sensation in her body. Evan's hand slipped into hers as he twisted around and brushed a strand of hair behind her ear. Feeling like she had lost all control of her body, Holly closed her eyes as she leaned forward.

Was this really going to happen? Was she actually going to kiss a man for the first time since before Hope's birth? She dipped her chin and tilted her head towards Evan, aware of the sounds of his breath, and her own pulse drumming hard enough to break free.

'Tell me you've got some ice packs in here.' The front door banged and Holly and Evan jumped apart as Tyler barged into the living room, his white T-shirt near translucent with sweat. 'Beer. I need a beer.'

'Make that two beers.' Naomi followed him in, limping as much as Holly had that morning.

'Make that a lot of beers.' Caroline flopped down onto the sofa. 'We need a lot of beers.'

Looking at the state of the intrepid hikers, Holly was more than a little grateful that she had escaped the day's trek, especially given how much better her ankle was now feeling. Every one of them, bar

Fin and Jamie, were dripping with sweat and sporting red faces, which could have been either sunburn or from exertion.

'You look like you had fun.' Holly's heart was racing as if she was sixteen years old again and had been caught snogging in the living room when she was meant to be working on a homework project. As subtly as she could, she slid off her stool and crossed the room to Caroline.

'Let me get you those drinks.' Evan said, instinctively moving in the opposite direction. 'Why don't you guys jump straight in the pool? I can bring them out to you.'

'God, I don't think I've ever needed a swimming pool so much in my entire life,' Zahida commented as she dragged her feet through the French doors and out onto the patio. 'Ten miles. We walked *ten miles.*'

'Ten miles, in this heat. Impressive.' Holly's pulse had dropped, but it was hard not to keep looking at Evan, just to see if he was looking at her too, though he had turned away so that his back was facing her.

'I can't believe how much you lot complained.' Jamie's first stop was the sink, where she filled up a pint glass with water. 'It wasn't like we did it all in one go. We stopped at least twenty times for Eddie to take photos. Not to mention every time Spencer whinged about another insect bite.'

'It's not whingeing if it's a genuine concern.' Spencer pouted. 'Those bugs were actively attacking me.'

As Holly cast another quick glance over to the kitchen, she caught Evan's eye and offered a quick, involuntary smile.

'Has everything been okay while we were away?' Caroline asked. 'Anything exciting happen?'

'Yes. I mean no. Yes, everything was completely fine. No, nothing exciting happened.' Holly spoke a fraction too fast, only to realise she had forgotten one important factor. 'Oh, wait, something exciting did happen. I got my luggage back.'

'That is exciting. Is that the only thing?' Caroline pressed.

Thankfully, Jamie appeared behind them before Holly had to suffer Caroline's unfeasibly scrutinising gaze for too long.

'Did I just hear you've got your luggage back?' She placed a hand on Holly's shoulder. 'That's good. It means you'll have something to wear on the yacht tomorrow.'

Holly still wasn't sure anything she owned was yacht worthy, but she didn't say that.

'What about the ankle? How's it feeling?'

'Loads better.' She lifted it into the air so they could see how much the swelling had gone down.

'That looks great.'

'Yeah, I can walk on it easier, too. I think all the time in the pool really helped. Talking of which, I think I might go in for another dip now.'

In the afternoon light, the pool was an even deeper shade of blue, matched perfectly by the azure of the sea. Grabbing her book from the sofa, Holly headed outside to one of the sun loungers, but had been sitting down for less than a minute when Caroline swept up beside her.

'So, what's going on with you and Evan?'

'What do you mean?' Holly adjusted the towel and avoided looking at her friend. 'Nothing's going on. Why would anything be going on? Nothing's going on. Not with me.'

'Well, I wasn't 100 per cent sure before.' Caroline smirked, 'But now I know for certain something happened.'

Holly wasn't sure if she was madder at Caroline or herself. She gritted her teeth and checked there was no one within eavesdropping distance before she lowered her voice and spoke.

'Fine, something almost happened, maybe. I don't know. But he's asked if we can go on a date when we get back to the UK.'

'This is amazing. You like him, right? Of course you like him. He's perfect. Why wouldn't you like him?'

'And I spoke to his mum on the phone.'

This was too much for Caroline. She had barely covered her mouth before she erupted in a shriek.

'Oh my God, that's so exciting.'

'Calm down. You're getting way ahead of yourself. It's nothing. It's really nothing.'

'This is not nothing. This is definitely something. Definitely, definitely something.'

Unable to bear her friend any longer, Holly pulled down her sunglasses and lay down on the sun lounger.

'We're not done talking about this,' Caroline said as she followed suit and lay down next to her.

'Yes, we are.'

Holly spoke as firmly as she could, but it was hard considering how much she was still smiling. With her eyes closed, her mind immediately returned to that moment. That near kiss that would, without any doubt, have been a full-on, earth-shattering smooch had they not been interrupted.

As she soaked in the afternoon sun, she wondered if there was some way she could make a habit of this. Coming somewhere warm, somewhere new and adventurous. After all, she needed to make the most of Hope being little. Soon, they would be bound by term dates and school holidays, and she wouldn't have the freedom to travel.

She was busy planning where some of these exotic, frugal holidays would take her when her phone buzzed.

Her mum's name on the screen.

Considering how often her mother sent photos of Hope when

Holly was at work, she had considered it strange that she'd not received a single message from her that day. But she knew how much her mother was hoping she would switch off, and limiting contact was obviously her way of doing that.

With a smile on her face, she answered the video call, ready to see Hope grinning back at her, but instead it was her mother who was staring at the screen and she looked anything but happy.

Holly sat bolt upright.

'Mum, what is it? What's wrong? Is it Hope? Where is she? Is she okay?'

'Hope's fine, darling. She's with Ben. He picked her up at lunchtime.' A sigh of relief billowed through Holly, only to evaporate almost instantly.

'What do you mean at lunchtime? She was meant to go back to his this afternoon. That's what we arranged. Is it Dad? Is his heart okay?'

'Your dad's fine, darling. But I'm afraid there's a bit of bad news.' She paused, causing the tension to wrap around Holly like a cloak. 'There's been a break-in at the shop.'

27

Holly stared at her mother's image on the screen before she shook her head, trying to make sense of what she just heard.

'There's been a break-in? At the sweet shop? At my shop?'

Caroline was staring at her, hanging on every word. And she probably had a right to listen in; she worked there too. But Holly was still having difficulty processing what her mother was saying. She walked into the house.

'What do you mean, a break-in at the shop? What did they steal?'

She'd never judge anyone for having a sweet tooth, but breaking into a sweet shop felt a little far-fetched even for her.

'They didn't take anything, love. Arthur had emptied the till last night and he'd taken the cash home to go to the bank this morning. They didn't find the safe either. They might have taken a box of Belgian truffles, but your dad can't remember if he restocked that shelf or not.' A quiet hiss echoed down the line, confirming Wendy's belief that Arthur should have absolutely known how many boxes of truffles were on the shelf before the break-in. 'If it makes you feel any better, you weren't the only one. They hit four shops last night, including yours. The jeweller lost quite a bit. Such a shame.'

It didn't make Holly feel any better that someone else's business had been stolen from, though it was a small comfort that they hadn't found the safe.

'What about the CCTV? Did we get a video of them?' She'd had the cameras installed when she very first moved there, after a shoplifting incident had left a sour taste in her mouth. They had been instrumental in proving Giles Caverty was responsible for planting a mouse by the chocolate hedgehogs. Though that whole incident felt so long ago, it was almost as if it had happened to someone else.

'We've told police they can have any footage we've got, though the culprits were all dressed in black and you can't make out much of their faces. Still, all the shops have cameras, so there's a good chance one of the others has got a clearer picture. The police think it's school children. You know. A prank gone too far. I'm sure they'll catch them.'

Holly felt sick. It didn't feel like a prank. It felt like somebody had invaded her home. And in Bourton, of all places. She would have expected it in a big city, or even some larger towns, but not a village like Bourton. More than once, when baby-brain and lack of sleep had been wreaking havoc on her, she'd got home from work to discover she'd left the back door of the cottage open all day. She wouldn't be doing that again.

'We had to close today,' her mother carried on. 'They made a bit of a mess with a few of the jars, so we cleaned that up and got the window repair man out. He did us a bit of a discount too, considering he's got to do several on the row. And Andrea came down too, helped us clear the rest up.'

'Thank you, Mum. Thank you for sorting it all out.'

'Really, it wasn't too much of a stress for us, though you should probably ring and thank Ben for picking up Hope early. We told him it was fine, that Arthur could do the clean up on his own, but he didn't want to cause us any extra stress.'

'I'll message him now,' Holly said with a pang of gratitude. It was a sign of how decent a guy Ben was that he still made such an effort with her parents. Then again, they were his child's grandparents.

'What happens now? What do I need to do?' Holly paced the dining area. The others had all headed outside to give the illusion of privacy, but the glass doors were wide open and when she glanced outside, she could see them listening in.

'You don't need to do anything, darling. It's all sorted, everything is with the police. I wasn't going to tell you at all until you got back, but I didn't want you to find out from someone else.'

The words of truth offered a fraction more comfort, though another bucket load of guilt. It had taken her mother a full day to pluck up the courage to call her, not wanting to ruin her day. If Holly could be half the mother to Hope that Wendy was to her, she knew she'd be on the right track.

'I guess I should just carry on and try to forget about it, then? Though I'm not sure that'll be so easy.'

'Don't be like that. I wouldn't have rung you if I thought it would bring you down. Promise me you're still going to have fun?'

Holly glanced back out the window only for the others to suddenly start chatting as if they hadn't been eavesdropping the whole time. Only one face continued to look straight at her. Evan's. His smile was ever so slight, but exactly what Holly needed.

'Don't worry. I'm fine. Just make sure that Dad isn't under too much stress, okay? The last thing I want is for this to put extra pressure on him.'

'Don't you worry about that. I've got a close eye on him. Now you go and have a couple of drinks for me. Love you, Holly bear.'

'Love you too, Mum.'

When the phone went dead, Holly moved over to the sofa, dropped onto the seat, and continued to stare at her phone. So much for thinking she should try to make holidays a regular thing. Perhaps she was just one of those people that was destined never to leave their home without disaster striking.

'Hey.' Jamie came over and sat on the sofa next to her. 'Really sorry. We all heard about what happened. That seriously sucks.'

Holly rubbed her temples, trying to ease the headache she could feel forming.

'Thank you. Mum says it's not that bad. They didn't take anything and I know it would have happened even if I'd stayed at home. But it puts them under extra stress, you know? And now Ben has looked after Hope for all these extra hours, and he's going to be stressed because he's behind on work.'

'And there is absolutely nothing you can do about that.'

Jamie was always blunt, so it shouldn't have come as a surprise that she was so matter of fact.

'So, you can either worry about things that you have no control over, or you can enjoy your holiday with us. Particularly as your ankle looks fine now. You know you were pacing the room like a caged tiger then, right?'

She was right, Holly realised. She had been walking up and down and hadn't even thought of her ankle.

'The boys are going to put on the barbecue in a minute. Why don't you pour yourself a big glass of wine and come outside and join us?'

'That sounds like a good idea.' Holly was about to stand up when Evan appeared in front of them.

'On second thoughts, Jamie, I need to get my towel from my room and message Ben to make sure everything's all right with Hope. You go outside without me.'

'Okay, but don't be long. We've said we're going to have a water polo game, and I need you on my team to make sure we win.'

It was a definite lie as Jamie would most likely thrash the boys without any help at all, but she appreciated the comment.

'You okay?' Evan said when Jamie was out of earshot. 'I feel like the afternoon has gone rapidly downhill since the others came back.'

He offered her a small, slanted grin. Holly knew she was meant to reciprocate, but she couldn't find the energy.

'I'm sorry. I'm not exactly the best company. Maybe I should go up to my room, have another afternoon nap.'

'Really? You've been inside all day. Perhaps what you need is to get out of the house.'

The thought of seeing a bit more of the countryside was definitely appealing but she wasn't sure she had the energy.

'Honestly, it's not exactly a tough house to be trapped in. Besides, my ankle's only just fine to walk on. I'm not sure I should push it.'

The slight grin that had graced Evan's lips lifted higher until it was an outright grin.

'Who said anything about walking?'

'Just give me two minutes. I want to make a phone call first.'

Evan headed towards the staircase, leaving Holly to wonder what on earth she had agreed to. Heading out of the house seemed like a good idea, but when Evan came back into the living room, the way he was grinning made her think this was going to be something different from your average drive.

'Well, that's all sorted. Now I just need to make sure I've got a helmet for you.'

'Helmet?'

'Of course. Safety first.'

Five minutes later, Holly was standing outside the house next to a baby-blue moped, which Evan wheeled out from his garage. A moped which he expected her to climb on the back of.

'Is it wrong that I'm scared?' she said as she pulled the helmet over her head, grateful for the snug fit. 'I'm not really into the whole motorbike thing.'

'It's a Vespa. Far, far less powerful than a motorbike,' Evan said. 'So I guess you've never been on one before?'

'You'd be guessing right.'

Other than a standard push bike, Holly had never been on anything that didn't have four wheels – not a motorbike, nor a scooter – and before now, she had no desire to. But as Evan slipped onto the front of the seat and patted the space behind him, the first tingles of excitement formed. It seemed like the bucket list was back on.

'Just hold on to me,' Evan said as the engine growled into life. 'I promise I won't go that fast.'

They drove higher and higher, weaving around the twists and turns of the road. At first, each bend in the road had Holly gripping Evan tighter and tighter, but gradually the fear began to recede and she even closed her eyes once or twice, enjoying the feel of the wind against her face. Not to mention the aroma emanating from Evan. It was probably the scenery adding to the mood but she couldn't remember a man smelling quite as good as he did. Hurriedly, Holly realised that the fact she could smell Evan was probably an indication that her head was far too close to his back, and as subtly as she could, she moved a fraction further away.

They were partway up the mountain road when Evan took a turn up a narrow track. The surrounding fields were blanketed with rows and rows of perfectly parallel vines which stretched out as far as they could see.

So many times, Holly wanted to ask him to stop so she could stare out at the view. Or perhaps take a photo to remind her that this place was real. During one of the times she was having that exact thought, Evan slowed to a stop and cut the engine.

'You doing okay?' he said through his helmet.

'This is amazing. I love it!'

'So, do you want to have a go?'

Holly frowned, wondering if perhaps her helmet was making it difficult for her to hear.

'Sorry, what did you say?'

'I said, did you want to have a go?'

'On the Vespa?'

She looked down at the vehicle beneath her. A Vespa had to be the most impractical vehicle for a single mother because she wouldn't be able to take her child on it. But Hope wasn't with her right now, she reminded herself. This trip away was about her, which was why her cheeks were once again aching as she looked at Evan.

* * *

Unfortunately, the confidence that Holly had developed waterskiing didn't transfer automatically to the Vespa, and she had a few false starts.

'I don't think I'm insured to do this,' Holly said after one particular wobble, but Evan was there behind her, holding on to the handles and steadying the vehicle.

'Don't worry, I won't let anything happen to you. And I have brilliant insurance.'

The knowledge that he was there to guide her and keep her on track helped, and soon she was turning in circles up and down the track.

When she finally stopped and pulled off her helmet, her hair was stuck to her head with sweat.

'A natural!' he exclaimed, his grin almost as big as hers.

For a split second, Holly thought he might be about to try to kiss her again, or that she might kiss him. Then she realised what a sweaty mess she was and hastily tried to straighten herself.

'I didn't get it as quick as the waterskiing.'

'You were brilliant, trust me.'

She beamed at the compliment, regardless of whether it was true.

'Do you think you can grab a photo of me on it?' She took her phone out of her pocket. 'So I don't forget.'

'Sure thing.' He took her phone before stepping back and taking a couple of shots, then handed it back to her.

'I think we should have a selfie together, too.'

His smile slanted as he crouched down by her side, while Holly stretched her arm out as far as it would go. She had never been one for selfies before Hope, but now Holly was determined not to forget any moments and had finally learned how to hold the phone and click the button at the same time. As Evan's and her face came onto the screen together, it was hard to deny how happy and perfect it all looked. And not nearly as sweaty or hot as she'd expected, considering the helmet and ride up. Thankfully, her bruise seemed to have gone down slightly too.

'A lasting memory of your first ride,' Evan said when she was done.

'And hopefully not my last.'

'Why should it be? You could get one.'

'Unfortunately, there's no way a baby seat can go on this thing.'

'Well, maybe you can save it for yourself. You get time on your own, don't you? When Hope is with Ben, right? Trips around the Cotswolds on a little thing like this, with the wind in your hair... sounds perfect to me.'

Holly imagined the thought. There were so many country lanes in her area, she'd have no problem travelling from one little village to another without needing to go near a dual carriageway. It would be tempting. That was when reality hit.

'What is it?' Evan's brow furrowed as he noted the sudden change. 'Did I say something wrong?'

Holly shook her head, though it took her a moment longer to find the words she needed.

'My life isn't like yours, Evan. I don't have a spare couple of grand to buy a Vespa. And I don't think I even have the money to put fuel in one. And it's lovely to think my life would be like this – road trips and adventures and amazing villas with beautiful swimming pools – but in two days, I'm going to go back to my real life, so I think maybe I should try to limit my daydreaming.'

She hoped the words hadn't come across as rude, as she certainly hadn't meant them that way, but as a silence spread between them, she feared she may have pushed Evan away, just as she'd started to want him closer. Yet, as she went to apologise, he placed his hand on her cheek.

'That may be the case back in the UK. But like you said, we've got two and a half days to go and I plan on making as many of your daydreams come true as I can in that time. Now, budge up; I need to drive or we're going to be late.'

'Late? I thought we were going back to the villa.'

'Not yet. I thought I might cash that date in a bit early. Now, put your helmet on.'

29

Back on the road, they continued onwards and upwards until eventually, Evan took a turning by a wooden sign with faded, white lettering.

Once again, the tarmac of the road quickly changed to gravel, although this time Evan didn't stop to ask Holly if she wanted to drive. She was fine with that, given how busy she was staring at the thousands of grapevines that stretched out around them. Finally, a large house came into view, nestled right in the middle of it all. No, not a house, she realised. A château. A genuine French château.

'This is a vineyard?' She finally put two and two together. 'You've brought me to a vineyard?'

'That's okay, isn't it? You were drinking wine last night, so I thought you'd like it.'

It took her a second to realise what this meant. 'Does this mean we're tasting wine? Because in that case, I like it. I definitely like wine, and I like some wines more than others, but really, I just drink whatever is on offer.'

Evan put his hand on hers, cutting the babble short.

'You don't need to know anything about it. That's the whole point of coming here. They teach you.'

'So we're doing a tasting?'

'You are. I have to drive. But I've done it before, so I'm okay with that.'

Adrenaline was skipping through Holly's veins. She'd seen wine tastings before on television shows. Sophisticated events, taking place in the most beautiful locations, just like this one she was in now. But just like waterskiing and luxury villas, it wasn't anything she had ever envisioned for herself.

She was about to thank Evan yet again when a tall woman with dark hair and a magnificent, long, red dress stepped out of the château, waving her hands emphatically.

'Evan. Welcome. Welcome.' She bounded across the gravel as if she was in a perfume commercial before kissing Evan on both cheeks. For a second, Holly felt like she should shift back a little and give them some privacy, but the woman didn't stop with Evan. Before Holly realised what was happening, the woman had grasped Holly's face and was planting equally expressive kisses on her cheeks too.

'And you must be 'Olly, I'm so glad you're here. Come, come. Edouard is just setting up.'

'Helene is the owner of the vineyard,' Evan said, offering Holly an arm. 'She took it over a few years ago and has done an incredible job. They've got awards coming out of their ears.'

Helene threw a scowl over her shoulder.

'You are exaggerating. We are still very small. But we are getting there.'

Everything about the way Helene moved screamed elegance and sophistication and, as they made their way up the steps, Holly couldn't help but feel underdressed. She was still wearing the shorts she'd had on in the afternoon when she was reading in the villa, and this didn't look like the type of place that let people in wearing shorts. It looked like the type of place people came to get married and yet Helene hadn't stopped her yet.

'Are you enjoying the villa? The view is beautiful, is it not?'

'Stunning,' Holly answered truthfully. 'I've never stayed anywhere like it.'

Still holding Evan's arm, she stepped into the hallway, where a large, copper chandelier hung from the ceiling, perfectly paired with turquoise wallpaper embellished with gold reliefs of peacock feathers. If Holly had attempted this kind of decoration in her house, it would've looked garish, but this was anything but. This was old-time elegance. The smell of wood varnish and red wine were embedded into the very floors of the building, taking her back centuries.

'I know we 'ave our group tastings in the cellar, but I thought we would stay up 'ere this afternoon. The view is too good to be shut away in the dark, don't you think?'

Holly turned back to the doorway, still mesmerised by the scenery. Vine-covered hills rolled away from them as the slightest sliver of sea glimmered in the distance. A strange flicker of guilt twinged within her. As much as her mother pretended she had no desire to travel, Holly knew how Wendy would love somewhere like here. Perhaps, if things at the sweet shop went well enough, Holly would bring them on a family trip in a couple of years' time. Once Hope was older. Assuming her daughter wasn't spending all her holidays with Ben and Georgia by then. Holly pushed the thought quickly from her mind.

'Please, take a seat. Edouard will be with you soon. If I'd 'ad a little more warning that you were coming, I would've been able to do it myself, but I am afraid I 'ave meetings I cannot miss. Ah-ha, right on time.'

With a nod of her head, she gestured outside, where a four-by-four was parking up on the driveway. Holly stared at the vehicle, fixated, not by the car, but by the driver. Large sunglasses covered his eyes and he wore a baseball cap pulled down low on his head, but there was something familiar about the way he was leaning back and holding the steering wheel, completely at ease. She had known someone who drove just like that back in England, and the thought was enough to tie her stomach into knots.

'We should let you go,' Evan said as he kissed Helene's cheeks and brought Holly back to the moment, although it was hard to ignore the tension that continued to hold fast within her.

She was being ridiculous, she reprimanded herself. Caught up in the grand gestures and lavish lifestyle, that was all. It was no surprise she found herself thinking of Giles; this was the exact type of place she could imagine him spending a weekend or taking his latest woman on a first date. With a quick glance back outside, she discovered the man had turned away from her and was crouching down looking at the wheel of his car in a manner that was distinctly un-Giles-like.

"Olly?' Holly turned back just in time to receive more cheek kisses. 'It is lovely to meet you. 'Opefully I will get to see more of you soon?'

'Yes... of course.'

A second later, Helene and her stunning red dress left, leaving Holly alone with Evan, and thoughts of Giles fading rapidly from her mind.

'She said we're in here.' Evan gestured to the room on their left.

'I think it's the reading room.'

'That would make sense.'

The walls were covered with floor-to-ceiling bookcases and the smell of vintage leather was almost as strong as the aroma of wine. Inside the room, a dozen wine glasses had been set out on a small table, next to a long couch, though there was currently no sign of the wine. Or any other people.

'Is this going to be a group thing?' Holly said, thinking of all the wine-tasting events she'd seen on television. They had always involved large groups of people, many of whom had arrived as part of a bus tour so that they could drive home safely.

'Yes,' Evan said promptly, before a slight smirk spread across his face. 'A group of two.'

'You mean it's just us?'

'This is the date you promised me, remember? Besides, this way you get to ask lots of questions. And I'm just interested to find out if you babble more or less when you're drunk.'

'Hey.'

She was about to nudge him playfully when a man entered the room, pushing a large, metal drinks trolly brimming with wine bottles. With his blond hair and bright-blue eyes, he was the antithesis of Helene, but nonetheless attractive and. once again. Evan was crossing the room, ready to exchange kisses.

'Edouard, how's it going? Helene was saying how busy you are?'

'Hopefully busy enough that she will employ some people to help me.'

Edouard's laugh was deep and throaty and immediately put Holly at ease. From greeting Evan, he moved across to Holly, but rather than kissing her cheek, he took her hand and placed it gently against his lips.

'Yes, very beautiful. Very beautiful indeed,' he said, before clapping his hands together loudly. 'And now, for the wine.'

30

After flicking out a white napkin, Edouard cleared his throat and made it apparent the lesson was about to begin.

'We are going to start with the white wine and then the red and the rosé and save the sparkling wines for last.'

'That sounds like a lot of wine.' Holly frowned as she stared at the bottles in front of her.

'You're most welcome to spit.' Edouard gestured to the silver bucket in front of him, offering her a twinkling smile.

Holly had seen people spitting out wine plenty of times in the shows she'd seen, but she couldn't imagine doing it for real. If nothing else, it felt like a terrible waste. Especially given this wine was likely to be substantially nicer than the average bottle of plonk she got on offer at Co-op.

'You can drink it,' Evan said. 'I would. I find spitting weird.'

She wasn't sure whether Evan was lying to make her feel at ease or not, but she was grateful. If this was a proper date, like he had implied, then she hardly wanted to spend it with him watching her spit in a bucket all evening.

'So, our first bottle is a Chablis.' He poured a small drop in the bottom of the glass. At least she didn't have to worry about getting too drunk. There couldn't have been more than a tenth of a normal serving there.

'You want to hold your drink by the stem, and swill it round, like this. 'Ave a good look at the colour. Then breathe in that aroma, like this.'

Following his instructions, Holly swilled her wine, then stuck her nose deep into the glass.

While some of Edouard's suggestions Holly had no problem with, one or two were slightly more unexpected.

'You need to hold the wine in your mouth for five seconds, then after you swallow, tilt your head forward and just appreciate the volume of saliva that gathers in your mouth.'

'I'm meant to be appreciating the volume of saliva?' Holly repeated, wondering if she had somehow misheard him.

'It is an excellent judge of acidity,' he explained. 'See for yourself.'

After a quick look at Evan, who nodded encouragingly, Holly took a sip of wine, held it in her mouth for five seconds before swallowing, then tipped her head forward. However weird it was, it was true; she could feel the saliva gathering under her bottom lip. By the time she was on the third drink, she didn't even think before tipping her head forward and experiencing it all again.

'So, do you have a favourite?' Evan asked, as Edouard poured her the final wines, which, as he promised, were sparkling.

'Is it wrong to say all of them?'

'Probably not wrong, though it won't help me know which ones I should buy you as a gift.'

Holly laughed, though it was tinged with awkwardness. Men showering gifts and money on women they barely knew didn't instil her with a sense of confidence. There was no way Evan could be as interested in her as he was making out. Could there? 'Trust me, I don't need any more. You have done more than enough. This place is phenomenal.'

'I know, I suggested it to Fin as part of the stag and hen do, but you know what he's like; his body is a temple and all that. Besides, he was worried Tyler and Spencer wouldn't behave. But now, I'm glad. I'm glad it's just been the two of us.'

'Me too.'

Holly could feel how hard she was smiling. Even with all her doubts, it was impossible to deny the fluttering in her stomach which increased with each millimetre he shifted towards her. Edouard had already wheeled the wine out, meaning they were on their own, and there was no one to come and disturb them this time.

Closing her eyes, Holly leaned forward and before she could even decide whether this was real life or a dream, they were kissing.

31

When they broke away from each other, Holly met Evan's eyes, only to find him smiling just as widely as she was.

'I wasn't expecting this to happen,' he said, running a finger across her palm before he kissed her again, just as tenderly. 'I wasn't expecting to meet someone like you.'

Holly shifted back, pressing her lips together tightly. 'You know, I'm really not that special. I'm incredibly ordinary.'

'You are definitely not,' he said, and kissed her yet again. 'I knew it from the first moment I saw you. I can't explain it. There was just something about you. And I'm so glad I trusted my instinct.'

She wanted to respond and agree. Or at least kiss him again. After all, it had been an incredible kiss. Even now, fireworks continued to erupt within her. Her whole body was alive with the tingles of excitement that could only come from a first kiss. But for some reason, her gaze shifted from Evan, back outside through the window. The car had gone and with it, a pang of disappointment. But did she really want Giles there? And what did it mean that now, when she was this close to moving past him, he was in her mind more than ever?

'We should head back to the villa,' she said, keeping her tone as neutral as possible. 'The others are probably wondering what's happened to us.'

The ride back to the villa didn't feel anywhere near as scary as the one to the vineyard, though whether that was to do with several glasses of wine, or the fact that Holly had her arms wrapped far more tightly around Evan than before, she couldn't say. All in all, though, she couldn't have imagined a better way to end the evening than watching the moon reflect off the water as they weaved their way back down the hillside.

When they reach the villa, Evan parked up inside the garage before the pair of them removed the helmets. Instinctively, he moved to kiss her, but rather than reciprocating the way she had done at the vineyard, she placed both hands on his chest and stepped back.

'It's not that I don't want to. I do. So much. But this is Jamie and Fin's trip, you know? If people know that we're... whatever we are... then that will detract from it and I don't want things to be awkward? Am I making sense?'

'You are making perfect sense. Honestly, I get it. I mean, it makes me like you even more and I hate you for that, but I get it.'

She smiled, trying to hide the flicker of guilt that she felt. No matter how much she'd enjoyed feeling herself pressed up against Evan as they rode home, it had been impossible not to let her mind wander back to the car at the vineyard. If that had been Giles, she wondered, what would she have said to him? Or would they need to speak at all? Perhaps they had been through so much together that they were past the stage of needing words. Again, she shook her head and forced herself to quash the thoughts. Giles was her past, and while Evan might not be her future, he was her present. He was kind, and funny and basically everything she could ever have dreamed of. When she went back to Bourton and reality set in, all this would be nothing but a fun memory and so it seemed a shame not to make the most of it.

They stepped out of the garage, but when Evan reached the front door, he stopped and turned to face her.

'As I'm going to spend the entire evening having to force myself to keep my hands off you, I might just need one more kiss before we get inside. Is that okay?'

Why was there something so lovely about a man asking to kiss her? Maybe it was the accent, or maybe it was because the newness and excitement was something she hadn't experienced for so long. Pushing aside all the doubts and uncertainties, Holly allowed herself to focus on the moment.

'I suppose one more kiss would be all right.' She stepped towards him and pushed herself up onto tiptoes, her lips finding his as if they were drawn there magnetically. And once they touched, she had no desire to pull away. No, what she wanted was for the world to slip away for a moment, just the way it had done at the vineyards. Yet no sooner had the thought occurred than a chorus of singing started from the balcony above them.

'Holly and Evan, sitting in a tree. K-I-S-S-I-N-G!'

As they broke apart, she looked up to the wrap-around balcony, where the entire group were there with drinks in their hands, looking down on them and laughing. A crimson blush flooded her face, as Evan slipped his hand into hers and squeezed.

'I guess this means we're busted,' he said.

'I think we are definitely busted.'

* * *

The strangest thing about sitting on the sofa with Evan was how comfortable he seemed to be with it. Not that it wasn't nice, having Evan's hand resting casually across her knee. Once or twice, she even forgot it was there, and moved to drop her shoulder onto his, only to jolt back upright and realise how ridiculous the situation was. She and Ben had been affectionate enough in private, and offered occasional displays in public, like a quick kiss on the lips when he popped into the shop at lunchtime, but never early on like this. And never with so many people around them. How was it that Evan had made her feel so comfortable so quickly? Especially with all the doubts she had.

As much as she didn't want it to be true, the only explanation Holly could see for the romantic haze she found herself in was that Evan was a game player. The type of man who made women feel completely at ease, then broke their hearts. Much the same way as someone else had done to her when she first moved to Bourton. But Giles had had good reason to try to make Holly think he was interested in her. Besides, if Evan really was that much of a Casanova, why didn't Jamie say something? And why had he introduced her to his mother? Whatever Evan's angle was, she was having a hard time figuring it out. Still, she was only there for a short while. It seemed silly to stress about it too much. After all, she was hardly going to fall in love with the guy in a couple of days, was she?

After several minutes of ribbing from the group, they had walked in hand in hand and sat down on the sofa by one another. Considering how much Caroline had pried about things earlier, Holly expected an interrogation, but so far there hadn't been the slightest bit of questioning. It would come, though. She knew her friends.

'Tell me that there's no walk involved tomorrow.' Naomi sat with her feet in a bowl of warm, soapy water. 'I can't do any more walking.'

'I promise, no walking. Just lazing on a boat.' Evan replied.

'Do I have to walk to the boat?'

'It's not that far. Just down a jetty. And I promise, when you're on the boat, that's it. I'm sure one of us will be okay to bring you your drinks so you don't even have to get up.'

'You know she's gonna hold you to that.' Holly tilted her head to look up at Evan.

'Don't worry, I'll bring you all your drinks too.'

With that, he leaned forward and planted a light kiss on the lips.

'No.' The cries went up from the group.

'This is not meant to be a romantic situation.'

'If anything, it's meant to be unromantic. An unromantic joint stag and hen do.'

'Exactly. We wouldn't have agreed to come otherwise. I'm not one for romance,' Zahida piped up, although Holly couldn't help but notice how she looked at Spencer as she spoke.

'I'm sorry.' Evan straightened himself up, though their hands remained entwined. 'There will be no romance at all. You have our word. Right?'

'Absolutely.' Holly's lips twitched involuntarily. Why was it so difficult to look at him without wanting to smile so much? It was as if she had slipped into a Disney film. Though there was one way to rectify that. Releasing Evan's hand, she stood up.

'I am going to leave you guys to it. I want to fall asleep before Caroline puts her frog music on.'

'Hey, it's not that bad. And it's whale music.'

'It's really not,' Holly said, before hugging her friend goodnight, then moving and hugging Jamie and Fin. Only when she had said goodnight to everyone did she move towards the staircase.

'Maybe I could walk you to your room?' Evan asked.

'That would be very nice.'

Ignoring the jokes behind her, Holly took Evan's hand, and they made their way upstairs.

'Are you sure you're comfortable with this?' Evan said as they stopped outside Holly's bedroom door. 'With everyone knowing, I mean.'

'Surprisingly, I am. Are you?'

'Absolutely.'

She knew another kiss was coming. And a good one. Her pulse raced, her breath grew shallower and shallower, like she wouldn't be able to breathe properly until they were kissing again. Finally, he placed his lips against hers.

When they separated, Evan planted another small peck on her forehead.

'Okay then, I shall leave you here and bid you good night.'

'Good night then,' she said, offering him one more quick kiss, before she slipped into her room, closing the door behind her.

32

After the excitement of the day, Holly had assumed that she would be awake all night. But as it happened, she had one of the best night's sleep since Hope's birth and when she rolled over and blinked her eyes open, a thin strip of sunlight was breaking through between the blinds. She stretched out a little, taking a moment to enjoy the soft sheets, when she became aware of the gentle tapping on her door. She twisted her head to the side, to where Caroline was still snoring away.

'Holly?' Evan's voice was a soft whisper. 'Are you awake?'

As Holly's mind cleared of sleep, a flicker of anxiety gripped her. People didn't generally wake one of their guests up when the entire house was still asleep unless there was a problem. Her throat dried. Of course. The kisses last night. He most likely wanted to speak to her in private to explain why it was best if it didn't happen again. Apologise for his temporary insanity brought on by the idea of an impending wedding. The disappointment struck her firmly between the ribs and caught her by surprise. Had she really fallen for him that much in such a short space of time? No, she couldn't have. Holly swallowed back the ache that was fixing in her ribs. She had expected this. A little earlier than planned, but she had still expected it. Ignoring the gnawing that continued to chew away at her, Holly kicked her feet over the edge of the bed and opened the door a crack.

'Sorry, I didn't wake you, did I?'

'I don't think so. I'm not sure,' she answered honestly. 'Is everything okay?'

'It's nice seeing you.' He leaned in, going for a kiss, when Holly jumped back and covered her mouth.

'I haven't brushed my teeth. Major morning breath.' The words came out muffled.

'I don't mind.'

'Well, I do.'

After a disappointed pout, Evan dropped the idea and carried on talking.

'I'm heading down to the bakery to grab breakfast. I didn't know if you wanted to come with me?'

Holly hesitated. One trip out when she hadn't realised it was a date could have been an accident, but going with him again now would be a conscious decision and make the disappointment of it ending even harder.

'On the Vespa?'

'If that's what you want?'

She pressed her lips tightly together. Whether she was setting herself up for a fall or not, she didn't want to give up another go on the Vespa. Not when she didn't know if she'd ever get the chance again.

'Give me five minutes to get dressed.'

'And clean your teeth?' Evan added with a hopeful smirk.

'And clean my teeth.'

The scenery looked entirely different in the morning. The sky was a powdery blue, dappled with the thinnest clouds, which would soon be burned through by the sun. Once again, Holly felt no concern as she wrapped her arms tightly around Evan and pressed her chest against him. This time they travelled inland, past yellow stones houses, and gated manors, until he brought them to a stop outside a small square.

While most of the shops were relatively quiet, one already had a substantial queue weaving its way out of the door and onto the square.

'Let me guess. That's where we're heading?' Holly asked.

'It's how you know the place is good. If there isn't a queue, skip it. It's like restaurants. You always go where the locals eat.'

Leaving the helmets on top of the Vespa, they headed over and joined the queue. All around them, people were chattering and Holly wished once again that she spoke a different language. Maybe when she went home, she would download one of those apps that promised to teach you. It would be useful if she was ever to come back with Evan. She stamped out the thought, almost as quickly as believing she'd seen Giles at the vineyard. Whatever this was with Evan, it would likely fizzle out the moment she stepped foot on the plane and she needed to remember that.

In what felt like no time, they were inside the shop and confronted with a range of pastries which caused Holly's eyes to bulge.

'So, do you see anything you fancy getting?'

'I fancy everything,' she said. 'I don't have a clue what half of it is, mind. But look at it all. Look at that cheese. I don't think I've ever seen a sandwich with that much cheese in.'

Evan pointed to the item in the cabinet and spoke to the baker in French. A moment later, she was handing him the cheese baguette.

'We might as well get a few things. I wanted to get some food to take on the yacht with us, anyway.'

'I love it. It's so different.' Holly was unable to contain her excitement. 'I know it's just a shop, but it feels so exotic.'

Evan let out a light chuckle.

'You're laughing at me.' Holly slapped his arm lightly.

'I'm not laughing at you. I'm laughing *with* you.'

'I'm not sure that can work if the other person's not laughing.'

'You're right, I'm sorry. It's just you're so cute.' As he kissed her again, Holly wondered if she'd ever been referred to as cute by anyone else before. It wasn't an adjective she associated herself with, but she wasn't going to object if that was what Evan thought. But she wasn't going to get used to it either. This was a holiday flirtation, nothing more. And she needed to remember that.

As he paid for the pastries, he hooked his hand into hers.

'If you're finding the bakery exotic, and you're in the mood for some cheese, we've got a spare half an hour. We could head to the supermarket.'

'Really? We can do that?'

He laughed again. 'Don't get too excited; it's just a shop.'

* * *

It was not just a shop. The smell hit Holly the moment she stepped inside. Rich and exotic, there were too many aromas to make sense of.

'Can we get some cheese?' Holly was bouncing as she spoke.

'You get whatever you want.'

'What about wine? Do we need more wine?'

'There's plenty of wine at the villa,' Evan replied, before seeing her face and changing his mind. 'But sure, why not? Let's grab a few more bottles.'

Holly pushed the trolley excitedly as she dropped in one item, then another. Only when she had selected half a dozen cheeses, three different types of crackers, and some strange crispbreads to add to Evan's selection, did she realise one important fact.

'I didn't bring any money with me,' she said, looking at the items piling up.

'It's not a problem. I was going to pay.'

'I'll pay you back.'

'You could. Or you could just pay for the first dinner when we're back in England?'

There was something about the way he spoke, the complete certainty that they would go for dinner in England, that made the tension fix in her muscles. All this insinuating that they were going to carry on seeing each other could get tiresome. Or worse still, she could start to believe it.

'I'll get the first dinner,' she agreed for the main reason of not knowing when she was ever going to make it to a cashpoint.

'Great. I'm just gonna head over to the deli counter. I want to pick up a couple of meats while I'm here. Are you okay with the cheese?'

'I am always okay with cheese,' Holly replied and immediately continued her browsing of the dairy items.

Letting her eyes wander, Holly thought about how they only had one more night in the villa. In one sense, she was desperate to get home so she could see Hope. Ben had messaged her to say she'd got up crazily early yet again, so he'd put her down for an early first nap. He said he'd ring Holly later in the day. And of course, she wanted to see her mum and dad, too. And check in on the shop. But she wasn't ready to leave Evan. Not yet. Not so soon.

After grabbing a packet of exceptionally blue cheese and two different types of goat fromage, Holly turned around to put them in her trolley, only to find it was gone. A second later, she spotted it, being pushed away by a short woman in a burgundy overcoat.

'Excuse me? I think you have picked up my trolley.'

The woman squinted, implying she'd not understood what Holly had just said.

'My trolley. This is my trolley.'

When repeating herself didn't work, Holly slowed her speech, and talked louder while pointing.

'This. Trolley. Mine.' She jabbed her finger in the air while she pointed at herself and attempted to take the handle, but the woman batted her away.

'*Non, c'est à moi. C'est à moi.*'

'Let go.' Holly tried to grab the handle again, but the woman swung the trolly away. Evan had put his favourite things in there. Things he wanted her to try. There was no way Holly was going to let this woman just walk off with them when they would have to spend another ten minutes gathering it all up again. No, she wanted her trolley back.

'This is mine!' Holly wasn't even bothering with the pointing now, but the woman was getting angrier and angrier.

'*Quel est votre problème? Vous ne voyez pas que c'est mien?*'

She attempted to push the trolley out of Holly's way, but Holly was ready. She jumped to the other end and made it impossible for the woman to move.

Back-and-forth pushing and tugging ensued, with both Holly and the woman continuing to shout at one another. As such, it didn't take long to attract a crowd.

'Fine!' Holly said, finally letting go. 'If you won't let me take my trolley, I'll just take the food instead.' Lunging forward, she plunged her hands in and grabbed out several packets of cheese, not even looking at what they were as she bundled them up. Crisps, crackers... her arms were almost completely full, but she'd just reached in for another item, when a voice called from behind.

'Holly?'

'This woman has taken our—' Holly spun around, trying to balance one of the blue cheeses on top of a jar of honey Evan must have picked out, expecting to see him there, equally cross at the theft of their soon-to-be-purchased items. But it wasn't Evan. It was Giles.

33

Holly couldn't breathe. The cheese was only seconds away from toppling, and her hands were trembling far too much to do anything about it. Fortunately, before she could even move to put the items down, Giles grabbed them from her. He stood less than a foot away. After taking the cheese, he then took the honey and the crisps. It was as if time slowed. All Holly could do was watch as Giles gave the items back to her in a perfectly organised manner, his fingertips barely even brushing hers as he did so. When he was done, he stepped back, and even though Holly knew everything was perfectly secure, she felt peculiarly unbalanced.

The last time she had seen Giles was in the hospital ward, just hours after Hope was born. And the last time she'd heard from him was when he'd sent a gargantuan gift basket as a farewell. She had spent the last eight months of her life convincing herself that she was better off without him. That letting him go had been the best thing for her and that her feelings for him had never been more than a mixture of hormones and fear. Yet her heart was hammering in her chest and those feelings suddenly felt far closer to the surface than she wanted.

'You seemed to be making quite a scene there.' He smirked in a typical Giles manner.

Holly opened her mouth, soundlessly at first, until she managed to choke out a small cough.

'My trolley...' she stuttered, only to turn around and see the woman walking away with it. All those items Evan had chosen for her to try were being pushed out of sight.

And she didn't even care.

As she turned back, Holly half expected Giles to have vanished, as if he was just an apparition of her overly tired mind, but it didn't happen. Instead, he was standing right there in front of her. His grey eyes unblinking. It took several seconds before she managed to clear her throat, and went to speak again, only to be cut off by the ringing of a telephone. Giles cursed under his breath as he pulled the device out of his pocket, and looked at the screen.

'Sorry, I really need to take this. Just... don't go anywhere? Okay? Don't go anywhere.'

Holly nodded. The way her feet were grounded and her leg muscles quivering she doubted she could've moved had she wanted to. Instead, her gaze remained fixed on Giles. How was he here? And why? What did it mean that he would show up now, just as she was letting herself relax with Evan? Holly continued to stare until a pair of hands grabbed her from behind.

Startled, she jumped around and found herself face to face with Evan. Just to the right of him, and slightly fuller than it had been, was a trolley.

'You picked up some other things,' he said, looking at the items in her hand. 'I think we've already got some of those cheeses, but no harm in having some more.' Holly was barely listening. Instead, she was staring at the trolley. Their trolley. A rush of embarrassment flooded her cheeks as she scanned the aisle again, this time looking for the woman. Thankfully, she seemed to be gone, though that did little to quench the humiliation Holly felt.

After taking the items from her and placing them in the trolley that was definitely theirs, Evan planted a kiss gently on her lips, although unlike the other times they'd kissed that morning, Holly couldn't respond and when he broke away, Evan was frowning.

'Are you okay? You look pale. Your ankle's not hurting again is it? I didn't think about that when I said we should come here.'

'No, no, my ankle's fine.' She fought the heat that was flushing her cheeks and almost involuntarily, twisted her neck to face the space where only moments before, Giles had been standing. Now, however, there was nothing but stocked chiller shelves and an old woman with a wicker basket.

Manoeuvring herself out of Evan's hold, Holly walked to the end of the aisle, looked both ways down it, then back again. She even took a couple of steps to see down one of the other aisles too. But as her stomach sank, she knew without any doubt the truth. Giles was gone.

'Holly? Are you okay?' Evan had moved the trolley beside her again and was looking at her with deep concern.

With a blink and a shake of her shoulders, she forced herself to smile. 'Yes, yes. I'm fine. We should probably go pay though, don't you think? The others will be wondering where we've got to.'

* * *

Holly's mind was a mess. Had she really seen Giles Caverty in a supermarket in France? She thought she had, but then he'd vanished. Gone without a trace. Even though he was the one who had told her to stay where she was. Why would he do that? Why would he tell her to stay put only so he could disappear? But then, why did Giles do half of the things he did?

It hadn't helped Holly's head that Evan continued to be the most perfect gentlemen, packing all the bags, offering his arm as he worried about her ankle. And when they arrived back at the Vespa and he handed her a helmet, it had felt entirely natural to kiss him again. Slightly longer and more intense than any time that morning. Perhaps just to check he was really there, and not a figment of her imagination too.

'Is it wrong that I wish I had you all to myself for today?' he asked, his hand on the base of her spine. 'We could let the others go on the yacht and stay at the villa?'

'You want me to miss out on a day on a yacht? You're nice and everything, but you're not *that* nice.'

'I'd miss it for you.'

'But you've been on yachts hundreds of times. Besides, it's for Jamie and Fin, remember? And you're the one that arranged everything. You can hardly plan a day and not turn up.'

She pulled on her helmet and climbed on without hesitation. It was crazy how quickly she had got used to being on the back of the Vespa. Almost as crazy as how quickly she had got used to being with Evan.

'Fine, but I will get you to myself, Holly Berry. I promise you that.'

When they returned to the house, the others were all downstairs.

'Thank God, we're starving.' Spencer grabbed the bags of pastries before Evan had even got into the kitchen.

'Holly gets the first pick,' Evan said, tugging them back away from him. 'It's her privilege for getting up early and going to the shops.'

'What shops did you go to?' Fin asked. 'You've been gone ages.'

'We popped to the supermarket on the way back from the

bakery,' Evan said, shooting Holly a sly glance to the side as he spoke. 'Things there were a little more hectic than anticipated.'

As she picked her pain au raisin, Holly was torn between wanting to glare at him and wanting to kiss him. But there would be plenty of time for that on the boat.

'Less talking, more eating.' Naomi snatched a croissant out of Spencer's hand before he had a chance to take a bite. 'I want as much time on this boat as possible now I don't get seasick.'

The morning excursion meant Holly had a fair bit less time to prepare for the boat trip than she'd expected. And given that she was now going to go on a yacht, in a bikini, with a man she was sort of dating, her outfit required some actual consideration. When she was sorted, she headed downstairs to find Hugo and the minibus ready and waiting.

Holly had planned on hanging back and getting in later so she could sit next to Evan, but the minute the door was open, Caroline grabbed her by the arm and yanked her onto the back seats like they were going on a school trip and wanted to talk about all the boys they had crushes on.

'Okay, I need all the details. Now,' Caroline started the minute they were sitting down.

Holly was aware that the minibus was filling up, and the last thing she wanted to do was discuss what had happened while Evan was within earshot, but if she didn't get this out she was going to explode. After a quick glance to ensure he was still outside, she lowered her voice to a near whisper.

'I saw Giles in the supermarket.'

'What?' Caroline's jaw dropped. 'What do you mean you saw him? Like, saw him in your mind, or actually saw him from a distance, so it might not have been him at all, or really *really* saw him?'

'I spoke to him. Briefly. He helped me straighten up my shopping and then he disappeared.'

'You're sure it was him?'

'Yes, I'm sure. I said we spoke, remember?'

It was difficult to explain why Holly felt so shaken up by the encounter. After all, she hadn't said more than two words to him. But it was the confusion he caused which had her so overwhelmed. 'Do you think it means something?'

'Like what?'

'I don't know. It's just Evan is the first guy I've really liked since Hope and everything—'

'So you do really like him.' Caroline cut across her. Her face beaming. Holly responded with a scowl.

'Don't look at me like that. It's not like anything real can happen between us.'

'Why not? He's clearly into you. He introduced you to his mum, for goodness sake.'

'I know but...'

'But what?'

Holly paused, trying to figure out a way of verbalising how she felt.

'Let's be honest, it's a bit too good to be true, isn't it? He's amazing, he really is, and amazing guys don't end up with women like me, do they?'

At this, Caroline's face dropped into a frown as she crossed her arms around her chest.

'Nope. No way. I am not letting you do that. I am not letting you talk yourself out of something that could be special because you're afraid. And forget about Giles. You saw him at a supermarket, so what? It's not like you're going to see him again. So before you go into all the reasons why it won't work, or it's bound to fail, answer me one question. Do you want to be with him? With Evan?'

It was such a ridiculous question, Holly thought as she tried to figure out what the answer was. She barely knew him. But he did have a way of making her feel like she could do anything. And the kisses... well, the kisses were fireworks.

'I guess I would like to get to know him more. And he's already said that we're going to meet up back in England.'

'Eek.' The noise Caroline made was ear-splitting, causing Naomi, Zahida and Tyler to turn around to face them.

'Sorry, I'm just excited about going on a boat,' Caroline lied flawlessly before turning back to Holly and lowering her volume.

'Right, no getting in your head, okay? No getting hung up about idiots from the past or worrying about the future. You need to enjoy this time, understand?'

Holly glanced out the window to where Evan was currently helping Sandra into the minivan. Not that Sandra needed any help, but she wasn't refusing it either. He was a genuinely good guy, and she understood exactly what Caroline was saying. But it didn't help erase the niggling nerves that were refusing to shift.

'I guess I don't want to get my hopes up. Yes. it's exciting, but that's what these things always feel like in the beginning. Don't they? It's how it feels six months or six years down the line that matters.'

Caroline squeezed her hand. 'Forget about the future for a day, will you? Let yourself live a bit. You're going to love it. I promise.'

A large slam confirmed that the minibus was full, at which point, Evan turned around from the front to the talk to them all.

'Okay, it's only ten minutes down to this marina. I hope you've all packed your sunscreen. Our chariot is waiting.'

'Eek!' Caroline let out another high-pitched squeal before facing Holly.

'That one really was about the boat.' She shrugged.

34

Holly felt as if she had fallen into a postcard. The way the light sparkled off the water couldn't possibly be real, and yet it was, and she was there staring straight at it.

The marina was different to where they had gone waterskiing, but once again, the boats were moored up on a series of long, wooden jetties.

'Make sure someone is holding Holly's hand,' Jamie joked. 'Evan, I guess that should be you, right?'

'I'm perfectly capable of walking by myself,' Holly replied, although she caught Evan's eye and the pair of them exchanged a sly smile. Caroline was right. From this point onwards, Holly was going to stop worrying about the future and focus on enjoying the present. With Evan. And her previous slip provided a nice excuse to hold his hand.

'You're sure this boat is bigger than the speedboat?' Eddie asked as he adjusted his hat so the back piece of fabric hung down to ensure his neck was covered. His nose, meanwhile, was white from sunscreen. 'It made me feel quite nauseous, all that bouncing around.'

'Don't worry, this is definitely not a speedboat. I've got you the full works.'

Evan slipped his hand into Holly's as he whispered so only she could hear, 'And it should be big enough that we can get a bit of space to ourselves, too.'

'That sounds nice,' she said, unable to suppress her grin.

'Where are we going?' Jamie asked as they stepped onto the jetty. 'Do you know what boat we're going on? You know, it would be helpful if you were guiding us, rather than hanging around at the back, snogging.'

'We are not snogging,' Holly said defensively.

'Not yet at least,' Evan joked, before turning to her. 'They're right; I should lead the way. Are you going to be all right to walk on your own?'

'Yes, absolutely.'

'I'll see you in a minute.'

'You will.'

He kissed her on the end of her nose, then bounded up the jetty to the front of the group with such ease, it looked as if he was walking on solid ground. Her heart ached unexpectedly as she found herself wishing he could have stayed with her a little longer. Then again, like he'd said, there would be plenty of time for them to be together on the boat.

'Ladies and gentleman, if you would like to follow me.'

As they ambled their way down between the boats, Holly alternated her gaze between looking forward and looking down at her feet, although she did stop to watch the shoals of white fish darting beneath the surface of the water. It was such a distraction that when she looked back up, she noticed the group had moved up ahead of her and were now currently stock still.

'Are you serious?' Naomi said.

'Does this meet your expectations?' Evan asked.

When Holly caught up with them, she finally saw what the fuss was about. The boat they were all staring at was wider than Holly's cottage and had two sets of steps going up the back. The white shone pristinely in the sunlight, and by the looks of things, it even had a balcony on the side, though why on earth a boat needed a balcony was beyond her.

'You really didn't have to do this.' Jamie squeezed Evan in the tightest hug Holly had even seen. Fin quickly followed suit.

'This is far too extravagant, buddy.'

'What's money for if not spoiling your best friend?' Evan replied. 'Besides, someone at my gym knows the guy who owns this and got us mates' rates.'

Mates' rates, Holly thought. She gave people bags of sweets at mates' rates, but the two did not compare.

'You okay?' Evan slipped back past the others to where she was standing.

'Well, I'm glad I didn't opt for a day with just you in the villa. No offence.'

Evan grinned. 'None taken. I better give the guy a ring and tell him we're here. We're a bit early, so he probably wasn't expecting us yet.' He pulled his phone out of his pocket, only to speak into it almost immediately. 'Hello, yeah, down on the jetty. Got here a bit early. Fantastic.'

He turned to face the group. 'Well, he told us to climb aboard. He's just on the bridge. He'll come and meet us.'

Naomi and Zahida didn't need telling twice, leaping onto the back of the boat. Holly, meanwhile, had no intention of rushing.

'Don't worry,' Evan said. 'There's no chance I'm going to let you fall twice.'

All the same, Holly waited until everyone was on board and, climbing up to the higher decks, then surveyed the ground in front of her carefully to ensure it was perfectly dry. With a deep breath, she took a wide step over towards where Evan waited on the other side to catch her. When she had both feet on the boat, he fixed his hands around her waist firmly.

'You're getting better at this already,' he said and kissed her.

'It must be the excellent teacher.'

As she stood there in Evan's arms, hearing the others' voices drifting into the distance, she couldn't help but think how nice it would've been to spend the whole day getting to know him. Now she'd made up her mind that she was going to give this a chance, she couldn't help but feel like she would miss him when this was over, and they weren't even separated yet. Hopefully, they'd meet up in England soon.

'Holly, I think you need to come here.' Jamie's voice came from an upper section of the boat and it had a peculiar pang of urgency.

'She probably just wants you to see the hot tub,' Evan said, moving to continue the kissing.

'Wait, there's a hot tub? That is way better than this. I need to go now!' She twisted towards the stairs before he tugged her back. The pair laughed as he pulled her into his chest. She was still there, tightly pressed against Evan, when a voice called from the top of the boat.

'Good morning, guys. If you want to get aboard then we can get the show on the road.'

Holly froze. She had heard that voice so many times in her life, in good times, and not so good times.

'I guess that must be the owner,' Evan said, releasing Holly from his grasp so that he was only holding her hand. But Holly didn't want to be released. She didn't want to move an inch, and she certainly didn't want to look up to see where the voice had come from.

Her heart turned a somersault in her chest as, against her better judgement, she lifted her head and saw his silhouette against the sun. Giles Caverty.

35

It was a strange scenario. Those who knew Giles, like Jamie, Caroline and Fin, had fallen deathly silent, while Zahida, Naomi, and Tyler were still gabbling away excitedly. Sandra seemed to understand somewhat and was trying to read the situation, trying to work out what was going on.

When they reached the top of the stairs, Evan's arm remained hooked around Holly's waist. She wasn't sure if she wanted to pull him in closer or push him away.

'Sorry.' Evan finally left Holly's side to shake Giles's hand. 'I was a little distracted. I'm Evan. I made the booking with you. Giles, right?'

His hand remained hanging in the air, as if Giles hadn't even noticed the man who was speaking to him. Given how he was staring solely at Holly, it was entirely possible.

Evan tried again. 'You are Giles Caverty, aren't you? I haven't made a mistake with the boat?'

'Oh, that's definitely Giles Caverty,' Jamie said pointedly.

'You guys know each other?'

'Oh, we all know Giles,' Caroline chimed in.

A burning lump was pushing its way up through Holly's throat. How? That was the only question that filled her mind. How could he be there? And why now?

'I wasn't expecting this again.' Giles looked solely at Holly as he spoke. 'I'm sorry about running off earlier.'

'It's fine.'

'No... I should have... I wanted to...'

He paused, dropping them into a silence that grew thicker and thicker with every breath.

'Is everything all right here?' Evan said. 'I'm feel like I'm missing something.'

Giles didn't reply; he was still staring at Holly and it wasn't just Giles who couldn't keep their eyes off her. Jamie, Fin, Caroline and the rest of the group had stopped their nattering and were staring at her expectantly. She needed to say something. She knew she did. But she couldn't think what.

'It's Fin and Jamie's hen do,' she blurted out. 'Stag do. Hen do and stag do. They're doing it together. A joint thing. In France. That's why we're in France.'

Giles nodded.

'I didn't realise with the booking. It was a different name.'

'Yes, Evan booked.'

'I see.' His voice was quiet. Barely audible above the waves that lapped at the side of the boat. 'How have you been? How's Hope?'

'Nearly eight months, if you can believe it.'

'Crawling?'

'Yes, she's into everything.'

'I can imagine.'

They paused, hundreds of unspoken words spiralling between them, and she was about to ask what he had been up to when Spencer spoke.

'So, are we actually going anywhere, or are we staying in the marina all day?'

Silence swelled.

'There are some other boats,' Giles finally said, breaking the immensely awkward pause. 'Or if you give me half an hour, I'm sure I can get one of my buddies to take you out, if that's easier.'

'I don't mind.' Jamie looked directly at Holly as she spoke. 'It's up to you. Are you okay with this?'

'I... I...'

She turned to look at Evan. She didn't know why, but she needed to see he was still there, but when she turned to face him, he was staring out at the water.

Did she want to go on a boat with Giles? Did she want to tell him everything he had missed in the last eight months and have him rib her for her failed attempts at baby-led weaning and horrendous nappy disasters? Did she want to open old up wounds that she had only in the last couple of days felt close to healing? No, she didn't, but this wasn't her day, her week, her holiday. This was Jamie and Fin's.

'Of course I don't mind,' she said, forcing her lips into the biggest smile she could. 'Now, are we going to get out of here or what?'

36

With Holly having given the go-ahead, the group started to move towards the front of the boat, where it didn't take Sandra long to yell about finding the hot tub, though Holly lingered back.

'I need to head up to the bridge. Getting out of the port is one of the tricky bits as far as my job goes.' Giles still hadn't moved from the same spot. 'But perhaps later, you and I could catch up?'

Holly nodded. 'A catch-up sounds good.'

'Okay, then I'll see you later. And I am honestly so sorry about earlier.'

'Really you don't need to explain.'

Giles pursed his lips as if he might say something more, but instead turned and disappeared, leaving Caroline and Evan standing on either side of her. Holly didn't want to face either of them, but one needed far more of an explanation.

'I'll join you in a minute,' she said to Caroline with enough pointedness that she hoped her friend would get the hint.

'Fine. I'll go find the drink. I think we're going to need it.'

A second later and Evan and Holly were alone.

'So if I'm not reading the situation completely wrong, I am

assuming you and Giles have some sort of history?' Evan started. 'Don't feel like you need to tell me. I don't want to pressurise you or anything, everyone has a past.'

'He's not... We do have a history,' Holly tried. 'But it's probably not like you think. He tried to ruin my business.'

'Okay?' Evan's eyebrow quirked. 'That certainly wasn't the history I was expecting you to have.'

'He tried to take it from me, but he didn't. Then he tried to make things up to me and turn over a new leaf, and he did. He became nice and we...' Holly couldn't work out how to finish that sentence. *We became friends?* It was true, but it didn't feel like enough to explain the situation. *We used to do our food shopping together?* No, that absolutely would not work. 'It got complicated for a while.'

Evan nodded and locked his eyes on hers.

'What I care about is if you are going to be okay today. I don't want this to affect your time here. I don't want things to be awkward for you.'

'No, they won't be. It'll be fine. It won't be awkward at all.' But even as she spoke, she knew it was a lie.

'Come on, I bet the others will have nabbed all the sunbeds.'

'Sunbeds and a hot tub? This boat is insane.'

The boat was immense, with two decks they could sunbathe on, the upper of which really did have a hot tub twice the size of any she'd been in before. As she took her place on one of the sun loungers, Holly quickly found out that Giles wasn't the only other person onboard. Two other members of crew beavered busily around them. One seemed to oversee the boat with Giles, dealing with the ropes when they cast off and ensuring all the buoys were correctly tied. The other person was there for the group, offering extra cushions and sun cream, while bringing them drinks and snacks. Holly and Evan's shopping trip, it appeared, had been superfluous.

After the morning she'd had, and the fact that holiday drinking times seemed entirely flexible, Holly was quick to grab the bottle of sparkling wine that the crew member had placed in a cooler in front of them. Only, when she pulled the bottle from the ice, she froze and gritted her teeth. The label shone out as clear as day. Of course the wine was from the vineyard she'd been to with Evan, meaning that it probably had been Giles she'd seen there. Which meant that every time she and Evan had been alone outside the villa, Giles had been there too. Holly didn't know if the thought made her want to laugh or cry.

'Your friend has good taste,' Evan said, as he plucked the bottle from her hand and poured them both a glass. 'Are you sure you're okay? You look a little shellshocked.'

'Just taking it all in,' Holly lied only to rebuke herself. She had meant what she said to Caroline. She did like Evan. He was without doubt the most generous man she'd ever met, not to mention attractive. So without giving herself time to stew on what it did or didn't mean that Giles was there, she took the glass that Evan offered to her, and clinked it against his.

'To the future,' she said, 'and to us.'

His grin was enough to set her whole heart a flutter.

'To us,' he said.

* * *

As wonderful as the boat was, it wasn't possible to relax fully as Giles kept appearing at all the most inopportune moments. Like when Evan was rubbing sunscreen on Holly's back, and when they were sharing a kiss. And when Fin's friends took it upon themselves to wind Evan up as much as possible about walking Holly to her bedroom at night. Every time someone made a remark about Holly and Evan being more than friends, Giles would appear right there beside them, checking their wine hadn't run out, or telling them something or other about the cove or village they were sailing past. And no matter how much Holly tried to pretend she was comfortable with Evan's hand slipping into hers or the little kisses he placed on her shoulders, they would cause her to flinch a little, as she cast her gaze over her shoulder in case Giles was there.

To make matters even worse, every time he appeared, Naomi would rush to his side to ask some question or another, or just to flick her hair in an overly flirty manner. Not that Holly was jealous or anything. After all, she was there with Evan. But it still didn't stop the knots that twisted her insides when she saw Giles smiling away at her, resting his hand on her shoulder and laughing in response. It was his job, obviously, to make all the guests feel comfortable, and Giles was an expert at making people feel at ease. Yet every time he smiled, her entire body clenched and it was hard to pretend she didn't care what he was saying or doing with reactions like that.

As the boat skimmed along the coastline, they sailed towards a small bay lined with golden and white houses.

Evan turned and spoke to her.

'Right, I don't want you to think I'm an old man or anything, but I don't like it when my feet are exposed to sea water and fish. It's a weird thing I've got. So I bought us all water shoes to wear.'

Even with Giles lurking somewhere in the background, Holly couldn't help but drop her head onto his chest as she laughed.

'You've got a foot thing?' It was hard to suppress a giggle.

'Wow. And no, I don't have a foot thing,' he corrected, 'but that laugh was amazing. You know, I think it's the first time I've heard it since we got back to the villa this morning.'

Holly was about to make up an excuse, or deny him altogether, only to change her mind. The more time she spent with Evan, the harder it was to deny how genuine he seemed. And he deserved the truth.

'I'm sorry. It's just this, us, it seems to be moving crazily fast.'

'And that's not a good thing?'

'I don't know. I've got a lot of past to work with and I need my head to catch up.'

'I get it. I can do slow too.' Shifting his position, he gently placed his hand around the back of her neck, and drew her face towards him. If the other kisses had been fireworks, then this one was a volcano.

As a burning heat rose through Holly, everything else disappeared from view, and once again, it felt like it was just her and Evan alone. And she didn't care what else was going on. All she wanted to do was kiss him like she'd done that morning when everything felt so easy.

She tilted her head towards him, only for a voice to call out from the deck above.

'Okay folks, this is where we're going to drop anchor. Who fancies a swim?'

'Your friend has impeccable timing, you know,' Evan said, as he shook his head.

'I don't know why you're complaining. This means you get to wear your water shoes, right?'

'I think you're mocking me.'

'Would I do that?' she said, and kissed him again before standing up and addressing the group. 'This way for water shoes, people. This way for water shoes.'

37

Much to Evan's delight, both Sandra and Zahida opted for a pair of his neoprene water shoes, although everyone else was either happy to go without, or had no intention of getting into the water.

'Water sports are different. For swimming, I am solely a heated pool kind of guy,' Spencer said with his eyes closed as he laid back on his towel.

'Sometimes I don't understand how we are still friends,' Fin replied.

'I'm worried about my skin with the sea water.' Eddie also had no intention of swimming. 'I had a reaction to a Himalayan sea salt bath one time, and I think submersion in salt water might result in adverse effects.'

'You can just say you don't want to go in the sea,' Tyler mocked.

As the boys continued to bicker, Holly scanned the view, only to spot Giles on the deck above her, though the moment she caught his eye, he turned hurriedly away. Good, she thought. That was good. Any time he was out of sight was time she could focus on enjoying Evan's company. Perhaps if he'd just stop lingering, it would be even better.

Evan's concerns about things brushing up against his feet when he couldn't see seemed completely unwarranted, given how crystal clear the water was. Once again, shoals of tiny, white fish danced around them, this time iridescent in the light.

'Is it deep enough to jump in?' Jamie asked Giles. Holly found it strange seeing him in crisp whites, rather than his typical salmon-pink polo shirt, though the white highlighted his tan exceptionally well.

'Absolutely. The currents are pretty mild round here too. It's a good place to swim. One of my favourites, actually.'

As he looked at Holly, she felt herself shrink away from his gaze. How could such an open space could feel so very penned-in? As enormous as it was, the entire boat felt claustrophobic. Then again, she realised, she didn't have to stay on it.

'Go on then, give me a pair of those shoes,' she said to Evan, taking the ones he was holding before turning to face Caroline. 'Are you up for it?'

'Those look bigger than you need,' Evan said, still rummaging in his canvas bag. 'Hold on a second and I'll find a pair that fits better.'

'It's fine. They feel fine.'

'Are you sure?'

'Absolutely.'

Less than a minute later, Holly was standing on the edge of the boat, right next to Giles. Her heart was pounding in her chest again, but she was certain it was just adrenaline from the impending dip in the sea. After all, since when had she been nervous around Giles?

'I can just jump off? I can just jump off here?'

'Yes, if you want.'

She did, and so she jumped.

The gasp that left her lips was a mixture of shock from the cold, and relief at the freedom that came with no longer being on a confined vessel with Giles and Evan. But as the water settled around her, all the peace of the open sea flooded through her. And it lasted less than a heartbeat.

'Cannon ball!'

Caroline's splash sent a wave up and it took several moments of leg kicking and flailing to wipe the salt water out of her eyes.

'So, that was interesting.' Caroline's head bobbed up and down as she kept afloat. 'I take it you want to talk?'

'Let's just swim out a little further.' Holly knew an eager listener could still catch wind of what they were saying. And so she kicked her legs and swam a steady breaststroke away from the boat. Only when she'd couldn't hear Eddie and Spencer bickering did she stop and turn to face Caroline.

'So you really did see him at the supermarket?'

'Why would I make something like that up?' Holly didn't have the mental capacity to be mad at her friend but she would definitely remember this next time Caroline doubted her about something. 'Can you believe it? Of all the boats in all the blooming world?'

'It could almost be fate.' Caroline smirked.

It was tempting to ignore the comment. Before moving back to the Cotswolds, Holly would never have considered fate a real thing, but if she hadn't caught Dan cheating on that exact day, she'd never have driven to Bourton and seen Maude, who would have sold the shop to someone else, and it was tough to believe that was just a coincidence. But this current situation? Well, if that was fate, then fate had some serious questions to answer.

'How does it feel, seeing him?' Caroline asked, kicking her legs beneath her to stay afloat. 'You know he hasn't been able to take his eyes off you. Not once.'

Holly didn't know if Caroline was saying that in some strange attempt to make her feel better, but she knew it was true. She, by contrast, had done everything possible to stop herself from looking in Giles's direction, though it had been far harder that she wanted to admit.

'I'd like to speak to him,' she admitted. 'See how he's been. Catch up, you know?'

'And would Evan be present for this catch-up or not?'

Holly swiped the water, causing a large spray to splash up into her friend's face.

'Hey, that's not fair! I was just asking. And you're the one who made us swim all the way out to talk. So talk. You and Evan looked very cosy together. Bizarrely cosy.'

Holly considered what Caroline had said. Yes, Evan made her feel comfortable, he made her laugh and he made her do things she never dreamed of doing before. But this wasn't real life. The only Holly he had ever met was one on holiday, scarily free of responsibility. And if fate was real, then seeing Giles like this couldn't be ignored.

Their conversation was interrupted by Giles himself, shouting loudly from the boat.

'Don't lose these or I'll charge you extra,' he said and threw a large rubber ring into the water.

Caroline and Holly weren't the only ones swimming now; Sandra and Jamie were heading straight for the inflatable.

'Look, you can't let your past dictate your future.' Caroline brought them back to the conversation. 'You never know, maybe the fate part is Giles being here, but maybe it's not. Maybe it's Evan?'

It was an idea Holly would never have considered, but if she was going to throw her hat in with fate, it only seemed fair she looked at it from both sides.

'However, now you need to relax and enjoy the water with your best friend, who wants to get a lilo.' Caroline started to swim back towards the boat as she spoke. 'Are you coming? Do you want one?'

The buoyancy from the saltwater was more than enough for Holly as she lay back in the water and kicked up her feet so that she was lying flat.

'You go fetch one,' she said. 'I'm just gonna float here for a bit longer.'

'Are you sure you'll be all right on your own? I don't want you to get swept away or anything.'

'Don't worry, I don't plan on going any further than this.'

As Caroline swam back towards the boat, Holly closed her eyes and felt the heat of the sun beating upon her face. This was a long way from paddling in the river that ran through Bourton, and as she floated there, she thought of her daughter. Hope would love this. She already had so much fun at the baby swimming classes they went to together. As soon as Hope realised they were at the pool, she would start kicking her legs, desperate to get in the water. Maybe Holly would try to take her more often.

She turned back onto her front, her thoughts still on Hope and swimming, only to feel her left shoe slide partway off her foot.

'Damn.' She reached down to pull it up, but the wake of a boat rippled past her, bobbing her up and down and knocking the shoe down to the end of her toes. Swimming in a circular motion, she tried to grab hold of it. If she lost a waterproof shoe, Evan wouldn't hold it against her – he could well own the factory that made them for all she knew – but she was certain she could grab hold of it. With a change in tactic, she picked her leg upwards, creating an almighty splash. It helped a little, although she was then momentarily distracted by the two figures diving off the edge of the boat. It was difficult to see who it was who had jumped into the water, but several other people were shouting loudly.

Only then did she note how far she had drifted.

She kicked her foot, and the shoe slipped off altogether, floating to the surface.

'Of course it floats.'

She was only grateful no one was there to see her moment of stupidity, although the two bodies were still swimming directly towards her, and fast.

It was then she realised who it was.

'Hang on, Holly! I'm coming!'

'Lie on your back. Stop kicking and lie on your back!'

Evan? Giles? They were racing toward her at an impressive speed, and before she could ask they were doing, they were both upon her.

'I've got you. You're okay now.'

'It's fine. I've got hold of her.'

'Holly, can you breathe? Can you breathe?'

Giles and Evan grappled at her from every direction, with Giles trying to get a hold of her waist, and Evan pulling her back by the chin.

Holly splashed and spluttered as she struggled to kick them both off.

'It's okay. I've got you.'

'What are you both doing? Get off me. I'm fine. I'm fine.'

'You're okay. You're going to be fine.'

It didn't matter how much she tried to shout, they couldn't hear her. Struggling to breathe, more from the lack of space than the water, Holly swung her feet and arms out simultaneously, clocking Giles across the face, and striking Evan squarely in the groin.

She hadn't planned on such a harsh action, but it worked and the two dropped away, finally giving her enough time to gather her breath and yell more forcefully.

'What the hell are you doing?'

38

'It was quite funny, now that we know you weren't in any danger.' Jamie handed Holly a towel. 'Giles didn't even bother to strip. He went in fully clothed. I'm impressed. I don't think I've ever had two men go after me like that.'

'You're impressed that they simultaneously almost drowned me while trying to save me?'

Holly wrapped the towel around her.

'When you put it like that, it doesn't sound perfect, I'll admit.'

'But it was still pretty romantic,' Caroline added.

'Holly, can I have a word?'

Holly glanced over her shoulder, only to wish she hadn't. There was Giles, his hair towel dried and scruffy, a dry shirt still unbuttoned, displaying his tanned body. She'd never seen Giles without a top on before, and it was an unexpectedly glorious image.

'Go on.' Jamie nudged her arm. 'I think he's earned a conversation at least. And we'll still be here when you get back.'

She looked across the boat to where Evan was showing Eddie and Sandra how to fish. He had already apologised profusely for the confusion and was probably even more embarrassed than she was. Not that there was any need for him to be at all.

Keeping the towel wrapped firmly around her, she stood up and followed Giles, going up and down various staircases until they came to the bridge.

To Holly, the word *bridge* invoked images of the stone structures which spanned across Bourton's river. But this was more like in science fiction films, with amazing spaceships full of flashing screens and colourful images.

It was a far more complex array of dials and screen on this boat than the one they had been waterskiing on. If anything, it was more like the cockpit of a plane. The view offered an even more impressive view of the coastline, which at this moment Holly pretended to be observing; it was an easier option than looking at Giles.

'I'm so sorry about that rescue thing just now.' He broke the silence. 'I thought I was being helpful.'

'I get it. There's no need to apologise. Really, there's not.'

'And sorry about walking off at the supermarket. I wasn't planning on it. I wanted to talk to you, but when I finished my call, he was there with you and I got flustered. It was cowardly, I know.'

'Yes, it was.'

Silence filled the air again, but Holly couldn't think of a way to fill it, although as Giles had been the one who asked to talk to her, it only seemed right he should be the one to speak. Thankfully, he did.

'So you and this Evan chap... He seems nice.'

'He is, though I've only known him three days.'

'Only three days? So it's not exactly a relationship, is it? Certainly not a serious one.'

The comment irked her slightly. Of all the people who were in a position to give relationship advice, she didn't think Giles was one of them.

'I like him. And he likes me, but it's difficult to know how serious any relationship is going to be within two days.'

'Unless you know that person is the one for you.'

He locked his eyes on her, and Holly could feel her pulse ticking higher and higher. Her mouth had grown inexplicably dry, and she tried to swallow, hoping that Giles would say something to alleviate the tension, only to discover she couldn't cope with the silence a second longer.

'You seem happy out here on your boat. It's a great boat.' The words left her in a stream. 'Not that I have much experience about boats, but I'd still be able to tell a good one. I have been on another boat this week, actually. We went waterskiing. And I was pretty good. Better than I expected, that's for sure.'

Giles's smile widened. 'I've missed you doing that.'

'Doing what?'

'Talking nonsense when you're nervous. You talking full stop, actually. I've missed you.'

Holly clamped her mouth closed, determined not to give him any more reason to compliment her, no matter how good it felt.

'I'd like to see you again,' Giles said. 'I know it's wrong, but I sometimes feel like I came out worst from the whole situation. You know, I lost the girl and my best friend. I've missed having you to talk to.'

Holly's heart ached. She had felt it, too. That loss of friendship without Giles in her life. And it hadn't mattered that there were so many other people to fill that void. It was a Giles-shaped gap, and nothing else could replace it. In the burgeoning silence, her mind drifted back in time eight months. To when she had been sitting in Giles's car and his hand brushed her cheek, and she had wanted nothing more than to kiss him.

'Holly? Where are you? Evan's just got the good bubbly out.'

Giles grimaced as Jamie's voice rang out. 'She's never gonna give me a break, is she?'

'Probably not,' Holly agreed. 'Although the hamper you sent for Hope earned you a few brownie points. And the stuff with my dad, of course.'

'Enough brownie points for her to let me in her house again so I can see you?'

'Actually, I don't live with her. I moved out. I'm renting.'

'That's fantastic. Still in Bourton, I assume?'

'Yeah, it's perfect for me. Us. Even closer to the sweet shop. Just big enough for Hope and me. I have no idea how Mum found it.'

'That's amazing. Cottages in Bourton are hard to come by. Perhaps I could come and see the place when I'm back in the UK? I'm pretty booked up with this over the summer, but maybe come autumn, I could drop in and see Hope and see how you're getting on? If that's okay? Unless you're free before then? If you have some time when you're here, I'd love to see you properly?'

'Holly, will you hurry up?' Jamie yelled again.

'I should go,' Holly said, apologetically. 'And I need to stay with the others today. It's our last night and everything.'

'I get it. I do. It's fine. And don't worry, I'm not out of your life yet, Holly. I can feel it.'

'Is that right?'

'It is. Now go find Jamie before she throws me off this boat, will you?'

39

They stayed on the water until sunset, long after the cheese and snacks she and Evan had bought had been demolished. How it had only been that morning that they'd gone to the supermarket, Holly couldn't understand. It felt as if she had gone through an entire year's worth of emotions since then. It didn't help that after the rescue incident, Evan had barely looked her in the eye.

She had thought things were fine when he was teaching the others to fish, but then he had sat across on the other side of the deck while they ate and drank and he'd spoken almost solely to Sandra. Holly had thought perhaps she was imagining it until they reached the marina and he was off the boat before she could talk to him. During the minibus ride back, he sat in the front and kept his eyes forwards the entire time.

'I feel like I've done something wrong.'

She and Caroline had taken seats in the back as the minibus rumbled towards the villa.

'You mean other than make him look like an idiot when he and Giles jumped in after you?'

'I didn't ask them to do that!'

'I know, but maybe if you'd just pretended you were struggling. You know how fragile male pride can be.'

Holly shrank back into the seat. Was Evan really one of those men whose pride was so easily wounded? He didn't come across like that, but then again, she didn't know much about him. Other than she really liked his mum, and he had lots of sisters and lots of money.

Finally, when they reached the villa and climbed out of the minibus, he seemed ready to acknowledge her again. He was standing at the minibus door, waiting.

'Can we talk?' he said.

Never had Holly been asked the same question by two men in one day, and never had it made her stomach plummet quite so greatly.

'You're fine,' Caroline whispered, quickly squeezing Holly's hand. 'You're completely fine.'

A moment later, Caroline disappeared into the villa with everyone else, leaving Holly and Evan alone.

'Today was amazing. Thank you.' Holly was speaking before she had even started thinking. 'The boat was phenomenal. And the scenery—'

'I don't want to talk about the boat or the scenery.' He gestured to a bench which overlooked the pool. The lights shone out from beneath the water, casting the trees and bushes in an ethereal glow. 'Can we talk for a minute?'

'Of course.'

Holly took a seat on the bench, and when Evan followed, it was hard not to notice the gap he left between them. It was a long way from how it had been the night before, with them next to each other on the sofa, her head accidentally dropping onto his shoulder like that was where it was supposed to be.

'I'm sorry about today,' Holly said, before the silence could take over.

'Sorry, about what?'

'You know. The shoes, and diving in...' She knew she needed to say the other bit, but it was hard. 'And Giles.'

Evan's smile widened knowingly.

'You don't have anything to be sorry about. I was the one who arranged the trip.'

'It was an amazing trip.'

'It just had your ex-boyfriend on it.'

'He's not—' Holly cut herself short. She didn't even know how to explain what she and Giles were to herself, let alone someone else. 'Evan, these last couple of days, they've been more than I could have dreamed of. You've been more than I could have dreamed of.'

'But...' he anticipated.

'I don't know. I don't even think there is a but. It's just romance has never come easy to me, and my past relationships – my relationship with Giles – there's a lot that's difficult to understand. For me, let alone anyone else.'

Evan nodded, his eyes moving back to the view.

'Holly, I don't want you to think I'm the perfect guy. I'm not. I will admit I've broken more than one heart in my life. Not on purpose, but because I didn't see what I had in front of me. But right now, I do. I see you. I see your humour, your kindness, your hard work and the way your friends love you. That says everything to me. You don't get friends like the ones you've got by being anything other than a brilliant person. And maybe there are a lot of things about each other we won't like. Maybe some of them will turn out to be deal breakers, but if I'm honest with myself, I don't think that's the case. I want to see where this goes. This is not a holiday fling for me, Holly. But if you have feelings for this other guy... I don't want to be second best.'

It was the most perfect speech, and her heart was close to bursting with how much it ached, but the problem was, it wasn't the first time someone had given her a speech like that.

'Evan, I think you're amazing...'

'Again, I can feel a but coming there.'

'There's no but. Except, I don't know you. And this... this isn't real life. Let's be honest, when we're back home, and I'm in my little cottage, running the sweet shop, co-parenting Hope and you're jetting off to LA or Paris, it's not going to be like this.'

'I'm thinking it could be better, if I'm honest.'

'Really? I'd like to know how.'

'You mean, you can't imagine how nice it would be to stay in a flat without Tyler downstairs snoring.'

'Okay, well, that's one thing.'

'Holly, there are things you don't know about me.' He paused. 'Parts of my life I don't tell people about, but I find myself wanting to share them with you. I want to share everything with you. But I'm scared of getting my heart broken. When I saw you with Giles today, I could see how he looked at you. I could see what you meant to him, and it terrified me. You might think that I'm some player, but I'm not. I've never fallen this fast, Holly, and I'm scared too.'

She took a deep breath in, following it with a low sigh out. Why could life never be simple? Why were men always like buses? And if fate really was real, why did it hate her so much?

'The thing about Giles and me, is we never were. Not really. There were feelings there, on both sides, but we never acted on them. I know how I feel about you, Evan, I do. But with him, I guess it's a case of wondering what could have been. I'm almost positive it would have been a disaster; he drives me insane most of the time, but it's...'

'It's the not knowing that makes it so hard?'

'I guess.'

He paused, his eyes looking directly into hers.

Had she really just said that to him? Had she really spoken about Giles to a guy she was kind of sort of dating when she couldn't even talk to her friends about him? She didn't know if that was a good thing or not. Though if that wasn't enough to surprise her, the words that came out of Evan's mouth next were.

'You should go and see him.'

'What?'

'You should go see him. Work out what these feelings are. If it's the only way you know for sure that you want me, then that's what you need to do.'

'I don't know...'

'I do. Besides, it's clear he's still crazy about you. You don't dive into the water in a shirt that expensive unless the girl is really worth it.'

'Evan, that doesn't feel right. I don't feel right doing that to you.'

'Why? This is best for both of us in the long term. Trust me, I'd rather find out now than in six months when I'm even more head over heels.'

The way he spoke made it sound rational, but could Holly really do that? Could she really see Giles after everything they had been through?

'No, no. Anyway, I don't have a way to get there.'

Standing up, Evan reached into his pocket and pulled out a key, which he threw to her.

'I guess you should take the Vespa?'

40

With the keys in Holly's hand, Evan headed back into the house, leaving her to decide what to do next. A chorus of cicadas were singing out into the night, while dense clouds drifted across the moon.

She was still contemplating her actions when her telephone buzzed.

'Hey, my baby girl,' she said after answering the call. 'How are you?'

Hope was wearing a denim dress, with a soft hairband across her head, while she chewed on her giraffe teething toy.

'Hi Mummy,' Ben's voice came from off screen. 'I am so sorry we haven't rung until now. It's been one of those days. Did you get the photos we sent?'

'I did.'

'We've just been looking at the pictures of you on the boat, and we're very jealous. Very jealous indeed. Did Fin pay for all that?'

Inside, Holly groaned. The last thing she needed was a reminder of Evan's generosity, particularly from Ben. Or a reminder of the boat trip. She put the Vespa key down beside her and focused on the conversation.

'No, it was his friend.' She kept things as simple as possible. 'What about you? How was your day? Busy, I take it?'

'Well, Hope met Georgia, didn't you, hun?'

'Oh, and how did that go?' Holly didn't know if her voice was neutral or not, but she was somewhat relieved when Ben appeared on the screen, grimacing.

'Well, first Hope was sick on Georgia's nice jacket, and then she threw a screaming fit when she tried to hold her. And then, last of all, she dropped the new teddy Georgia gave her into the river.'

Holly's lips twitched. 'So, a good start.'

'We are going to try again next week. If I'm honest, I think she was playing up because she missed you.'

'I miss you too, Hopey. I miss you so much. But I'm going to see you tomorrow. I can't believe how quickly the trip has gone.'

'But it's been fun. You've had a chance to relax?'

'At times.'

He nodded.

'I know you were worried about all the business at the shop, but you really don't need to be. The insurance will cover all the costs, and they've already caught the people who were responsible.'

'That was fast.'

'Well, apparently one of them mooned a camera in the jeweller's and had a very identifiable birthmark. Not the smartest tool in the box.'

She was probably meant to laugh, but her mind was still elsewhere, and it didn't help that she could hear Hope grizzling away.

'I should probably get going,' she said, heavy pressure building in her chest. 'Last night and everything.'

'I understand. Give the others my love. And be careful. We don't want any more disasters before tomorrow morning.'

'Don't worry. I'll be fine. Can you put Hope back on for me? I want to say goodnight.'

Hope had dropped the giraffe and was now chewing her sleeve instead.

'I miss you, baby girl.' Holly's eyes filled with tears. 'I love you more than anything in the whole universe. You know that, don't you?'

Hope gurgled before proceeding to wiggle uncomfortably on Ben's lap.

'You should go,' she eventually said, wiping her eyes as she felt a tickle of a tear slide down her cheek. She told Hope she loved her one more time, before hanging up.

When she put down the phone, she noted the Vespa key still there on the bench beside her. She picked it up and marched into the house, down to the kitchen where the group had just started pouring drinks.

'Caroline. Jamie. I need you. Now.'

'Now?'

'Now.'

It must have been a testament to the urgency with which she spoke that Caroline immediately stopped pouring. Jumping from their seats, they both followed Holly up to the bedroom, where she closed the door behind them.

'I'm thinking of going to see Giles. To be sure there are no feelings left there. I need you to tell me I'm not insane.'

She looked between them, waiting for a response. It didn't take long.

'Nope, can't do that.' Jamie was straight in with her opinions. 'You are 100 per cent utterly insane. He was a pig. A liar and a manipulator. And you are on to a good thing with Evan.'

But Caroline was quick on Giles's defence. 'You're forgetting the fact that Giles is crazy about her. And people change. Even you have to admit that he's changed.'

'Okay, so he had some mildly redeeming features,' Jamie conceded, 'but where does this leave Evan?'

'Evan is the one who told me to go.' Holly interrupted before the girls got too absorbed in their own conversation and forgot about her.

'What?' Both flinched in disbelief as the spoke in unison. 'Why?'

Holly shrugged. It had sounded sensible when Evan had suggested it. Romantic, even. But now she was saying it aloud, she felt more than a little insecure.

'He said I should know the truth about how I feel about Giles. Before he and I take things too far. That he wants to make sure I'm all in.'

'That sounds sensible,' Jamie said.

'Or it sounds like a test,' Caroline countered.

'A test? What do you mean, a test?'

'Like he doesn't want you to go. Clearly, he only said that because he wanted you to pick him immediately. No person in their right mind would send the woman they like into the arms of another man she had feelings for.'

'Once had feelings for,' Jamie stressed. 'Unless he's completely secure. And genuine.'

Holly considered what Caroline had said. 'I don't think he's manipulating me like that. I don't think that's what Evan's like.'

'Well, if he is, then he's not the type of guy you should be with. I say go. And I love you and Evan together, I do. But I don't think you'll ever let yourself be with him properly until you've got this Giles thing out of your system.' Caroline folded her arms to demonstrate her certitude.

'Jamie?'

'I don't know. I don't, Holly. I'm sorry, this is a decision you need to make on your own.'

Holly nodded. It was hardly the answer she wanted, but deep down, she knew it no longer mattered. She knew what she was going to do.

41

Holly Berry was driving a Vespa on her own. Less than twenty-four hours ago, she had never even sat on one, but now she was going solo down a very winding hill. In fairness, she was driving very slowly, her hand barely touching the throttle as she let gravity take her down, and could probably have jogged as fast, but she wasn't taking any risks.

The scariest parts were when a car or motorbike flew past her, and it felt as if her heart leaped out of her chest. But finally, the lights of the marina came into view.

Of all the crazy things she had done in her life, this one had to be up there. Higher even than buying a sweet shop on a spur-of-the-moment decision. She was borrowing her current fling's vehicle to see her past fling, and for what? To see if she still loved him? If she ever loved him in the first place?

She hadn't seen Evan before she left. If she had, she would have second guessed herself, and ended up not going. What she wanted was to go back to the way things were the previous night, but now she had seen Giles, that couldn't happen. Not now a seed of doubt had been planted.

At the signpost for the marina, she flicked on her indicators and turned off the main road into an even narrower and steeper one. She had thought some roads around the Cotswolds were steep, but these were crazy, so after deciding she didn't want to risk her neck, or Evan's bike, she found a place to park up and walked the rest of the way.

The marina was an entirely different place at night. Even before she reached the waterfront she could hear the music and laughter filling the air. Taxis were lining up in the taxi rank, mostly having dropped people off, while couples and families spilled out of little side roads, chatting and laughing.

If this week had felt like something out of a romance movie, then this place was where the final big scene would take place. All around the water's edge, restaurants had set up their tables, with candles flickering on white, linen tablecloths. Fairy lights hung around windows while large parasols remained open from the heat of the day. But the edge of the water was nothing compared to the water itself.

The water lapped a gentle, slow rhythm accompanied by the clinking of sails against masts. And though the water was dark, it was mesmerising, reflecting all the light that fell on it and casting it back in sparkling pinpricks as if it was made of diamonds.

The beauty of the scene momentarily distracted her from the nerves that were bubbling away inside. When she had been driving down here, she had assumed that staying on the Vespa and not causing any accidents was going to be the trickiest part of the trip, but now she had arrived at the marina, she saw just how wrong she was. The trickiest bit was still to come.

But first, she had to find the boat.

It didn't help that Holly hadn't paid a great deal of attention to where they'd walked that morning, although, in her defence, her priority had been not falling off the jetty again. Now, however, she wished she had paid more attention to exactly which jetty the boat was on.

There were three different routes she could take, and each of those had boats on either side. After a moment's deliberation, she decided her best option was to go down the middle. That way, even if Giles's boat wasn't on that jetty, she could hopefully see which one it was on.

What a way to live, she thought as she passed a boat filled with women scantily clad in bikinis clinking champagne glasses together. It didn't look like they had to budget for how many glasses of wine they had to make sure they could still afford the taxi back.

As she reached the end of the middle jetty, she let out a groan. Not only was Giles's boat not moored on this part of the marina, but she realised, with a sense of sickening dread, that he might not be here at all. Boats were still heading out, so it would be perfectly reasonable to assume he may have gone out for a night trip some-where, or perhaps he didn't moor there permanently. He could have taken another trip out for the evening, or sailed off somewhere to get away from her and the terrible memories of the day.

'I'll give myself five more minutes looking,' Holly said to herself, only for a couple to pass her with an extra-wide berth. As if talking to herself was the worst thing she could do.

Back at the end of the jetty, she started again down one of the different wooden walkways. It was made of identical planks of wood, but for some reason, this path seemed more familiar to her. Some of the boats looked vaguely recognisable, as if she had already passed them that day. Then, when she was halfway down, she saw him.

Holly had seen Giles Caverty in many situations during their friendship. She had seen the ruthless, cut-throat and downright nasty Giles who had been utterly vile to her when he wanted the sweet shop. But that had been a long time ago. Since then, she had seen the Giles who took pizza to his sister and her colleagues at the maternity ward in Cheltenham hospital. And the one who had driven to Moreton to tell her that her dad had had a heart attack. She had seen him help her with her shopping, week in and week out, and offer her all the words of comfort she could need.

But she had never seen him with a bucket and sponge, cleaning.

A laugh caught in her throat as she stood there in silence and watched as he washed the back of the boat, dipping the sponge in to the bucket and pulling it out again, sodden and soapy. Oh, she loved this. Mr Glamorous doing the cleaning. Even if it was a massive yacht, it still made her chuckle. With her knot of nerves loosened by the sight, she headed forwards, opening her mouth to speak, when she spotted another person on the boat.

Both of the crew members who had been with them that day had been men, but this was a woman, with long hair tied in a high ponytail, who was wearing the type of skinny denim shorts that would look like underwear on Holly. Giles was absorbed in his cleaning and had not yet noticed the woman above him. He was busy dunking the sponge into the bucket when she reached down and grabbed it out of his hands. As Giles turned around to face her, the woman slapped the sponge straight into Giles's face.

Holly watched on in disbelief as his eyes bugged in shock. Then, before the woman could stop him, he had grabbed the sponge back out of her hand, but rather than soaking her with it, he threw it back into the bucket, wrapped his hands around her waist, pulled her in and kissed her.

42

It felt as though a vice had clamped around Holly's lungs and yet she couldn't stop watching. This wasn't a casual peck on the lips. This was a full-on, bodies pressed together, no coming up for air kiss. Giles picked the woman up so that her legs were around his hips and still the kissing continued. And Holly was only feet away, but Giles hadn't noticed her. He hadn't noticed anyone except for the woman in his arms.

Holly backed away, the horror she had felt at seeing Giles in this situation replaced by a wash of embarrassment. What was she thinking, coming down here? It had been eight months. Of course he was seeing someone.

As she stepped back, her foot caught on the edge of the jetty.

'Crap,' she whispered as she lurched forwards and dropped onto her hands and knees with a thud.

The laughter coming from Giles's boat stopped.

'Is someone there?'

Holly didn't move, remaining crouched on the wooden planks. Her heart was all the way up in her throat. The only thing that would be worse than her turning up to find Giles with his girlfriend, would be Giles finding her here, crouching on the wet ground as if she had been spying on them. She held her breath, willing the moment to pass.

'Come on, I need to get out of these wet clothes.' Giles's voice cut through the silence. 'You can help me.'

With her heart pounding, Holly listened to the footsteps retreat, though she still didn't move. The cold from the damp wood seeped into her knees and she shivered against it. Only when she was certain no one was there did she push herself onto her feet and head back to the marina.

So much for her holiday being a chance for her to get her head straight. She was going to head back in even more of a state than she had left.

What was so infuriating was that she hadn't even known how she'd wanted the night to go. She had gone to see if she was over Giles, but how did you know when you were truly over someone? With Dan, it had been easy; there had been no way she was going back there, not after how he treated her. And with Ben, it had just been a case of growing apart, possibly before they'd even grown together. But with Giles, she had never thought she needed to get over him. Because she and him could never be. But now Evan had swept in and made her feel like she was ready for another relationship; it was just who that relationship was going to be with that was the issue.

When she reached the cobbled stones of the marina, she placed her hand on the wall and looked out at the boats.

'Argh!'

Her lungs rattled with the scream just as a couple scurried past. They muttered in French, yet Holly didn't bother apologising for her moment of insanity. She was insane. Jamie had said it, and now it had been confirmed. One thing she knew, though; she couldn't go back to the villa now. What would she say to Evan?

Sorry, I don't know if I'm over him or not, but do you still fancy hanging out?

His whole concern had been around being her second choice, and this would make him exactly that. She could lie and say she had spoken to Giles, but then starting a relationship on a lie didn't feel like a good thing to do. What she needed was time to get her head straight.

With the decision made, she headed into the outside seating area of a restaurant and dropped into a chair. Instantly, a waiter was at her side, offering her a menu.

'Water? *L'eau?*' Her voice hitched.

She thought she'd got the term for water right, but the waiter looked at her with pure confusion.

'*Du vin?*' he said, instead.

'Vin, no, no. I'm driving. No vin.'

'*Du vin, oui. Rouge? Blanc?*'

'*Blanc?* No. *L'eau. Wasser?*'

Holly wasn't sure what was going on. Her own ears hurt at her abomination of one of the most beautiful languages in the world and she was pretty sure she'd slipped some German in there, but the waiter was smiling happily.

'*Oui, mademoiselle,*' he said, before disappearing back into the restaurant.

Left on her own, Holly looked up at the hills, wondering whether it was possible to see the house from here. What were the others up to? Had Eddie got his way and finally persuaded the group to succumb to the board games he had brought all the way from the States? Was Tyler already snoring?

Mainly, she wondered about Evan. What was he thinking about? And what did he think about the fact she had come to see Giles? If this was a test, like Caroline had suggested, then she had well and truly failed it.

She was still lost in these thoughts when the waiter appeared with a tray, upon which was a carafe of wine.

'*Vin rouge*,' he said.

'Uhm, *non*. No, water. Water. *L'eau. L'eau*.' Holly tried several variations in accent, hoping it might make her words more intelligible, but the waiter placed the wine down on the table and walked away. So wine it was.

Suspecting that she was going to have to pay for it now, regardless of how much she drank, Holly poured herself a tiny drink, took a sip, pulled out her phone and looked at the time. Maybe she could ring one of the others and see if they wanted to join her. Naomi had said she liked the look of the bars here and Holly did owe her for the loan of the clothes.

She went to dial Caroline's number when her phone rang.

'Hi Mummy!' Ben said, his image distorted and pixilated, although there, sitting on his knee, was Hope.

'What are you ringing for? I've already spoken to you tonight.'

'I know, but you seemed a bit down, so Hope wanted to say an extra goodnight, didn't you, Hopey? We've just had our bath and we're about to have an extra big bottle of milk.'

'Extra big? Has she not been feeding properly today?'

'It was just an expression. She's going to have the same size as always,' Ben responded. 'Although I think she's going through a growth spurt. She devoured the mashed avocado I gave her today. Didn't you?'

Hope gurgled. The denim dress was gone. Instead, she was wearing lilac pyjamas and was shaking a soft toy, with which she seemed far more intent on hitting Ben over the head than listening to Holly. That was fine, though. She loved watching her play like this. So innocent and happy.

'Where are you?' Ben asked. 'Are those boats behind you? Are you out?'

'Umm, yes. Just for a drink.' She turned phone around so that he could see the scenery.

'Are you there on your own?' he asked, as Holly panned around the view. 'Where are the others?'

She took a sip of her drink before flipping the camera back to herself.

'Oh, they just headed for a walk. I'm manning the table, that's all.'

She didn't like lying to Ben. After everything that happened with Giles, she had promised herself she would never lie to him again. But telling him why she was there would just complicate things further.

'Well, we've got another fun afternoon planned for tomorrow,' Ben started. 'I've booked to get out of work early, and so we're going up to the falconry centre at Bourton-on-the Hill. Have you ever been there?'

'No.' Holly's brain took a moment to catch up with what Ben had just said.

'Maybe we should all go together if you're back in time? I can't remember what time your flight gets in?'

'We leave just after midday. I'm not sure when we land.'

'Well, you can let us know.'

Holly took another mouthful of wine. It wasn't as nice as the ones from the vineyard, but it was far from terrible. Maybe, if Evan had time in the morning, he could take her to the supermarket so she could stock up on some bottles as gifts for her mum and Ben, or better still, head back to the vineyard and grab some of those. Then again, they were probably out of her price range. And who was to say that Evan would even want to take her?

'So, what do you think? Holly? Earth to Holly?'

'Sorry, what did you say?'

Ben stared at her.

'I'm sorry. We should let you go. It's your last evening. Enjoy yourself. We can tell you about the bird centre when we see you tomorrow, can't we? Now say goodbye to Mummy, Hope. Give her a big wave.'

Ben lifted Hope's hand, waving it goodbye, and Holly had just raised hers to wave back in response when the screen turned black.

'Okay, bye then,' she said to the air, and picked up her glass, only to find it was already empty. That's what happened when you poured yourself a tiny measure.

'I guess I'll just have to get a taxi back,' she said to herself, as she picked up the carafe and this time filled the glass to the top.

43

A bottle of wine normally felt like a lot of wine. It *was* a lot of wine. Ben had told her countless times how many units of alcohol were in one. But she hadn't had a full bottle, or even the full carafe's worth, so maybe French wine was stronger. Or maybe it was the heat, but as Holly poured the final remnants into her glass, it was hard to ignore the way the water was swaying in front of her. She squinted at the boats, wondering if perhaps a storm was coming in and that was the reason they were rocking from side to side so much.

She was still staring at the boats when the waiter appeared.

'*Un autre?*' Holly didn't understand what he was saying, though he looked concerned. And he had a kind face. The type of face that made her want to pour everything out to him. And she had a lot to pour out.

'My life is a mess,' Holly replied. He tilted his head to the side, which Holly assumed meant he wanted her to continue. 'This holiday was meant to be a chance to switch off, you know? Forget about real life for a bit. And I did. I really did. I mean, I met Evan, and he has been perfect at helping me forget about real life, because let's be honest, he doesn't live in the real world.'

'*Excuse-moi?*' The waiter was staring directly at her, his big, wide eyes imploring her to keep going.

'So why would he be here? What kind of trick of the universe is it to put Giles Caverty in my path this week? He's been everywhere. Everywhere I've turned. And it's not like I think about him all the time or anything. It's not like I have time to think about him. Maybe a bit. When I'm on my own. Or when I go food shopping. I do think about him when I'm shopping. Or when I get pizza. I guess that's quite a bit, isn't it?'

'*Un autre carafe du vin?*'

'Awesome *vin*? Yes, yes, you're right. It was lovely wine. So do you think it is? Do you think it's fate?'

The waiter smiled politely and nodded, although rather than replying, he turned around and headed back into the restaurant.

'That's okay! We can chat when you get back!' Holly called after him, although much to her disappointment, he didn't return. Instead, a middle-aged woman with a surly face appeared and dropped a carafe of wine on the table in front of her.

'Oh, I don't think I ordered that?'

The woman walked away, and after a brief consideration, Holly decided the polite thing to do was to have another glass. She topped up her drink to a reasonable level, then kept going until it was so full, she had to lean down and take a slurp from the top of the rim. The couple at the table next to her turned and scowled, but rather than apologising, as Holly would have done under normal circumstances, she simply took an even longer slurp than before, then lifted the glass up and took a proper full mouthful.

'Holly?'

With the wine glass still up to her mouth, Holly swivelled her head, sloshing drink over the tablecloth.

'Giles?'

She scanned around him, looking for any sign of the long-legged woman who had been with him, only to find he was on his own and looking straight at her. If he had looked gorgeous on the boat, this was something else. It was as if the moonlight had transformed him into a Greek god. His hair shimmered, while the corner of his untucked shirt wafted gently like a sail in a breeze. He moved towards her, his eyes narrowed.

'Are you here with someone? Evan?'

'No.' She took another mouthful of wine, trying to moisten her drying throat. 'No, it's just me.'

'How, come? Where are the others?'

She opened her mouth, only to close it again several times.

'Umm, I... I...' She struggled to think of what she was going to say. Before the wine, she'd had the vague outline of a speech prepared, but even then it had been sketchy. And that was before she'd seen him and the beautiful woman kissing. That was before she realised what a complete and utter mess she was making of her life. And so she said the only thing she could say.

'Do you want some of this wine?'

44

Holly wasn't sure what surprised her more. The fact that Giles sat down on the seat opposite her without a moment's hesitation, the flawless French with which he spoke and got himself another glass for the wine, or the way the previously grumpy waitress's face lit up when she spoke to him. It was far from the surly attitude the woman had had when she dumped the carafe down on the table for Holly. Judging by the way the pair of them laughed together, they could have been old friends.

'You know each other?' It was hard not to think about how many women Giles had around the marina to fetch him wine glasses at his beck and call.

'It's a close-knit community here. Maria's brother owns another restaurant over in Èze. I used to go there regularly with my uncle. But he sold it last year. She doesn't need to work here. Not financially, anyway; she just does it for the social side.'

Holly stayed quiet. Evidently, the lack of needing the job clearly translated to a lack of needing manners, too. Still, even with the way her head was spinning, Holly could feel that wasn't something she should say.

A moment later, Giles had been given a wine glass, which this time the waitress topped up, before saying something else Holly didn't understand. From the way she laughed and fluttered her eyes, though, she was definitely flirting with Giles.

Finally, after some less-than-subtle throat clearing by Holly, the waitress took her leave.

Giles took a long drink from his glass. 'How did you get here? Did someone drop you?'

'Actually' – a broad smile stretched out on Holly's face – 'I drove here. On a Vespa.'

'A Vespa!' Giles's jaw dropped. 'Since when did you drive a Vespa?'

'Since tonight, on a road at least.' Holly was feeling very pleased with herself. 'I hadn't even been on one until the day before yesterday. Evan took me up to a vineyard on one. Then he let me have a go on it. And according to him, I'm a natural.'

'According to Evan?'

'Yes.' There was something about Giles's tone that made her stop. The glint that had glimmered in his eyes had also gone, and the lightness that had been filling Holly took a sudden weight.

'Why did you come down here, Holly?'

The cool night air stirred with a heat, which caused a clamminess to fix to her skin.

'I don't know. Closure, I think. But then...' She paused, debating what to say next. 'I came to your boat. You said you wanted to talk, but I came to your boat and...' Her words trailed into nothing, though her eyes bore into Giles's and she knew he understood. For a moment, they stared at each other, the bond between them so strong it was almost as if the world had stopped swaying. The pair simultaneously took a sip from their drink before they spoke in unison.

'That girl—'

'You and Evan.'

They stopped, and Holly tipped her glass to Giles, gesturing for him to continue.

'She's not what you think.'

'You don't have to explain.'

'I know I don't, but I want to.'

'It's fine. Please. It was stupid of me to even come down here.'

'No, it wasn't. It was what I wanted you to do. I asked you to.'

He reached out to grab her hand, but she backed away sharply, knocking her knees against the underside of the table. Without a second's pause, Giles leaned forward and grabbed the two wine-glasses before they could topple.

'Reflexes from the boat,' he said with a narrow smile that dropped almost as quickly as it formed.

'Why did you ask me to come and see you?' Holly said. 'Why did you say you wanted to talk if you already had someone?'

She pressed her thumbs into her temples, trying to push away the throbbing that was building.

'Cecile is not my girlfriend. It's not that serious. It's just a casual thing.'

'It looked like you have fun together.'

'We do. We have fun. And then we stop having fun and I stop seeing her, and then I get lonely and she comes back, and it starts up again. It's easy. Predictable. But sometimes... sometimes I want more than that.'

He was looking at her with those eyes again. The ones that could melt her inside. And she hated it. She hated that he could do that. But what she hated even more was that she didn't have the strength to look away from him.

'I should get going.' She stood up – this time without knocking the table – and held out her hand to Giles, as if they were parting after some formal business meeting. But he didn't take it.

'Holly, we should talk.'

'There's nothing more to talk about. Really. It was nice to catch up. To see you doing well. I need to get back now.'

His lips pursed as he sucked them inwards. 'How are you getting back? You're not planning on driving the Vespa, are you?'

'No, I was going to get a taxi.'

'And leave the Vespa here?'

'I thought I'd get it in the morning.'

'But you're leaving in the morning.' His questioning was starting to irritate her.

'I know I am. It'll be fine. I'll get someone to give me a lift down early.'

'Okay, just give me your keys.'

'What? No, I don't need to give you the keys.'

'You do. I don't trust you when you're drunk like this.'

'You don't trust me? That's rich.' She could feel her volume rising, but she didn't care. 'You're the one who keeps messing with my life. Who comes back into it the moment I feel like I've got my head straight. Who keeps filling up my damn thoughts.'

She hadn't wanted to say these things. She hadn't even known she was going to. But now she had started, she couldn't stop.

'You know, it broke my heart. I wanted to choose you. My heart wanted to choose you, but my head couldn't.' She was crying now. Tears rolling down her cheeks. And people from the table next to her were looking over too. 'And then when you left, I lost you, and I lost Ben. I lost my two best friends. And I've been so lonely. And seeing you... it just reminded me how damn lonely I've been feeling.'

The tears burned down the back of her throat. There was no stopping them now.

Giles reached across the table and took her hand.

'Come back to the boat with me, Holly.'

45

Walking was far harder than Holly remembered it being. For some reason, it didn't matter how much she concentrated; her feet wouldn't go where she wanted them to. On the rare occasion they went in the right direction, then her arms and torso would start flailing, and she would wobble to the side, or backwards. Maybe all the wine had shifted her centre of gravity. Or maybe it had been the bike. Maybe she was now such a seasoned Vespa driver that her body preferred it to walking, though that seemed unlikely.

'Come on. Slowly does it.' Giles hooked his arm around her waist, the same way Evan had when they walked together.

Holly's mind locked onto the image of Evan and his Vespa. She had told him she would bring it back and now he was probably going to be mad at her. As soon as the thought formed, it switched again. Evan didn't really do mad. He did charming and sophisti-cated and unfeasibly mature.

'Watch it. You were nearly in the water there.' Giles's grip around her tightened as she stared at the water. Not that she could see much. Other than a few glimmers of reflected light, the sea was entirely black.

'Can I drink this? I'm thirsty.' She bent her knees, only for Giles to tug at her arm and pull her back upright.

'Drinking seawater is not a good idea. Come on. Let's get you onto the boat. I'll get you some water. And probably a strong coffee, too.'

'Coffee? I can't have coffee, I won't sleep.'

'Honestly, I don't think that's going to be a problem.'

Smacking her lips, Holly took a few steps forward, only to stop suddenly. Giles jumped back and grabbed her hands and pulled her into the middle of the jetty.

'What are you doing? You nearly fell in.'

'We have to go back.' Holly said, trying to turn around. 'I need you to take me back to the restaurant. I didn't pay for the drinks.'

Giles loosened his grip.

'It's fine, I got it. I paid for them.'

'You did?' Holly went to frown, only to find it caused her head to ache. 'When? I didn't see you pay? Are you tricking me? You tricked me before.'

'I promise you, I paid for the wine. Though given how drunk you were, I expected the bill to be a lot higher. You are a lightweight.'

Even though Holly knew Giles had just insulted her and that he would, at some point, require a rebuke, she still couldn't let go of the question of who'd paid for the drinks.

'When did you pay? I didn't see.'

'No, you wouldn't have because it was while you were dancing with the lamppost, singing. Just a word of advice. Please don't give up the sweet shop for a career on the stage.'

Dropping her frown, Holly pouted instead, though only partly because of Giles's insult. The other issue was that she really couldn't remember singing around the lamppost. And that felt like something she should probably remember, particularly if it had only been a few minutes ago.

When they reached the boat, Giles stepped on board and offered her a hand.

'You're going to be okay. Just take it slow.' His hand remained extended, but Holly had stopped again, her eyes on the bucket placed by the back.

'Is your girlfriend on board?' The humiliation of the day had already been bad enough. There was no way she could cope with that, too.

'No, she went home. She's jetting off for a shoot in Milan tomorrow. Early morning. And she doesn't sleep well on the boat.'

'A shoot? Like shooting animals?' Holly stumbled back in alarm. 'Why would she do something like that?'

'No, not shooting animals. A modelling shoot.'

'She's a model? Of course she's a model.'

She took another step back, only for her foot to catch on the edge of the jetty. In one leap, Giles was off the boat, grabbing her.

'Come on. Let's get you inside and get you a coffee.'

Her entire weight flopped onto his shoulder as he pulled her up the steps.

'Okay, that's it. I've got you.'

He opened the doors to the large dining area.

'Right, I'll get you below deck before I make you a drink.'

'Below deck?'

'Downstairs?'

'There's a downstairs! How's there a downstairs? It's a boat!' Holly turned in a circle, banging her hips against the side of the table as she moved.

'You saw the downstairs already, remember?'

'I did?'

'You did. It's where the toilet is.'

'There's a toilet on the boat?'

It was safe to say she sounded drunk, though it had hit her so quickly, she was still having trouble admitting it.

'Come on, you need to sit down,' Giles took her by the hand.

'No, I don't. I'm fine.'

'You're wobbling everywhere.'

'That's because I'm on a boat. Boats are wobbly.'

To reinforce her point, Holly swayed back and forth, only to overestimate her ability to stay standing. A moment later, she toppled into Giles's arms.

'Here, it's okay, I've got you. Now please, sit down. Jamie hates me enough as it is. She would never forgive me if you cracked your head open.'

'She doesn't hate you as much as she used to,' Holly said, flopping down onto what felt like the comfiest sofa in all existence. 'She still hates you, but not as much. I think she realised you couldn't be completely horrible. Not when I missed you so much.'

'You missed me that much?' Giles's voice was quiet and low, his eyes looking straight at her. Unfortunately, it was hard to meet them, because they kept shifting from side to side, and a lot of the time it looked as if he had an extra third eye in the middle of his forehead too. Closing her eyes, Holly tried to battle all the thoughts that were competing in her head.

'Of course I missed you. I loved you,' she whispered.

A moment later, she was snoring.

46

Holly blinked. A flash of light burst through the crack in her eyelids. Blindingly fierce, it sent a bolt of pain shooting to the back of her skull.

'What the hell!' She squeezed her eyes tightly closed again.

Her head was on fire. And something was hammering behind her temples. It felt like thousands of nails were piercing the back of her skull. This was not good. Not good at all.

She sat up, still, with her eyes closed, hoping that a vertical position might abate some of the swaying and nausea. It didn't. If anything, it was even worse.

'Good afternoon, sleepy head. I was getting worried there. I thought you weren't going to wake up.'

The sound of Giles's voice was all it took for Holly to drop back down again.

'Do you need to speak so loud?' She clutched her head. 'How much did I drink?'

'I have no idea. Too much, I would say. Definitely too much.'

She groaned again. It wasn't just her head that was the problem. Every muscle ached, as if she'd just run two marathons back-to-back. Not that she'd ever even ran one. And what was that taste in her mouth? It felt like she'd been chewing on a dry flannel.

'I need another ten minutes.' Vaguely aware of the fact that she was now on a bed, she sank further into the mattress, only to bolt upright. 'Did you say afternoon?'

Giles smirked. 'Thought that might wake you up. I might have exaggerated a little. It's quarter past ten.'

'What? No!' She scrambled onto her hands and knees. The white sheets tangled around her feet and legs. It was only one sheet, and yet the more she tried to pull it off, the tighter the knots became. 'I need to get up. We're leaving the villa at eleven for the airport.'

'Here, let me help.' Giles sat on the end of the bed and untwisted the fabric. When her first leg was free, Holly noticed she was no longer wearing her own clothes, but an oversized white shirt. The nausea swept through her again, but she didn't have time to think about it.

'Where's my phone?' She dove for her bag on the floor. 'I need to ring Hope. I'm meant to speak to Hope in the morning.' Her hands were in her bag, tossing out her wallet and packs of tissues and sanitary towels, but there was no sign of her phone. 'I must have left it in the restaurant. We need to go and get it. I have to have it.'

Now on her feet, she marched towards the door, only for her balance to fail three steps in. Giles caught her by the arm and lowered her down onto a chaise longue that was conveniently placed.

'It's fine. Your phone was out of battery, so I put it on charge. And...' He paused. His eyes shifted. Holly may not have seen Giles for a long time, and she may have been as hungover as hell, but she knew that look meant he had done something. Something he probably didn't want her to know about.

'Giles.'

'Ben kept ringing. I assumed he was calling so you could talk to Hope.'

A layer of dread cemented itself in Holly's alcohol-filled stomach. Yes, Ben had a girlfriend now, but she could only imagine the way he would respond to Giles answering her phone.

'Please tell me you didn't pick up?' The sound of her voice was enough to make her head pound even harder.

'Of course I didn't pick up. I'm not a fool. But I sent him a message from your phone. Said you'd got on an early-morning sailing trip and the reception wasn't good enough for a video call. Then added a photo from the other day, too. Just so it was believable. You know.'

'Wow,' Holly replied, needing a minute to take it all in. That was a lot to unpack. It was no wonder Giles had fooled her so well during those early months at the sweet shop if this was how well he could cover things up.

'How did you know my password?' she said after a pause. She had taken a moment to think about her photo roll, and whether there was anything incriminating on it. But other than half a dozen photos of cracked nipples from when Hope was first feeding, everything was very much U-rated.

'Hope's birthday,' Giles responded to her question. 'Though I tried yours first to be fair.'

'You know my birthday?'

'Of course I know your birthday.'

With a long sigh, Giles took a seat on the couch.

Now that she was fully awake, she could see just how amazing the room was. Everything was sleek and white, accented with dark navy blue. The large bed was surrounded by built-in cabinets, and the marble ensuite glinted in the distance.

'Holly, I'm sorry about last night. About you turning up. If I'd have known you were going to come...'

'You'd have told your girlfriend to make herself scarce?' Holly laughed. 'Don't be ridiculous. It's me who should apologise for turning up unannounced. And then being so drunk, you had to bring me back here.'

'It wasn't an easy feat. You've no idea how many times I thought you were going to fall off the jetty and into the water.'

'It wouldn't be the first time.'

'That doesn't surprise me.' He chuckled again, only to stop abruptly. 'Holly, last night, before you passed out, you said something.'

'Oh, God.' She covered her head in her hands. This was why she hated getting drunk. If the physical effects of the hangover weren't bad enough, the mental torture of wondering how much of a fool she'd made of herself was even worse. Of course, she knew already she'd made a fool of herself in front of Giles, but the soberness of his tone now made her worry just how bad she had been.

'What did I say? I'm so sorry. I honestly don't know what I was thinking. I can say horrible things when I'm drunk. I don't mean to. I think I'm being funny.'

Giles took a deep breath in before he spoke.

'It wasn't anything bad. I promise you. Or at least, I didn't think it was. I just need to know if you meant it.'

'If I meant what?' The nausea that struck was only partly to do with the drink. Giles's eyes were locked on hers, and his hands, she realised, were still holding hers too. This closeness wasn't something they'd shared that often, even when they were seeing each other every week.

'You said that you loved me. Was it true?'

47

Holly was having difficulty locating the exact source of the spinning that was going on in her head. Given that she was on a boat, it could well have been the water beneath her. Equally, it could have been the drink. Yet deep down, she couldn't help but think it was the third and final option. She had told Giles she loved him. How? When? And why? It didn't make sense. But as the gnawing crept from the pit of her stomach, she knew he was telling the truth.

'I... I was drunk,' she said.

'Yes, I'm aware of that,' Giles chuckled. The laughter creased his eyes, though the creases faded as he continued to look at her. 'What I did before – putting you on the spot when you were with Ben – that wasn't fair of me. I'll be honest, I don't get many things right when it comes to you. But that doesn't mean what I felt wasn't real and true. You're not with Ben any more, Holly. There's no one here you need to protect. It's just you and me.'

Just Giles and her. Her mind returned to the car journey to the airport, where Caroline had asked her about the other one. Not to mention Evan's response. And the way her mum had brought him up more and more. Holly had assumed it was because her mother thought a reconciliation with Giles was the swiftest way to ensure Holly wasn't on her own, but perhaps it was because she had seen how much Holly had missed him.

'I think I did,' she said, finally voicing the words she hadn't allowed herself to speak or even think. 'I think I loved you.'

Giles's lips parted, his eyes unblinking as he looked straight at her.

'And now? Do you still feel the same way?'

Holly took a deep breath in. What was she doing? How did she manage to make a few relaxing days away into such an absolute mess? For a moment, she tried to steady her breath, though she hadn't realised her hands were covering her face until Giles's fingers gently prised them away, and wrapped them in his own. Even then, she kept her eyes closed. Only when she finally opened them did she see that his face was only inches from hers.

'Holly, this is not pressure. I learned my lesson about putting pressure on you the hard way. But I wouldn't be able to forgive myself if I let you get off this boat without knowing the truth. If there is any chance you still feel that same way, then I am here. I am here to try. We could have a future together, Holly. I think I knew that from the first time we sat at dinner together, and I didn't want the evening to end. And now, years later, you are the only woman I can't get out of my head. So if you think there is any chance, any chance at all, that you can see a future with us, then now's the time to say.'

A loud squall of a sea bird rang through from outside, disguising the silence that formed between them. Holly's throat had constricted so much, she could hardly take a breath. Why was it that men, like buses, always seemed to come into her life in pairs? There was Dan finally deciding he wanted to propose when she was trying to get things together with Ben, and then when she finally thought things were straight with Ben, Giles was there on the scene, making her doubt their relationship (which had undoubtedly been a good thing in the long term but had still been pretty terrifying at the time).

And now she was here, in the most fledgling relationship possible with a man who couldn't be more perfect. A man who was so perfect, he had sent her to see her ex because it felt like the right thing to do. A man who had introduced her to his mother on video call, a man with whom she somehow felt utterly excited and yet totally relaxed at the same time.

'Giles, thank you. Thank you,' she said, standing up. The excitement pulsed through her as she placed her hands on his cheeks and kissed him on the top of his head. 'Thank you so much.'

'Does that mean... What does that mean?'

He was looking up at her, his eyes bulging with expectation. It reminded her of that moment, in the hospital, when Hope had arrived and her life had changed inexplicably.

'Giles, I loved you. And I will always love you. But I don't think I'm in love with you any longer. Maybe, maybe had we bumped into each other a couple of months ago, or maybe even a week ago, I wouldn't be saying this. But...'

'But there's someone else?' He pressed his fingers against the bridge of his nose before forcing his lips into a smile that didn't quite reach his eyes.

Holly nodded, the guilt rolling through her.

'I'm sorry, I'm so sorry, but I have to pray I haven't messed this up. Thank you. Thank you for everything. But I need to go. I need to go now.'

It didn't matter how much alcohol was still running through her veins. Suddenly, Holly was thinking with the most clarity she'd had in the last twenty-four hours. Possibly longer.

She stood up and pecked Giles on the cheek before running to the door, only to be struck by the same bout of nausea and dizziness that had been afflicting her since she'd woken. She rested her hand on the doorjamb, closed her eyes, and prayed for the moment to pass.

'Do you want a lift?' Giles said from behind her.

'That would be great.'

48

Holly would have preferred it if Giles had dropped her by the road so she could walk down the driveway to the villa without him having to come with her, but there was the small added inconvenience of the Vespa in the back of his pickup truck, and Holly didn't trust herself not to end up taking a tumble, even if she was just pushing it down a slope.

'This was definitely an unexpected turn of events, but it was a fun one. I'm glad we got to talk,' Giles said as he lifted the Vespa down from the truck bed.

'Me too.' Holly nodded.

'I've got a couple of business things to see to when I'm back in the Cotswolds, but maybe we could catch up for a drink? Or dinner? I'd love to see Hope again. And see how this worked out.' As he said the last comment, he nodded his head towards the house, leaving Holly in no doubt as to what he meant.

'That sounds good,' she said, then kissed him once on the cheek. 'See you around, Caverty.'

Time wasn't on her side, but all the same, Holly waited until

Giles's truck had disappeared up the driveway before she headed to the house.

She opened the front door to chaos.

Every member of the group was running back and forth in various states of dress, some holding their suitcases, others shouting out to one another. Tyler was rubbing his eyes, indicating he had been even later waking up than she had, while Fin was hurriedly collecting up any rubbish. For a split second, Holly thought she might be able to slip in unnoticed.

'You're back!'

Caroline pounced before Holly had even seen her. 'What the hell? Giles Caverty? You spent the night with Giles Caverty?'

'No, I didn't.' Holly tried to keep her voice low. 'Well, technically, I spent the night on his boat, but I didn't *spend the night*, spend the night with him. Listen, Caroline, I need to talk to Evan. Where is he?'

Holly edged towards the staircase as Caroline opened her mouth to respond, but before she had got a word out, thundering footsteps came hammering behind her.

'Holly! Oh my God. What the hell?' It was Jamie speaking, with Zahida and Naomi standing behind her, looking like a group of schoolgirls desperate to catch up on a piece of juicy gossip. 'I thought you were going to miss the flight. What does this mean? Are you two together now?'

'This is the yacht guy?' Naomi said. 'I can't believe I tried to flirt with him. I am so sorry. I didn't realise you and him were a thing.'

'We're—'

'So you're properly together now?' Jamie asked. 'I'm guessing that's what you staying the night on his boat means. So I promise I'll try not to judge, but it might take a bit of practice. You know I've despised him for a very long time.'

'This is so exciting!' Zahida joined in. 'You'll need to fill us in on the taxi journey. It's going to be here any minute now.'

'I wasn't actually—'

'I packed your suitcase for you,' Caroline continued. 'I thought it would be best to be prepared. Don't worry, I kept all the dirty and clean washing separate, though you might want to do a quick last-minute check in case I missed anything in any of the cupboards.'

They were talking in every direction. Over one another, as well as over Holly, and it was impossible to keep track of it all. Her head had barely stopped spinning from the hangover. If they didn't stop yelling at her soon, it was going to push her over the edge.

'Did anyone pack my speedos?' Tyler stood at the top of the stairs as he spoke. 'I looked by the pool and I can't find them?'

'Will you all stop talking!' Holly squeezed her eyes closed and clenched her fists as she yelled. It was a toddler-esque shout and the type she could never remember making as an adult, and yet it worked. Everyone fell silent. Every pair of eyes, including those of Tyler – who evidently still hadn't found his speedos, or any other pieces of clothing, for that matter – were now looking on.

Steadying herself with a deep breath, Holly looked first at Jamie and then at Caroline before she spoke.

'Thank you for sorting my luggage out, Caroline,' she said. 'Now, will someone please let me know where Evan is? I need to speak to him. Now.'

The silence that had descended when she raised her voice extended far longer than Holly had expected, and suddenly all the people who'd had so much to say had lost their tongues. And whether it was her imagination or not, they seemed to be avoiding her gaze, too.

'Caroline. Jamie?' She focused her attention on her closest friends. 'Where is Evan? I need to speak to him.'

Another second of silence remained, and in the end it was Fin who cleared his throat and finally spoke.

'He was pretty gutted if we're honest, Holly. He tried not to show it, but I know the guy. He thought you and him, you know... that you might have something.'

They were all still staring at her with an expression she couldn't quite read. Was it guilt? No, pity.

'So, where is he? I need to talk to him.'

'Holly, you spent the night with another guy,' Jamie cut in.

'But I didn't. That's what I'm trying to say. When I got the boat, Giles was there with a girl, and I felt like an idiot, and drank loads.'

'Giles was with another girl? Then whose car was it we heard dropping you back?'

'I thought you and him were fate?'

It was taking all Holly's willpower not to snap again. Had her friends always been this infuriating?

'Giles dropped me back. He found me at the bar, already drunk. Look, I really want to talk to Evan. I didn't choose Giles. I didn't want to choose Giles. I chose Evan. It was always Evan. I just needed to be sure. Now will one of you please tell me where he is so that I can let him know this too?'

Her question was met by a silence more consuming than before. And now there really was no denying it. They were definitely avoiding looking at her.

'I'm sorry,' Jamie said, as she stepped forward and took hold of Holly's hands. 'I'm really sorry, Holly. He's gone.'

49

Holly stared at her friends as they surveyed her with a look of deep, unwavering pity.

'You know what? I think I remember where I left my speedos,' Tyler said and made a sprint for the nearest staircase.

'Let me help you look for those, buddy.' Eddie hastened after him. Even Naomi and Zahida slipped away, their need for gossip satiated.

'What do you mean, he's gone?' Holly said finally, directing her question at the remaining people in the room, her core group of friends. 'Where has he gone? This is his house. Besides, I thought he was getting a flight back with us?' She closed her eyes and rubbed her forehead and temples with a pinched finger and thumb. 'Where is he?'

'Apparently, it was work,' Fin said, although the lie was so poorly veiled that Holly didn't even bother acknowledging it.

'Where is he?' she said again.

Finally, it was Caroline who stepped forward and spoke.

'We got up this morning, and he said he had to go. He needed to get an early flight out.'

'What?' Holly was having trouble putting all the information together. 'I didn't think there were any other flights. There's only one a day.'

'Out of Nice.' Fin answered. 'He can charter a helicopter whenever he likes out of Monaco.'

'Of course he can.' A heavy weight pressed down on Holly's chest as she waited for someone to say more. To say something that would make this situation even slightly bearable, but none of them had anything.

'He waited up all night, Holly,' Jamie said eventually. 'I think... we all thought...'

'That I'd chosen Giles.'

Her friends nodded. A lump had lodged itself in Holly's throat, forcing out tears she didn't want to shed. Especially not in front of people. After all, it wasn't like she'd even known Evan for long. Could she really cry for a man she had only known for three days? Already knowing the answer, she sniffed back her tears, trying to think of something jovial to say, when a car beeped in the driveway.

'That'll be the taxi,' Fin said. 'We need to get going. We don't want to miss this flight.'

It felt as though everyone was moving around her. As if she had someone slipped into another dimension. One that was full of numbness and self-doubt. Caroline fetched her suitcase, Sandra did a double check in all the rooms, and then that was it. They were driving away.

'Don't worry.' Jamie huddled herself up in the seat next to Holly. 'Fin will message Evan and make sure he knows you came back for him. We'll sort out something when he's back in the UK.'

And when would that be? Holly wanted to say. After Hope had been born, Giles had moved to a different country to get away from her. Evan might well do the same. It could be months until she got to see him. Besides, why would he believe her? She had already sent him six messages, all of which had been left unread, and his phone went straight to voicemail. She had ruined things the moment she had been too blind to see what was standing there in front of her and gone off chasing a ghost. A ghost, it turned out, she was no longer in love with anyway.

With her head pressed against the window of the minibus, it was hard not to think of the journey over. How Evan had been so patient with her on the plane. And how he'd done everything to ensure he was the perfect host. Maybe if she'd let her guard down and been open to the possibility of a little fun earlier, they would never have got into this position.

'Did you hear that, Holly?' Jamie tapped her on her shoulder.

'Sorry, I was lost in my thoughts.'

'Fin said that they're having a function in London later in the year. At the Shard. Maybe we could all go to that. Evan will definitely be there.'

'Maybe,' Holly replied.

By the time they reached the airport, Holly was numb. She couldn't even say she was looking forward to going home. Of course she wanted to see Hope, desperately, but even without being able to speak, her daughter could read Holly's mood better than anyone. She would know that something was off. And then, she was going to have to face the reality of Georgia and Ben. He had probably moved her in by now. And got her a jumper with *BEST STEP-MUM IN THE WORLD* sewn on it.

They stood outside departures, unloading the minibus one by one, before collecting all their luggage. All around her, people were getting in and out of cars and taxis. The midday sun was burning now, though it didn't bother her. It would be the last time she felt this type of sun for a very long time, and she wanted to remember it all.

Before she could get her phone out for one last photograph, the minibus was driving away and they were heading inside, lining up in the baggage drop queue.

'You know, I get it's tough.' Fin sidled beside Holly in the queue. 'But you two had something special together. Right off the bat I could see it, just like Jamie and me. At some point, this will be a silly story you tell the children.'

'I'd like to think so,' Holly replied.

'It will be. Trust me. You know I've got your back. Just let me know if there's anything I can do and I'll be there for you.'

She nodded and cast her gaze around the large hall. There were so many people, just like her, lining up, ready to head back to their real lives, but there were so many others too. People hugging and laughing as they greeted one another. People squeezing their loved ones goodbye as they prepared to leave them. And outside, through the big windows of the departures lounge, she could see the row of white taxis waiting to take people off on holiday, or back to their loved ones. And all of a sudden, a thought struck her.

'Actually Fin, there is something you can do for me. You can lend me your credit card.'

Fin tilted his head to the side.

'Any chance you can elaborate? I'm not saying no. I'm just asking why?'

Holly took a deep breath in. 'I need to go to Monaco. I'm going to get Evan back.'

'Well, if that's the case, I can't possibly say no.' His eyes glimmered as he reached into his pocket and retrieved a black card, which he promptly held out.

Holly hesitated. 'Just so you understand, I have no idea when I'm going to be able to pay you back for this.'

'It's fine,' Fin said. 'I'll take unlimited free sweets for a lifetime.'

'You've got it.' Holly jumped up onto her tiptoes to kiss him on the cheek, before turning back around in the queue.

'Sorry, excuse me.' She squeezed her way past Eddie and Sandra, who were stuck in a deep conversation, and Zahida and Naomi, who were busy taking the last selfies of the trip. Only when she reached Jamie did her friend grab her by the wrist and stop her.

'Holly, what are you doing?'

'I'm going to find him.' If Holly had needed any confirmation that she was doing the right thing, the way her heart leaped when she spoke said it all. 'I'm going to find Evan.'

'What? How?' Jamie was straight in with the logistics.

'He's gone to the heliport in Monaco, right?'

'Holly, that's insane. He left early in the morning. He could be anywhere in the world by now. He didn't even say where he was going.'

'He went so he didn't have to see me.' Holly didn't know for certain but, she reasoned, it had to take a couple of hours to charter a helicopter. After all, there would be forms to fill in. Tickets to get. She was going to find him. She could feel it in her gut.

Though Jamie still wasn't onboard with the idea.

'Holly, you don't have to do this. We can tell him it was a mix-up. We can tell him you wanted to do this.'

Holly knew it didn't make sense, but nothing about the week had so far, so why should this be any different? Besides, she needed to do this. From the moment they met, Evan had been nothing but the perfect gentleman. He had even introduced her to his mother, for crying out loud. She wanted to show that she could be the one who did the big gestures. Just like Dan had done with his badly thought-out marriage proposal in her back garden, and like Giles had, turning up at the hospital, and Ben when he had outbid Dan at the charity auction all those months ago. Big gestures mattered. And it was time she was the one doing them. She just hoped her attempt didn't go down in flames like theirs all had.

'I can't explain it. I can feel it. I can feel it, Jamie. This is the right thing for me to do.'

'And what about Hope? Ben is expecting you back this afternoon.'

Holly stopped in her tracks. Given that Hope had been at the forefront of her mind the entire break, it was ridiculous that now, the moment she was getting ready to leave was the moment she had slipped from her thoughts.

'I'll ring Mum. She's been nagging me about having Hope for a sleepover forever. Now she'll finally get her chance.'

'And I can make sure she's got everything she needs.'

Only then did Holly see Caroline standing there, looking at Holly with tears glazing her eyes. Not sad tears, but glowing, happy tears.

'If anyone deserves this, Holly. It's you. Go get him.'

Jamie looked between the two of them before shaking her head and letting out an exaggerated sigh.

'Fine. Go. We'll sort everything else out.'

'I love you guys.'

With the tightest squeeze she could, Holly pulled her two friends into her. It was hard to know what she had done to deserve two women like this in her life. Women who would be there for her no matter what, no matter when, but she was forever going to be grateful. Wiping her eyes, she finally let go and stepped back away from them.

'Wish me luck, ladies. I'm going to get my man.'

51

Holly didn't even bother taking her suitcase. What did it matter? It was old anyway, and it was hardly like she was going to need a silk sarong and sequined flip-flops any time soon. What she needed was a taxi.

With countless apologies, she weaved her way out of the baggage drop queue, past the same tourist police stand she had seen when they arrived and outside into the sun, where for the first time, she stopped and considered what her next move was going to be. Before she had left, Jamie had offered to come with her, but this was something Holly needed to do by herself. Now she needed to work out how.

While taking Fin's credit card had felt sensible in the moment, she was hit by the realisation that she had no idea how much a taxi to Monaco was going to cost. Or even how far away it was. But she wasn't backing out now.

Not giving herself time to second guess her actions, she raced towards the taxis. Without even heading to the front of the queue, she opened the nearest back door, jumped inside and opened a search engine on her phone, ready to work out where to go next.

'Monaco,' she said, without looking up.

'Where in Monaco? What is the name of the hotel?'

He may have only spoken one sentence, but something about the man's tone made Holly look up from her phone.

A mixture of shock and disbelief hit her. There, sat in the driver's seat, was a round-faced man wearing aviator sunglasses. This was the same taxi driver who had insisted he didn't speak a word of English when he had taken two hundred Euros of Evan's money from her and raced back to his cab. And now he was sitting there, speaking to her with a flawless accent. Even with the fans blowing on full, his cheeks were unusually red, while a small soul patch made his large chin look even larger.

'You speak English?' Holly spoke through gritted teeth. 'I should go to the police about you, right now.'

'And say what? That you were foolish enough to let me walk off with your money?'

He spoke with a confident lilt, though Holly noticed the way his Adam's apple bobbed up and down as he swallowed. If she had to make a bet, she suspected she wasn't the first tourist he'd ripped off.

'I'd tell them the truth. That I didn't even see the meter and when I asked you how much the trip was, you took the money from my hands and drove off before I could stop you. You're lucky I don't have any time to waste or I'd be dragging you to the tourist police now.'

He emitted a loud sigh. '*Merci. Merci.*'

'Just drive, will you? And put the meter on now. I'm not letting you get away with it again.'

His eyes glinted as he switched on the engine.

His initial cocky talkativeness was replaced by complete silence and they were several minutes onto the highway before he finally spoke again.

'You still didn't tell me what hotel?'

Holly looked up from her phone.

She had been worried, given her limited knowledge of luxury locations like Monaco that she would have difficulty finding out where Evan was planning on departing from. In the films she watched, it looked like every posh hotel had a helipad on top. But a quick internet search told her this wasn't the case. At least not here. Monaco, she discovered, was only 1 square mile and the second smallest country in the world, and as such, had only one heliport.

That was where she was going.

A constant stream of questions whirred through her head, although she kept coming back to the same one: was she doing the right thing? It was certainly the craziest thing she had done. Even when she'd made a spur-of-the-minute decision to buy the sweet shop, she'd had some knowledge of how to run the place. Not to mention she'd bought it in a country she had lived in all her life with family around her. But in this moment, she was alone in the back of a taxi with a man she knew was untrustworthy with only a distant B-grade GCSE in French to get her through.

'Will you stop that, please?' The taxi driver glared at her in his rear-view mirror. 'Your foot. It keeps banging on the floor. You're going to ruin my suspension if you keep going like that.'

Holly doubted it was true, but he was right. Her knee was bouncing about like crazy. Unfortunately, she couldn't stop it. Even when she tried and held her knee down, the tapping resumed somewhere else, like her hands.

'Do you need the toilet?' The taxi driver spoke with a hint of fear. 'These seats are only just cleaned. You'll pay extra if you make a mess.'

'I don't need the toilet,' Holly said indignantly. 'Besides, I wouldn't pay you extra for anything. I'm just nervous, that's all.'

'About the helicopter? You should be nervous. Scary things. Never liked them.'

Holly was starting to think she liked the taxi driver better when he was pretending he didn't understand her. But at least talking to someone was helping to diminish her endless rollercoaster of thoughts.

'No, not about the helicopter. I'm not going on a helicopter. I just need to speak to someone who is there.'

'A pilot? Helicopter pilots are the worst. The way they look down on our taxis. My brother-in-law, he is a helicopter pilot. You should hear him at Christmas. Easter. Every time: helicopter this, helicopter that.'

While the taxi driver continued to rant about his brother-in-law, flicking between French and English, Holly questioned again and again whether she had lost her mind. What if Evan really had needed to go early? What if it hadn't been an excuse not to see Holly? What if she got to the heliport, found he had already gone, and she was stuck there, entirely on her own, with only Fin's credit card? She shook her head and tried to push the thoughts from her mind. She didn't know how to explain it, but she could feel it in her gut. Evan was going to be there. They were meant to be together. Never in all her days had she felt it before, that certainty that she was meant to be with someone. The assurance that the fates would align to make sure it happened.

Several toll roads slowed their pace, but it didn't take long until the taxi was twisting and turning through the narrow roads of Monaco. The land of the rich and famous.

'Are you sure you're going the right way?' Holly said as they weaved past designer shops and luxury cars, and closer to the sea.

'Only one heliport in Monaco.'

She was about to question him again as they were heading right towards the water, and it didn't seem as though there would be enough space for a decent-sized car park, let alone a full airport, and yet, as the car slowed, the rust red and cream building came into sight.

'This is you.'

Holly's heart flipped in her chest.

'Do you want me to wait for you?' the taxi driver said, as Holly paid for the fare and opened her door.

'No, I'll be fine.' She could just imagine him keeping his meter running for the half hour it took her to find Evan and get back outside and then charge her extra, too. This taxi driver had got enough money from her. Besides, Evan might not want to head straight back to the villa.

With a deep breath, she straightened her dress, combed her fingers through her hair and stepped through the double doors.

52

The air-conditioning inside was a stark contrast to heat of Monaco, and cold enough to raise Holly's arms into goosebumps. She stepped inside, scanning from one end of the building to the other. A queue had formed in front of a coffee shop, while people wheeling designer handbags – some of which had small dogs in – were heading towards the check-in counters. Which, she decided, was where she needed to go.

It took far less time than expected to reach a desk, where a woman with bright-red lipstick and perfectly applied winged eyeliner smiled.

'Good afternoon, *mademoiselle*, may I have your passport for check-in, please?'

Holly reached into her handbag where her passport was stowed, though she didn't retrieve it.

'I'm not actually here to check in,' she said.

'Oh?' The woman's red lips formed a perfect circle. 'If you need to purchase a ticket, you will have to go to one of the counters over there.' She pointed to the far side of the building, where chairs were placed in front of sleek, wooden booths.

'Thank you, but I don't actually want to buy a ticket either. I want to know if someone has already checked in. Evan. Evan...' It took her a minute to recall his surname. 'Evan Roth?'

A thin line creased the skin between the woman's perfectly plucked brows.

'You want to know if someone has checked in?'

'Yes, is that possible?'

'No. No, it's not. Madam, our passenger lists are entirely confidential.'

'I get that, I do. And I don't want to know about anyone else. Just him. Just Evan Roth. I think he might still be waiting to fly. Can someone check? Please?'

The woman's lips were now tightly pursed as she pressed her shoulders back.

'Madam, I cannot tell you any details about other passengers.'

'He knows me. I'm a friend. Please.'

'Madam this is the check-in. You do not have ticket so you cannot check in. If you wish to purchase a ticket, you can do so from one of the counters at the other end of the building, but right now, I must ask you move away from the desk.'

She wasn't smiling any more. In fact, she was doing the exact opposite. Her dark eyes had diminished into small, angry ovals. Holly opened her mouth, ready to try again, only to close it again immediately afterwards. There was no way this was happening. Not at this desk at least.

'Thank you. You're right. I should go. I apologise.'

She stepped back and noted several men rolling suitcases to the far end of the room. With a glance at the wall above them, Holly saw the sign. Departures.

She wanted to run. She wanted to sprint, the same way she had done leaving the airport, but this wasn't the place to do that. The woman from check-in had moved on to the next passenger, so as stealthily as she could, Holly stepped towards the departure lounge.

'Ticket.' The man who spoke to her was dressed in a sharp black suit, and had it not been for the small silver badge fastened to his lapel, Holly would have assumed he was a passenger, not an employee. But his sharp glower said it all. 'Madam, can I see your ticket, please?'

'Actually, I'm just looking for someone.' Holly fixed her best smile, trying to mimic the woman on the counter.

'You cannot go through here without a ticket.'

'I don't need to go through. I don't want to go through. I just need to ask you something. Have you been working here all day?'

The man's eyebrows furrowed into a deep frown as he looked at her.

'Since seven a.m.'

'Perfect.' She let out a deep sigh of relief. 'I'm looking for a man. My boyfriend, sort of. I just wanted to know if he's been here.'

Opening her phone, she flicked through her photos to the selfie they had taken together on the Vespa up by the vineyard. She hadn't noticed at the time how the sun had splintered on the horizon behind them, or how Evan was looking at her, but studying it more closely, she could see what a perfect photo it was. The type she could imagine having framed and put up next to all the ones of her and Hope.

'Do you know if he came through here today?' She held up the photo to the guard. 'I need to know if he got on a flight.' The guard had barely looked at the image before he shook his head.

'I do not recognise him,' he said, turning away.

'Please, can you have a proper look? He's very tall. Six-foot four. Taller than most people. I'm sure you would remember if you saw him.'

The man ran his tongue over his bottom lip, which Holly hoped meant he was about to have another look. But instead, his eyes slid past her and the photograph. Holly twisted around to see the previous woman from the counter walking towards her, with two security guards by her side.

* * *

Holly had never been thrown out of anywhere before. At least, not in a very long time. There had been one incident with Caroline when they were seventeen and had tried to get into a pub in Bath and she had nearly died of embarrassment then. But it was nothing compared to this moment.

Escorted. That was the word that was best to use. Forcefully escorted.

The woman from the check-in counter looked on with smug satisfaction as the two oversized guards stood either side of Holly and led her back towards the exit.

She stepped out into the warm air and lifted her head to the sky. What the hell had she been thinking? And what the hell was she going to do now? She picked up her phone and for a split second, considered trying Evan again. But he had ignored her previous calls. She doubted this time would be any different. Sweat was already beading on the back of her neck and she hadn't had a single glass of water all day. A dull throb from the previous night's wine continued to pulse behind her temples. The way she was going, it would be heatstroke and a hospital bill if she wasn't careful. As much as it pained her to do so, she knew there was only one option. Giles.

No sooner had she formed the thought, than a car beeped loudly.

Holly spun around and saw the taxi. It wasn't waiting in the taxi rank like the others were and its light was switched off, indicating it wasn't taking any passengers, but as she stood there looking at it, the window wound down. A round face with aviator sunglasses appeared from the driver's seat.

'I thought I would wait for you,' he called.

53

Holly didn't speak as she climbed into the back of the car.

'I'm not paying for this trip. This makes us even. Got it?'

The driver looked at her in the rear-view mirror though he didn't agree to Holly's terms. He didn't argue either.

What did it matter now anyway? She had far bigger things to deal with. Like what the hell she was going to do. Once again, it would be down to Giles to save the day. Assuming he was still at the marina. God, how could such a romantic – admittedly naïve and un-thought-out, but romantic – idea turn into such an unmitigated disaster? And Hope. Crap, how had she thought leaving Hope for an extra night would be the right thing to do? She wouldn't blame Hope if she hated her after this. It must have been the drink, she decided. The only explanation for her absolutely ridiculous behaviour was the fact that she had still been drunk when she'd decided to run off on this scheme. At least that would help explain why she was feeling so bloody tired.

As she stared at her phone, a series of messages buzzed through from the girls.

Just boarding

Hope you got him

Can't wait to hear everything

She turned off her phone and rested her head against the window, watching the scenery pass by outside. A whole heap of emotions took hold as she closed her eyes, and she allowed herself a moment of wallowing. Stray tears ran down her cheeks, one after another. Stray tears that lulled her into a well-needed sleep.

'We are here. Madam? Madam, we are here.'

Holly could hear the voice, yet it took her a moment to realise it was talking to her. Even when she opened her eyes and saw the taxi driver staring straight at her did it take her a moment to recall what had happened.

'Where are we?' She sat up and wiped the side of her mouth in case a stray spool of dribble had escaped while she was sleeping. 'This isn't the marina.'

The effects of the sleep were clouding her thoughts, and as she looked out of the window at the white-brick building, all her brain could process was that she wasn't at the marina with Giles where she needed to be. A second later, and she realised where she was.

'The villa? Why are we at the villa? We should be at the marina.' Her pulse soared.

The driver frowned. 'You didn't ask to go to the marina.'

'I didn't?' Holly tried to remember what she had said to him before she'd fallen asleep, only to realise she hadn't said anything at all.

'This is where I came before, yes? With the suitcase?'

'It is. Only...'

'Only?'

She buried her head in her hands.

'It's fine. Here is fine. I can walk from here.' Even as she said the words, she wasn't 100 per cent sure they were true given that she had been on the Vespa the previous time she'd made the journey. But it couldn't be that hard. It was just a case of following the coast.

'It will take you a very long time,' the driver insisted. 'I will take you.'

'It's fine. It's not like I have anywhere else to be.'

With her body feeling like a dead weight, she stepped out of the taxi.

'Madam, here.' He handed her a card with his number on. 'I will finish around ten. If you would like to get a drink, maybe? I know some good places?'

'Really?' Holly laughed, then looked at the card again. 'Maybe I'll call you,' she said.

Holly's body experienced a strange sense of disassociation as she stood in front of the large doors of the villa, watching the taxi drive off. At some point, she would have to ring home, though she wasn't sure who she wanted to call to tell of her disaster. Jamie would get Fin involved, who would try to contact Evan, and that was the last thing she wanted. And she could hardly explain to her mum that she had gone off chasing a man her mother had never met. It would fall to Caroline again; what was a best friend for, after all?

With one more look at the double doors, she let out a sigh and turned back to the driveway.

'Excuse me, can I help you?' Holly spun around in shock, only to find that the door to the house was still closed. 'Holly?'

She looked up. Evan was standing there on the balcony, a towelling dressing gown draped over his swim shorts.

'Evan?'

'What are you doing here? You had a plane to catch.'

'What are *you* doing here? They said you'd got a helicopter. I went to Monaco.'

'You went to Monaco? Why?'

She was shouting up to him, not sure if he was questioning her because he didn't understand or because he simply couldn't hear her.

'I went to Monaco to find you.'

'You did? But I thought...'

Holly was looking up at the balcony as she spoke, squinting against the bright sun that gleamed behind him. Her heart throbbed.

'Actually, do you mind if I come up? Or you come down? It's pretty hard to talk this like this.'

'Of course. Just give me one minute.'

A moment later and she heard the thundering of footsteps inside before the front door swung open.

'I can't believe you're here.' Evan shook his head in disbelief.

'Me neither.'

Neither of them moved.

'You stayed the night with Giles. On the boat.'

'I stayed on the boat,' Holly agreed, 'but not with Giles. At least, not in that sense.'

'But you two talked?'

'We did.'

'And?'

Holly's stomach was a flutter. Never had she felt so excited and so terrified at the same time. Evan was there, standing less than three feet away from her, and all she wanted to do was reach out and touch him, but she couldn't. She couldn't yet. Not until she had said what she had needed to say.

'And I skipped a flight, took a dodgy taxi all the way to Monaco on Fin's credit card and got thrown out of a heliport. Does that answer your question?'

His eyes glinted as he stared at her.

'You did all that for me?'

She nodded. Her actions sounded crazy in her head, but they sounded even crazier now that she had said them aloud. 'I thought...'

All that certainty she had been feeling before, all the crazy notions of destiny and fate and maybe even soul mates, felt so childish. Until there he was. Standing over her. Looking down with a smile toying on his lips.

'You thought right,' he said.

54

Holly caught the flight out of Nice the following morning. Just like the flight in, she sat beside Evan, although there were two key differences between this flight and the one from London. The first was that she wasn't vomiting constantly. The second was that she was holding Evan's hand.

'This was not meant to happen,' she said, as she rested her head on his shoulder, gazing out the window as the city disappeared beneath them. 'I was meant to go away to relax and step away from life. Not to come back to England with a new boyfriend.' She lifted her head up and looked straight at him. 'Is it too early to use the word boyfriend? I don't want to if you're not comfortable.'

Evan shifted back in his seat and viewed her quizzically. 'I introduced you to my mother before we'd even kissed. I think I can handle the whole boyfriend thing.'

She tilted her chin up so he could kiss her softly on the lips. This wasn't how she expected finding her one to be. So easy. So natural. But now that it had happened, she couldn't have imagined it any other way.

'So, I need to head back to London when we get home, but I thought I might visit at the weekend, if you're okay with that?'

'The weekend? As in two days from now?'

'If that's okay?'

'I think I can cope with that.'

'Great, and I was also planning on coming back here next month. You know Mum said she wanted to come across, and she loves decorating, so I thought maybe we could combine it. I could book you and Hope flights if you're okay with that.? That way, I'd be able to meet her properly. I know we'll need to sort out a crib and play things—' He stopped, noticing Holly's tightly pressed lips. 'It's too fast, right? Am I taking things too fast? Tell me to slow down if you want. I should slow down. I should probably meet her before I start arranging her a room, right?'

As Holly felt her hand in his, and the pressure of his grip around hers, her heart ached. She should be terrified, she thought as she stared up at him. Putting her heart so openly on the line like this could easily end in disaster. But for the first time she ever could remember, she had no doubt about this relationship at all.

'I think everything is going at exactly the right speed,' she said.

ACKNOWLEDGMENTS

Holly has been on an incredible journey during these books, and so have I. But I have not done it on my own, and there are lots of people I need to thank.

To the wonderful team at Boldwood, who really are the most fabulous publishing group, thank you for all your support and publicity. In particular, Emily Yau, my editor. She is simply marvelous.

To my amazing cover designer, Alex Allden, there are no words to describe how beautiful you make these books look. I really do smile, each time I look at them.

To my friends and family, in particular Elsie, who loves the stories of my time at the shop, and to Jake, who I love so dearly, even though he still won't let me have a sweet shop of my own.

And lastly, to my readers. I would not be here where I am without you, and I am grateful to every last one of you. Thank you so much.

ABOUT THE AUTHOR

Hannah Lynn is the author of over twenty books spanning several genres. As well as signing a new romantic fiction series, Boldwood is republishing her bestselling Cotswolds Candy Store series inspired by her childhood.

Sign up to Hannah Lynn's mailing list here for news, competitions and updates on future books.

Visit Hannah's website: www.hannahlynnauthor.com

Follow Hannah on social media:

f facebook.com/hannahlynnauthor

instagram.com/hannahlynnwrites

tiktok.com/@hannah.lynn.romcoms

BB bookbub.com/authors/hannah-lynn

ALSO BY HANNAH LYNN

The Cotswolds Candy Store Series

Second Chances at the Cotswolds Candy Store

Love Blooms at the Cotswolds Candy Store

High Hopes at the Cotswolds Candy Store

Family Ties at the Cotswolds Candy Store

Sunny Days at the Cotswolds Candy Store

The Wildflower Lock Series

New Beginnings at Wildflower Lock

Boldwood

Boldwood Books is an award-winning fiction
publishing company seeking out the best
stories from around the world.

Find out more at www.boldwoodbooks.com

Join our reader community for brilliant books,
competitions and offers!

Follow us

@BoldwoodBooks

@TheBoldBookClub

Sign up to our weekly
deals newsletter

https://bit.ly/BoldwoodBNewsletter